THE MURDER OF MISS PERFECT

WHO REALLY KILLED ABBIE MORAN ?

MARK EKLID

PROLOGUE

They needed to get out of there as soon as the verdict was delivered but became swept up in the surge of bodies, all heading for the main exit.

Jim Pendlebury, from his position towards the back of the court, was dumbstruck. All he wanted was to slink into a dark corner and hide, unnoticed, left alone. He had to try to make sense of what had just happened.

But when he noticed them, two terrified faces being jostled in the middle of the pandemonium, he understood he had a duty to fulfil first.

He bumped and barged through to reach them and extended his long, thick arms as barriers while he glanced around in search of a haven.

'Over there,' he said and guided them towards a small pocket of calm by the side of the public gallery.

Pendlebury used his large frame to shield them as the flow of people bustled towards the bottleneck of the exit. He looked anxious, edgy, grey.

He felt bad, but what about them? It was a million times worse for the parents.

Shane was beyond shocked. He and Kerry clung to each other as if it was the only thing stopping them from being picked up by the swirl of confusion and hurled into the abyss. Tears rolled from her eyes and she did nothing to hide or dry them.

Eleven months earlier, they could only watch helplessly as their hearts were torn from their chests and ravenously devoured. Those barely-healed wounds were gaping again but this time there was nothing left to gorge on. All that remained was their still-empty shells.

Pendlebury could give them no comfort. There was no comfort. None at all. There was nothing he could say and nothing more he could do. All he could offer was his body as a physical barrier to save them from being injured.

The only way he could have served them the smallest solace, the tiniest possibility that they could pick up the pieces of their shattered lives again, was to deliver them a guilty verdict. He hadn't been able to do that.

He had let them down.

They should be bitter about that. They had every right to be. They trusted him and he failed them.

But bitterness was for another day.

Not this day. Not now. All he saw in those frightened eyes now was the empty pain of another unanticipated wound, like a family pet cowering after a savage, undeserved beating. Those eyes will never trust again. Never give unreservedly again.

The surge had slowed. Pendlebury checked over his shoulder to see if they were able to move away from their sheltered space.

'Let's get you out of here,' he said.

Shane nodded, eagerly, desperate to get away.

'There'll be a scrum outside, cameras and such. Did you want to say anything to the press?'

Kerry glanced at her husband. She was immaculately dressed, as she had been every day during the case, this time wearing an all-white suit with a pale grey blouse. She was a beautiful mid-forties woman, honey-blonde hair lapping over her shoulders. The media loved her, borderline obsessing over her through the course of this wretched ordeal.

It was easy to see where their daughter had got her looks from.

There was a flash of panic in her wide blue eyes. Shane recognised it too, like they had both just realised another small horror had still to be faced.

'I was going to,' he said, reaching to the inside pocket of his dark blue suit jacket. He pulled out a folded sheet of paper. 'I wrote a speech. But it was for when they found him guilty. I didn't...'

Pendlebury bowed his head. None of them saw any other verdict coming.

Shane peered at him, almost pleading. 'I don't think I can face it now. I just don't...'

'It's OK,' Pendlebury said, attempting to convey all the calm assurance he could muster. 'I can do it, if you'd like? I can say something to them.'

They both nodded, eager to accept the offer. Their continued faith humbled him.

Say what? The family could say what they wanted – what they truly felt – but he had to be more careful. More professional. Pendlebury tugged at his tie to straighten it. He'd think of something. This was part of the job.

'Come on, then. Let's get it over with.'

He led the way towards the banks of glass doors at the main entrance to Sheffield Crown Court. He was in his early fifties and balding but there was a natural menacing swagger to his walk. He was six foot five and as powerfully-built as a rugby second-rower, though one whose waistline had long since expanded to match the width of his shoulders. As the steeliness of his expression hardened with every step he took towards his next, unenviable task, Pendlebury still looked as if he could brace himself and stop a small car at full speed if the situation demanded.

The Morans followed closely, gripping each other tightly. They huddled behind the protection of the large man ahead of them, but then the confined building opened into the vastness of a warm blue-sky summer day and they were exposed again. Shane pulled his wife closer still, as if fearing a colossal silent raptor might swoop as soon as it spotted they had given up their sanctuary.

A bus passed by on the road in front of them and a passenger on the upper deck glanced idly around, wondering what it was that now stirred the huddle of people and cameras to the right of the imposing brown stone and brick court building.

Calls came from the crowd. There were thirty of them waiting, maybe more. They knew the routine and had gathered, chatting nonchalantly about the verdict or sucking on long-awaited cigarettes. Minds were turning to what they would soon write or say but first they needed this final judgement. The last act of what had been a great story. The people they were waiting for emerged through the main doors and a crackle of nervous anticipation spread among the pack, in case the parents were ushered quickly away to a waiting car without giving them what they wanted.

Pendlebury saw and heard the assembled media and turned towards them. He knew the routine as well. In defeat as well as victory, it was best to play the game.

Five metal stands, holding microphones protected by foam or fur windshields, had been set up to mark where they were expected to make their address. Beyond the microphones, handheld voice recorders were raised in expectation and photographers fired off their first shots. Voices fell respectfully silent. There was nothing to be gained by yelling out questions.

As he reached the gathering, Pendlebury saw familiar faces.

Many of them had been covering the case from the early days, long before it went to court. He nodded recognition to one or two of them and they smiled back weakly, acknowledging that this was not the outcome any of them anticipated. Others might be less sympathetic. Pendlebury was prepared for that.

He turned towards the Morans.

'OK?' he asked and they grimaced their assent. This was torment for them.

'Good afternoon. For those of you who don't know me, my name is Detective Chief Inspector Jim Pendlebury of South Yorkshire CID.'

It was unlikely any of them didn't know who he was. So many press conferences. So much coverage.

'Mr and Mrs Moran have decided they would prefer not to speak to you at this time. As you can imagine, this has been a distressing end to what has been a deeply traumatic eleven months for them and I would ask you to respect their need for privacy in the days ahead. However, I will try to answer your questions on their behalf.'

Several voices sounded but one rose above the rest to be heard. 'What is your reaction to the verdict, Detective Chief Inspector?'

He shuffled and stared at his feet before answering.

'I think it's fair to say we're all shocked and disappointed by this verdict,' he said at last and there was a whirring burst of motor wind shutter clicks as he raised his eyes again.

'Obviously, we felt the evidence we had presented warranted a conviction, but the jury disagreed with us and we have to respect that decision.'

'But do you think the jury got it wrong?'

Pendlebury bit his lip. All the strength in his body was beginning to feel as if it was draining into his size twelve shoes, leaving his legs unable to support the rest of him. He breathed deeply and attempted to shake himself back to full power.

Jesus! This is no time to go all weak-kneed.

'Look, I'm not going to say this is a miscarriage of justice, or anything like that. We have a system and it works. We present the evidence, the jury considers its merits and, sometimes, they come to a verdict we don't agree with. I have no doubt the jury weighed up the evidence carefully and impartially but they didn't come to the decision we hoped they would. That's the way it goes sometimes.'

'Some people feel the judge's summing up may have swayed the jury towards a not guilty verdict. What are your thoughts on that?'

'I have no issues with the judge's summing up and I don't think the jury would be so easily swayed.'

Pendlebury tried to point towards where one of the local reporters, one of those he had built up a rapport with over several years, was waiting patiently with a raised hand. It took more effort than expected. His left arm felt heavy as hell.

'Yes, Carol,' he said. Beads of sweat were forming on his brow.

'Do you think there was more the police could have done in the presentation of the evidence? I'm thinking particularly about the failure to find the ligature that was used. Do you think that left too much room for the element of doubt?'

'Obviously, we would have preferred to have located that key piece of evidence, but I still feel we were able to present a compelling case and so did the CPS.'

His mind was beginning to drift. It was taking too much effort to draw the warm air into his lungs. He needed to wind this up, quickly.

'Just one more, please. Mr and Mrs Moran need to be allowed to go home now.'

'In light of your failure to get the conviction, do you intend to resign, Detective Chief Inspector?'

The question deserved only a terse reply but the words were stuck in his throat. Pendlebury's head was swimming, the faces in front of him melting into one and the click of the cameras echoing in his ears.

Tightness clamped his chest, blackness filled his eyes. His huge frame crumpled like a vast cooling tower yielding to the press of a detonation button.

CHAPTER
ONE

Former Detective Chief Inspector Jim Pendlebury sat in his armchair, his newspaper folded on his lap ready to do the crossword. He had become very good at crosswords.

He had not made much progress with today's. He was not in the mood. He was waiting for his eldest daughter, Heather, to arrive.

Normally, a visit from either of his girls was a treat. They were less frequent these days, but then both Heather and Natalie were young women in their twenties with their own lives, so that was fair enough. More often, since Olivia was born, he and Kate made the short drive to Heather's. That was fair enough, too. Any trip away from home for Heather these days seemed to involve packing enough spare clothes, nappy changing gear, toys, feeding supplies and equipment to kit out an entire nursery.

Pendlebury did enjoy being a new grandad. Kate had taken to being a new grandma more enthusiastically, it was reasonable to say, but he did love little Olivia. That's not to say he didn't also feel an enormous sense of relief – and not feel guilty about it – when it was time to go home.

He could see nothing wrong with that. There's only so much squawking a person can take, after all. And Olivia certainly could squawk.

Kate bustled into the living room. 'Don't get carried away with that crossword, they'll be here in a minute,' she said, without breaking stride, on her way to the kitchen.

Pendlebury belligerently ignored the instruction and brought the end of his pen to his lips, as if deep in concentration. He wasn't. Three down was an anagram and he usually cracked those straight away. He wasn't seeing it today.

Some might consider his behaviour a tad childish. Others might say he was sulking. Pendlebury thought he had a valid reason to show his displeasure.

They had been building up to this morning for a few weeks, since Heather told her mum she was going back to work. Only part-time. Three days a week at first.

'Would you be able to look after Olivia?' she had asked, when the two of them were alone. 'It's just that private day nurseries are so expensive and I don't feel comfortable leaving her with strangers.'

'Of course we will!' Kate had replied. 'We'd love to!'

No 'I'll have to talk to your dad about it first, though.'

None of that.

'*We'd* love to.'

Pendlebury most certainly did not want to. Especially when he realised two of those three days were the ones when Kate volunteered at the local library in the afternoon.

That meant for two afternoons a week, every week, it would be just him. Left alone with a nine-month-old baby girl who, in full cry mode, could pierce sheet metal at twenty yards. Handed full responsibility to entertain, feed and change her.

Change her. He had never changed a nappy in his life. Kate always saw to that sort of thing.

Kate had told the people at the library she would not be in this week, while they adjusted to the new routine, but was adamant she would not give up her volunteering for good. Pendlebury had not asked her to, in fairness, but that didn't stop him hoping she would.

He could see no other way of escape.

'Come on, Jim, shake yourself,' Kate said with an edge of exasperation as she re-plumped and re-straightened cushions on the sofa that had not been touched since she plumped and straightened them quarter of an hour earlier.

'I can't do it,' he declared, slapping his pen and newspaper down on the table at the side of his armchair.

'Don't start with that again.' Kate stared sternly at him, hands on hips. 'We've been through this. We're doing it and that's that.'

He gave no response, allowing his silence to say everything about how he felt.

'We'll be fine,' said Kate, more conciliatory.

'You'll be fine. You're used to it. I've no idea. You raised our girls because I was always at work and I'll always be grateful to you for that. I don't know what I'm supposed to do.'

'You'll learn, Jim.' She walked to him and perched on the chair arm, stroking the back of his head. 'It's not the labours of Hercules, it's looking after your baby granddaughter. You'll love it, honestly. You'll see what you missed out on with our two when you were out there, working all hours. You'll be there to watch her grow and see her personality develop, which is magical. And it's not as if you're going to be stuck in the house all day. You'll be able to take her for walks in the park in her pushchair. It'll be good exercise for you.'

Pendlebury's face did not soften.

'Can't we just get a dog instead?'

Kate stood and stomped away. He knew he had irritated her. He wanted to irritate her.

'I'll pretend you didn't say that,' she huffed.

It was not only the new childcare arrangements that had

caused Pendlebury's bad mood. It was June the twenty-first. It was on June the twenty-first three years ago that he had been talking to the media outside Sheffield Crown Court one moment and, the next thing he knew, he was in a hospital bed, surrounded by machines and with tubes coming out of places he never imagined tubes could go into. As he blurrily became aware of a crushing pressure on his chest and realised Kate was sitting beside him, red-eyed and haunted as she cradled his hand in hers, he knew something had cracked off.

Like being given CPR by a consultant anaesthetist who just happened to be passing by the court the moment he collapsed. Like officially dying three times in the ambulance on the way to hospital while the paramedics fought desperately to restart his heart. Like being stabilised by a crash team in A&E at the Northern General Hospital while the theatre was prepared for an emergency operation. Like nine hours in surgery having a quadruple bypass. That sort of thing.

He was so lucky to be alive – and thankful for that – but as he began the long recovery process he began to realise his career in the police was over.

So the coming of June the twenty-first would forever be a reminder of the day he had to give up the job he loved. The job that was so much a part of everything he was. That was still hard to deal with.

On top of that, Pendlebury had still not been able to bury the bitter regret of that final day in the job and the final case he took to trial.

The Miss Perfect Murder.

Abie Moran was eighteen, the same age as Pendlebury's youngest daughter, Natalie, at the time. That was part of the reason why the case felt so personal to him.

Abie was a sixth form student at one of the new Academies in one of Sheffield's more respectable areas. She had just taken her final A Level exams and was expected to earn the highest grades before going on to study at one of the top universities. She wanted to become a doctor.

With her long blonde hair, slim build and soft, fresh, innocent features, she was a beautiful young woman well-liked by all her fellow students. Friends gravitated to her because she was completely unaffected. It was impossible not to like Abie.

Her biggest flaw – her fatal flaw – was that she had developed a secret infatuation for one of her maths tutors.

David Bales was thirty-six, no more than average height and build and had features that some might have considered handsome. *He* certainly did. He was also well aware of his ability to charm the hind legs off a donkey. It made him a constant target for teenage crushes and, it has to be said, he loved the attention, though there had never been any allegation of serious misconduct made against him.

That was, until Abie Moran started to make her interest known.

Bales could not resist her and she allowed herself to be lured by him. On July the eighteenth, 2017, a couple of days before the official end of term, she went to his home, which was a short walk from the school. It appears she went there to deliver a small present, a show of gratitude for his guidance as a tutor. There is no evidence to suggest her visit was down to collusion on his part.

Bales invited her in and Abie, in her naivety, accepted the offer.

He then tried to get her drunk by giving her beer and she was coerced into having sex with him. There was no evidence of rape or of her being restrained but who knows what manner of threats or misdirection were used to get her to agree to his debauched advances?

After the act, the scale of his impropriety must have dawned on Bales. He realised the only way he could guarantee Abie's future silence, to save himself from the inevitable consequences after she reported his appalling behaviour to the appropriate authorities, was to kill her.

Abie was murdered by strangulation, using a ligature. It was believed he used his own necktie because fibres of blue silk were recovered from beneath Abie's fingernails where she had clawed at the restraint to try to release the pressure on her throat. Several witnesses reported seeing Bales wearing a woven silk tie in pale blue with a repeating pattern of six small white dots earlier that day. The tie was not recovered during a thorough search of the house and grounds. Its whereabouts are still unknown.

After he killed her, his preparations for the disposal of the body were twice disturbed.

Firstly, he received a phone call from a work colleague who was in a state of distress over an incident at the Academy. The length of that call was later timed at twelve minutes and thirty-eight seconds.

Secondly, the call was cut short because Bales' wife, Gemma, arrived home unexpectedly. It was she who discovered the body and ran into the street to alert neighbours. The police were summoned and Bales was arrested at the scene.

Despite the overwhelming nature of the evidence against him, Bales denied the charge of murder and pleaded not guilty in court.

The jury found in his favour. The missing tie was, as it turned out, a crucial gap in the evidence against Bales, allowing scope for doubt which his defence exploited. They argued there was insufficient opportunity in the timeline for Bales to have disposed of the tie so effectively and that it had been taken from the scene by a person or persons unknown.

No viable theory was presented to suggest who the 'real murderer' (in the view of the defence) was or why Abie Moran had been targeted by them. In the end, however, the jury chose to be swayed by the defence's argument.

In the eyes of the police and the public, Bales was an unscrupulous predator who had taken advantage of a vulnerable young woman, breaking every professional code of conduct, and had callously ended her life. Only the timely intervention of Mrs

Bales had prevented him from covering his tracks by disposing of the body.

Shortly after her death, Abie's distraught father, Shane, issued an impromptu statement to the large pack of media gathered outside his home.

'She was the perfect daughter, the perfect big sister, the perfect friend and the perfect student,' he told them. 'She was simply perfect.'

His words were a headline writer's dream.

In the manner in which they often apply a soundbite tag to a running story, Abie Moran was from then on popularly referred to in the media as Miss Perfect.

The case became the Miss Perfect Murder.

CHAPTER
TWO

A beer was a treat these days and Pendlebury savoured every sip like it was a hundred-year-old single malt.

An occasional pint was not breaking the new set of rules set for him since the surgery but it had become a sort of secret indulgence. He knew Kate disapproved. She had taken the cardiologist's grudging acceptance that one beer every now and then would not do any harm as a tacit suggestion that giving up completely would be far preferable and had tried to encourage her husband to make that sacrifice.

Pendlebury did not want to go that far. He knew Kate had the best of intentions. He knew he had given her an almighty scare by nearly dying and he understood why that had made her overprotective.

He had agreed to give up smoking. He didn't especially mind that he would never again tuck into a large fry-up and that the days when he could go to the pub to swill down a gallon with his mates were behind him. He had even learned to accept that kale and spinach would become an almost constant presence on his dinner plate and to chew it down without complaint.

But he did not believe the price of cheating death was to give up living completely and a beer every now and again was one of the few little pleasures he was not prepared to surrender.

Kate understood that and they dealt with this small area of conflict through a truce of silence. He didn't tell her when he was going out for a pint and she didn't ask, though she certainly guessed every time he invented some flimsy pretext that required him to pop out for an hour and came back smelling of mints. She trusted him to set self-imposed limits.

Today's story was that he was catching a bus into town to have a new battery put in his watch and to maybe look in the shops for a new jacket, but Pendlebury had ventured no further from the bus station than the Old Queen's Head, no more than a couple of hundred yards from where the bus stopped at the end of its route.

He had arranged to meet someone. A former colleague.

The pub was quiet now, just the way he liked it. He deliberately arranged the meeting for a time when food was unavailable and only a handful of drinkers were still around. He had the smallest of the pub's three rooms to himself and sat contentedly, leafing through his paper, eking out his beer, waiting for Clare Larson to arrive.

On that anniversary, three days earlier, he had felt an urge to contact the Morans. Kate was in the front room, trying to quieten the baby with cuddles and cooing, and Pendlebury had escaped into the back garden. Maybe any excuse was good enough but he did genuinely want to call them again, to see how they were. It would have been too much to expect them to be fine – to have got over it – but he wanted to show them he had not forgotten either.

It had been a while. The Morans, he was told, were good enough to call several times to ask how he was while Pendlebury lay, barely able to do anything except let the machines keep him alive, in his hospital bed, but neither he nor they had tried to keep in touch since. He could understand why they would not want to talk to him, to be reminded. He had thought about them from time to time, but hadn't previously felt it appropriate to follow up his thoughts by re-establishing contact. It wouldn't have been right.

This was different, somehow. It felt like it was time. Maybe their scorn for his professional abilities would have dimmed by now. Maybe the reminder of his failure would not hurt them quite so much.

The phone rang three times before a voice, tentative and guarded, answered.

'Hello?' It was Shane. The number had not been recognised, it seemed.

'Shane, hi. It's Jim Pendlebury.'

The name echoed in the space between them. There was no response for a few seconds, enough silence to make Pendlebury wonder if a bitter rebuke was forming in the tormented mind of the man at the other end of the line.

'Jim. Hi.' The delivery was flat, forced. 'How… how are you?'

'Not so bad.' Pendlebury was already beginning to regret having made the call, like he was intruding. 'What about you two? How's Kerry?'

The line fell quiet again. A response was being contemplated, rather than formed.

'I'm OK. Fine really. Kerry's…' He hesitated again. 'We split up.'

Pendlebury sagged. It was not a development he had seen coming. They were so dedicated. How they could have got through everything otherwise, he had no idea.

'I'm sorry to hear that, Shane.' He could think of nothing else to say.

'Yeah, well.' Shane let out a resigned sigh. 'It just got too much. We couldn't be the same people anymore. When we lost Abie we lost what bound us together. We drifted apart. We could barely even stand to talk to each other in the end. Splitting up was for the best, I guess.'

Nothing in his tone suggested Shane believed the last part of what he said.

'That's…' Pendlebury's voice tailed off. It was many things but none of the words he could think of felt adequate. 'Look, I know I'm probably one of the last people you wanted to hear from but the reason I called was to say I'm still thinking about you – both of you – and if there's anything I can do…'

'Appreciate that, Jim.' It had become a stock reply, to offers of support that could never be taken up. How could anybody help? They couldn't begin to understand.

'I'm a bit out of the loop now,' Pendlebury added. 'Have the police been able to come up with anything, do you know? Anything new?'

Shane let out a long and loud exhale of breath.

'I haven't heard from the police for, what? Months? Years? Are they still bothered? I don't know. They've probably given up.'

Pendlebury wanted to say something to encourage him not to lose faith but he knew how it worked. The trail had gone cold. They had devoted a lot of resource to the Abie Moran case and had suffered a defeat. Unless anything new came to light, it was hard to justify devoting limited manpower to digging aimlessly. There was never a shortage of new serious crimes which presented a more realistic chance of a positive outcome.

He wrapped up the tortured conversation with a promise to contact a few old colleagues but even to his own ears it sounded like a hollow pledge. What good could it do?

The call had been a mistake. The motivation for it was selfish, he now saw. What was he expecting? Reassurance? Vindication?

All he got was a reminder. His failure had made an appalling nightmare even worse.

What could he possibly offer to make up for that? He was not even a policeman anymore. Pendlebury stood, facing a garden that had never received as much attention as it had in the last couple of years, and felt useless. Neutered.

Then he decided to call Clare Larson.

Clare came in through the main door, the one Pendlebury had positioned himself to be able to keep an eye on. She scanned the larger room to the right of the bar first, then smiled when she turned and saw him, folding his paper and grinning sheepishly.

'Hello, sir,' she said as she moved towards him, with that same long stride and assured sense of purpose in her step he remembered. In full flight, Clare cast quite an intimidating figure as she bore down on whoever she locked in her sights, especially when her expression hardened and her eyes narrowed, like a security dog spotting an intruder. She was taller than most women and had powerful broad shoulders, a legacy of the days in her late teens, fifteen or so years ago, when she had been a good enough freestyle swimmer to reach the national championship finals. Even the cockiest of minor offenders were cowed by her. Not even the most hardened of criminals could unnerve her.

When Clare was a newly-qualified Detective Sergeant and their boss decided to pair her with Pendlebury, some of their colleagues latched on to the physical similarities and took to calling them the Heavy Mob. Never to their faces, mind you.

They were well matched in other ways, too. They shared the same nagging determination to get to the bottom of whichever case they were assigned to and they both willingly embraced the social side of being part of the CID team. Pendlebury said she was the best Detective Sergeant he had ever worked alongside and a person he had grown as close to as anybody on the force.

'It's Jim,' he said, rising to his feet to greet her. To his surprise, she wrapped him in a firm hug.

'Old habits,' she replied as she released him, a broad grin spreading across her face. It had been a long time since they had met up.

'How much weight have you lost, you skinny sod? Look at

you.' Clare took half a step back to size up the frame of a man who had almost certainly never been accused of being skinny in his life.

He laughed at the suggestion.

'Three and a half stone. I can't say as I recommend the method, though.'

Pendlebury reflected that Clare seemed to have found a fair proportion of the weight he had lost but knew better than to say so.

She glanced at his half-full pint glass.

'Can I get you another?'

'No thanks.' He looked down at the beer ruefully. 'This is my ration these days.'

She nodded and turned to the bar. He neither expected nor wanted her to feel sorry for him. He wasn't good at handling sympathy. It annoyed him.

Pendlebury sat and picked up where he had left reading his paper until Clare came back to the table with her pint. She took a gulp as she lowered herself into a chair.

'So I hear you got made up to DI at last,' he said. 'About bloody time.'

She wrinkled her nose. 'You know how it is. It's sometimes better if you're made to wait for it because then there's less chance people are going to resent you for it.'

'True enough.' He had never been the most tolerant through his career when he saw officers he considered less able than others rise quickest through the ranks.

Risen without trace, he used to say.

'How've you been? Ticker still holding up?'

Pendlebury slapped his hand to his chest, pressing his fingers on the still prominent long scar which started just below his throat, where the surgeons had needed to saw down the length of his sternum to fix his suffocating heart.

'Think so,' he answered with a smile.

Clare took another mouthful of her drink.

'So what was important enough for you to want to blow your entire beer ration with me?'

He grimaced. He didn't like the implication he had only set up the meeting because he wanted something but, in truth, that was the reason.

'It's the Abie Moran case.'

'I'm not on that anymore,' she replied, dismissively.

'I guessed not. Is there anything going on with it at all?'

'It went cold, Jim. We haven't had a new lead on it for ages.'

That was the answer he anticipated.

'I talked to Shane the other day,' he said, watching for the flicker of response in her eyes.

'Yeah?' She picked up her glass again.

'It sounded like he was in a mess. Him and Kerry split up.'

There was proper anguish in her expression. They had both grown very close to the couple during the investigation.

'What a pity. It's surprising how often that happens. As if what they had to go through wasn't enough.'

'Aye,' said Pendlebury and reached for a sip from his pint.

'The thing is,' he added, 'it still gets to me.'

Clare's brow knitted. 'What do you mean?'

'Losing that case. The fact that the bastard got away with it.'

'It still rankles with me as well,' she nodded. 'But you have to let it go, Jim. We didn't have the evidence to make it stick, or so the jury decided. Maybe they were right. Maybe we had the wrong man.'

'We had the right man and we both know it,' he snapped back, with more venom than he intended. 'There was no other suspect. You can't possibly buy that defence bullshit about some unknown assailant nipping in through the conservatory, can you? It had to be him.'

'But we couldn't prove it,' she retorted.

'Aye,' he said, calmer. 'I'd like to give it another go.'

She stared back at him blankly, not understanding where he was about to go with this.

'I want you to tell me where Bales lives now so I can do a bit of digging. You know, see if I can come up with something new so the case can be reopened.'

It took her a moment to absorb the suggestion. It stunned her.

'No, Jim,' her tone was emphatic. 'Absolutely not.'

He expected her resistance to the proposal.

'Hear me out. I'm not talking about anything complicated, just a bit of good old-fashioned legwork. If you tell me where to find him, I can do some low-key asking around – neighbours, shops, pubs, workplace. See if he's mentioned anything that might seem innocent to them but which could be a new break for us. You know what he's like. He's such an arrogant bugger he's bound to have said something to somebody. He wouldn't have been able to resist. He got away with murder. His type can't keep that to themselves.'

'You're not a copper anymore, Jim. You can't do this sort of thing.'

'Nobody else is doing it, are they? I won't overstep the mark and if I do find anything, then I bring it straight to you. I'm not going to try to arrest him or anything.'

Clare's opposition to the plan was not waning.

'There's no way. Rightly or wrongly, the court found him not guilty and we have to live with that. Bales left the area to start again, as he was entitled to do because, in the eyes of the law, he is innocent. For all we know, he's taken on a whole new identity.'

'You're not telling me we haven't kept tabs on him. I know if you wanted to get hold of him, you could find him in two minutes.'

She was not about to deny that.

'That's not the point. What you're suggesting is wrong. If it ever came out that I gave you the details of where he is and what he's calling himself now, I'd be thrown out.'

'Nobody has to know,' he pleaded.

She snorted, scornfully, and took another large mouthful of beer.

'I need this, Clare.'

He was wilting before her eyes, broken. She had never seen him so vulnerable.

'I feel useless, not doing anything, day after day. I'm a copper. I've still got something to offer. I still find it difficult to deal with losing this case and I feel like I could make a difference, get the bastard locked up for what he did. Give her poor parents a bit of closure. They deserve that, don't they? It broke my heart again, talking to Shane the other day.'

She was softening. She saw his pain.

'You have to let go, Jim. Enjoy your retirement. Enjoy spending a bit of time with Kate. God knows you didn't do enough of that when you were working.'

'Retirement!' Pendlebury cast his head back and looked to the ceiling. 'She's got me bloody babysitting now.'

Clare tried to suppress a smile.

'I'm not meant for bloody babysitting. I'm not ready to give up.' He leaned forward.

'For all intents and purposes, I should have died in front of the court that day. They told me I actually did die three times in the ambulance on the way to the Northern General, but I survived. I owe my life to the consultant who was first on the scene, to the paramedics and to the skill of a surgeon but, I don't know, maybe I'm still here because it wasn't my time. It makes you think a great deal about a great many things when you have that sort of experience, believe me, and I'm not saying I have any of the answers but I know this: I wasn't spared just to be wrapped in cotton wool and be told what I can't do for the rest of my time. I need to find a reason to still be alive and, for me, that means being a copper. It's what I am.'

Pendlebury drew a deep breath.

'Look, it's just this once. I have to try. I have to work some of this frustration out of my system or it's going to wear me out. I promise not to do anything stupid and I promise that if I don't find anything, I'll drop it. A couple of days, that's all I'm asking for. A couple of days of being a copper again and then I can go back to bloody babysitting. I know I'll be able to come up with something if I just ask around.'

Clare shook her head. She trusted him, but he was asking too much. She would be risking too much.

But what if he did come up with a new lead?

'This is a stupid idea,' she said and checked her watch. It was time to head back to the office. Clare swilled down the last of her drink and stood to go.

'Let me think about it. I'm making no promises.'

CHAPTER
THREE

As usual, for a Sunday afternoon, Kate was busying herself with her routine of household chores and, as usual, Pendlebury was in his armchair watching sport on TV. This time, however, he was distracted. He was trying to pick the best time.

Clare Larson had called him on his mobile the day before.

'If I do this, you've got to swear to me not to do anything daft,' she said, sternly.

'Absolutely.' He was encouraged. It was not a straight no.

'No direct contact with Bales. Nothing in anything you say can even remotely give anyone the impression you're a serving police officer or that you've ever been a police officer. You do nothing that's even remotely illegal. No deep digging. If you find even the smallest scrap of information that might be relevant to the case, you bring it straight to me and me alone and that's the end of your involvement. Understood?'

The terms were set. He would have agreed to whatever she demanded.

'Understood.'

Clare hesitated, still not convinced this was a good idea.

'Have you got a pen?'

Pendlebury scribbled down an address.

'Scarborough?' he repeated.

'Apparently so. Maybe he thought the sea air would do him good.'

He snorted. 'Should have bloody thrown himself off the cliffs and done us all some good.'

There was no conspiratorial signal of agreement. Maybe he should lay off making jokes which could be misconstrued.

'Has he taken another name?'

Clare was quiet on the other end of the phone. This was it. The point of no return.

'David Wilson.'

There. It's done.

Pendlebury wrote down the name and underscored it with a flourish.

'Got that. Thanks Clare. I owe you one.'

Silence again. The doubt was still there.

'Just don't make me regret this, Jim.'

And so he sat in his armchair, not really watching the rugby. The news that Bales had relocated to Scarborough presented a difficulty initially – how to come up with an excuse for spending a couple of days in Scarborough on his own without arousing Kate's suspicion? – but he got lucky.

The cricket festival. Yorkshire were due to play against Lancashire in a four-day match at the North Marine Road ground in a couple of weeks. Kate had encouraged him to take himself off to watch some cricket, partly, he suspected, to get him out of the house and have it to herself again for a few hours. He had often mentioned he would like to go to the Scarborough Festival. Kate would be happy to let him go alone. She didn't share his appreciation for cricket.

It was a good plan but the deception did not sit easy. It was a lie. He would have to tell Kate a lie to make it work and he never lied to Kate. There were many things, through his career, he had held back from telling her, because sometimes that's what a policeman has to do, but he had never been unfaithful and he never lied.

He still felt this was something he needed to do for the sake of his peace of mind in the future – just one more stab at bringing the Morans the justice they deserved – but now the plot was hatched, he felt guilty at not being honest about it with his wife. For all he tried to justify his secrecy with the knowledge of the anxiety it would cause Kate if she knew, he could not get past that guilt.

She came into the living room with a basketful of dried washing, still warm from the embrace of the gentle summer breeze.

'Here, let me do that, love,' said Pendlebury as he shot to his feet.

He snatched the basket from her and emptied its contents on to the sofa, like he had noticed her do countless times without ever being stirred to action himself. He picked through the clothes, attempting to match socks, like an explorer sifting through discovered tribal artefacts.

She watched his fumbling efforts with bemusement. Jim had brought many qualities to their marriage over the years but he never helped out around the house. She had often been censured by her daughters for allowing him to escape his share of the chores, but she had not gone back to full-time work after having the kids and had got used to it. Even though her husband no longer worked all hours, she had no appetite for change. She was no downtrodden housewife, she just liked everything done properly, that's all. Her way.

Pendlebury picked up a pair of her knickers and peered at them, trying to figure out how this tangle of material could be reformed into an article of clothing and then flushed with embarrassment when he realised he was holding them by the gusset.

'Do you want a hand with those?' she offered.

'No, I'll manage,' he replied with determination, folding the knickers without noticing they were still inside-out.

'You have a sit down, if you like. I'll put them away when I'm done.'

A frown formed on Kate's brow. Either her husband was experiencing a miraculous late transformation into a new man, or…

'What are you up to?'

He stopped rummaging and attempted to muster a look of indignant surprise.

'What do you mean?'

'I know you, Jim Pendlebury. You're up to something.'

He put down the black T-shirt he held in his hands. She could always see through him like he was made of Perspex. It was time to tell her.

'Bloody hell, I wish I'd had you in with me in interview rooms sometimes.'

She smiled and folded her arms, waiting.

'I was thinking about going away for a couple of days.' He looked up, watching for the reaction, and her eyebrows arched. 'On my own.'

'Oh!' There was a small trace of hurt in her expression.

'I wanted to go to watch some cricket. In Scarborough.'

Kate was unmoved.

'You know I've said for ages I'd like to go to the cricket in Scarborough and you've said I should. Well, they're playing the Lankies in two weeks and I fancy going.'

She held her pose for a few moments more as Pendlebury tried not to show how on edge her silence was making him.

'I think that's a good idea,' she said, at last.

'You can come as well, if you'd like,' he felt obliged to offer.

'To watch cricket? No thanks!'

'You wouldn't have to go to the game. You could, you know,

have a day on the beach or something.' He was conscious of not putting too much into the selling of the idea.

Kate appeared to be pondering the thought.

'We could take Olivia with us,' she suggested.

She watched his expression closely to fully appreciate the horror he could not keep from it, wickedly delighting in his sudden alarm.

'Well, I'm not sure that would be…'

He glanced and noticed her devilish grin.

'I'm joking, Jim. Of course I don't mind you going away for a couple of days to watch the cricket, as long as you don't gorge yourself on fish and chips without me there to keep an eye on you.'

He laughed, nervously. 'No. No, I won't. Thanks, love.'

'It'll do you good.' She took hold of his hand. 'Which days are you thinking of?'

'Monday and Tuesday,' he replied. 'It'll mean you'll have Olivia to yourself.'

Kate took a deep breath.

'Is that what this is about?' she asked. 'Wanting to get away from your granddaughter?'

'Not really.' The timing had not been in his control. It was dictated by the fixture list. He certainly hadn't regarded it as unfortunate, however.

She appeared unconvinced.

'I know you wish I hadn't offered to look after Olivia for Heather but you will grow to enjoy your grandad days, you know.'

It was his turn to betray doubt.

'You will!' she insisted, enthusiastically, gripping his hand more firmly.

Pendlebury tried to appear as if he had been rallied by her attempt.

'Yeah, you're probably right. It's just that…'

'What?'

He hesitated. 'Well, it'd be better if she wasn't such a mardy little bugger.'

Kate laughed and put her arms around his broad chest.

'She is a bit, isn't she? But then, so was her mother and she didn't turn out so bad.'

Pendlebury drew back from the embrace and stared at his wife. 'Was she?' He had no such recollection.

'Oh God, yes,' Kate replied. 'I seriously contemplated leaving her in the ladies' toilets at Coles once in town when she was playing up particularly badly. It's a wonder we had another after dealing with Heather's constant misery for the first year of her life. It's a wonder she made it to her second birthday. Thankfully, Natalie was different again.'

This was a revelation to him. How on earth was he shielded from that? It made him realise just how little he had to do with the raising of his daughters and he was shamed by that.

'I had no idea,' he muttered.

'Of course you didn't.' There was no sharpness in her tone. 'You were out doing your job and I was doing mine. You didn't bring your work troubles back home with you and I didn't think it was right to burden you with my problems. It wouldn't have been fair.'

He saw then how wrapped up in work he had been, how all-consuming it had become. He knew he had not always been around to help out but hadn't been aware how much he had missed. He hadn't realised how much he had under-appreciated Kate and what she had given up for the sake of their family.

'It's hard work bringing up a child, Jim. You need all the help you can get and that's why I said we'd take care of Olivia for three days a week. It gets easier, as they get a little older and start to be able to interact properly, and it's so rewarding, building a bond with them and seeing them grow up at close hand. You'll see.'

Pendlebury was contrite.

'I haven't been much use to you, have I? I haven't been much of a father.'

Kate hugged him again.

'We did perfectly fine between us and that's what counts,' she said. 'Besides, you were doing an important job and making a difference for all of us. I was always proud of you for that.'

He kissed the top of her head. 'Thanks.'

'What do you say we have a few days away in a bit? Just the two of us.'

She looked up at him and grinned. 'No Olivia?'

'No Olivia,' he smiled back. 'We could look at places to go for days out when she gets a bit older, though. You know, kiddie farms and playgrounds and such.'

His lack of base knowledge when it came to entertaining children amused her, but at least he was showing willingness to learn. That was good.

She squeezed him once more and released him, turning to the still unsorted pile of dried washing.

'I'd like that. Now, I'll do this. You watch your rugby.'

He lumbered back to his armchair without protest.

Scarborough was on. The lie left him uneasy, but it had to be done. He would make it up to Kate.

CHAPTER
FOUR

Pendlebury was puffing hard by the time he reached the
summit of the third flight of narrow stairs. He set down his
small overnight bag and leaned against the wall, bending his large
frame to rest his hands on his knees as he attempted to draw deep
drafts of air into his lungs. His dismissively confident response
when the landlady asked, over the phone, if the room on the top
floor would be all right had proved misguided.

He was more out of shape than he had been prepared to admit
to himself. The surgery could not be blamed. The cardiologist had
discharged him after fourteen months and said he could lead a
relatively normal life. He had advised Pendlebury to join a gym or
take an alternative form of regular exercise, but that's the kind of
thing they do say, isn't it? The suggestion hadn't been seriously
considered. Perhaps it hadn't been such a bad idea.

When he felt capable of doing something other than just trying
to breathe, Pendlebury dipped into the pocket of his jacket for the
room key. It and the smaller front door key were attached by a

ring to a bulky hard plastic fob with a number five etched on it. Clearly, the intention was to make it as difficult as possible to absent-mindedly drive away with the key still in a pocket at the end of your stay.

It also proved a challenge to make the key actually open the door.

The long stem of the key rattled loosely in the well-worn keyhole but it would not turn. He tried pulling and pushing the door, shaking the key and, finally, swearing at it, but it did not budge. If there was a knack, then clearly he didn't have it.

Just as Pendlebury was contemplating the least attractive of his limited options – ignominiously trudging back down the three flights of stairs to ask the landlady for help and, therefore, having to haul himself back up the three flights of stairs again, the lock ended its resistance with a satisfying click and he was in.

The room was a converted attic space, which meant Pendlebury would need to crouch under the slope of the ceiling to open the one small window, but it was cheerily decorated and appeared invitingly comfortable. He spotted, with a note of relief, that there was no solid board at the feet end of the single bed, meaning he would be able to stretch his full length without restriction.

Having recovered his breath and his temper, he glanced around and nodded. It would do nicely for a night. Seaside bed and breakfasts appeared to have upped their game since the last time he stayed in one.

He put the bag on the bed and sat beside it, enjoying the inner peace of rest at the end of a two-hour drive and absorbing his new surroundings. He considered using half of his meagre ration of long-life milk pots to make a cup of tea and thought about emptying his bag but, in the end, decided to do neither.

It was time to go to work.

———

The address he had been given, the one where Bales now lived, was less than a mile away but Pendlebury decided to drive there.

It was the time of day when the sun would have been at its highest in the summer sky. Instead, it was shying away, unseen, behind the thick sheet of baleful, pale grey cloud that hung over the resort, barely stirred at all by the gentle cool breeze off the North Sea.

Pendlebury prised himself out of the driver's seat and sniffed the sea air, practically tasting the saltiness. He was close to the South Cliff but away from the main concentration of Esplanade hotels and guest houses. This was an area for residents, not tourists.

The curved Victorian terrace of Regents Crescent loomed over him, almost threatening to close its great arms and envelope him. It must have been grand once, with jutting, proud stone bays on all four storeys and the high ornate carved detail that would be dismissed as simply unnecessary by builders these days. They must once have been homes to the fairly well-off, in their tall top hats and long ruffled skirts. Now, the buildings had been split into flats and their cream-fronted façades were flaking and chipped. Faded glory.

Pendlebury had found a parking spot around fifty yards along the Crescent from the flat he was looking for. The sign beside the marked parking area said it was for permit holders only but he reckoned he wouldn't be stopping for long enough or venturing far enough to be risking a ticket.

He locked the door. Further along the sweep of the terrace he noticed a young woman with a pushchair, bumping it cautiously down the dozen steps from the front door to the pavement. It seemed as if she might be coming from the same block he was looking for.

This could be a first chance to gather information. He quickened his pace as the woman reached the bottom of the steps and turned to head away from him.

'Excuse me, love,' he called, but she either did not hear him or ignored him. If anything, she began to walk more quickly.

Pendlebury had to almost break into a trot to catch up. 'Excuse me,' he said again as he stepped alongside her.

She slowed but didn't stop and glanced suspiciously at him from the corner of her eye.

'Could I just have a quick word?' he persisted as she trundled on, the small boy in the pushchair, with his tangle of blond hair, gripping an opened packet of crisps with one hand and feeding himself with the other. Pendlebury had to virtually step in front of the wheels to make her pull up.

'It'll only take a second,' he added.

She appeared to be contemplating trying to barge past him but stood still at last. She, like the buildings beside her, had long since given up trying to look their best, even though she could not have been much older than her early twenties. She looked warily, challengingly, at him with the air of a person who had been let down and deceived one too many times in her short life. She said nothing.

'I noticed the house you came out of and I'm hoping you might be able to help me. I'm looking for a man who I think lives in one of the flats around here.'

He reached into his inside jacket pocket for the photograph.

It would be useful to have a photograph, he decided, so he had done a Google search for images of Bales and had found one he thought would be ideal. It was a smiling picture with him at the centre, surrounded by the pixelated faces of fourteen- or fifteen-year-old girls. Taken on a school trip, maybe. Going by the source of the image in the search, whoever took the shot must have made it available to one of the national papers in the build-up to the trial.

It made his skin crawl. He detested the bastard and what he did to Abie. Did to her parents, too. He could barely stand to look at that arrogant, conceited grin but, cropped down, he reckoned it could pass as an ordinary family snap and so he had sized it as he wanted it and printed it off.

'This is him,' he said, presenting the photo for her to look at. 'His name's David Wilson.'

The woman barely allowed her eyes to settle on it. 'Don't know him,' she mumbled and tried to move away but Pendlebury did not budge.

'I know it's not a very good picture and it's a few years old now but could you please have a good look? It's very important.'

Her curiosity was sparked. 'What do you want him for?'

'He's not in trouble or anything,' he said, attempting to reassure. 'I'm his step-dad and we lost touch four years ago. Had a bit of a row, you know how families are sometimes.'

She gave no response but he guessed that scenario probably resonated with her.

'Anyway, something's happened that means we have to talk to David. I've been trying to track him down for ages and I think this is where he lives. Please. I've come all the way from Sheffield.'

The woman's resolve appeared to be waning. She took a proper look at the picture but then said 'Sorry, can't help you,' dismissively.

She bundled past him this time and Pendlebury let her go for a few steps before calling after her again. It was time to go all-in with the play of desperation.

'His mum's really poorly,' he said, walking after her. 'They used to be close but he took it hard when his real dad died and he couldn't forgive her when she started seeing me a few months later. That's when they fell out. But she's sick and she's not going to get better. I'm trying to give him the chance for them to patch up their differences before it's too late.'

She slowed and stopped.

'Please,' he added.

The woman sighed.

'He lives in the same block of flats as me. He's on the second floor.' She rushed the words out before she could change her mind.

'Thank you,' he said, peering towards the door the woman had emerged from.

'Have you got to know him at all? We don't even know if he's got a family now or whatever. Does he ever talk about us?'

'I hardly ever see him,' she added. 'We pass on the stairs sometimes, you know. He never says anything, just kind of minds his own business. I've never seen him with anybody. I think he lives alone in the flat. Never hear from him, really. He's quiet.'

Pendlebury was pulling his best concerned face, reacting as if every scrap of information was a dagger to the heart. 'I see,' he uttered at last.

'I've got to go,' said the woman suddenly and he made no attempt to stop her this time.

'Thank you,' he called after her, then adding 'Oh, just one more thing.'

Her shoulders sagged as she pulled up again but she turned to face him.

'I'd appreciate it if you didn't mention anything to David if you do see him. If he hears I've been around he might run off again and then I might be too late. I'd like to wait until I can see him face to face and explain.'

She nodded briefly before scurrying away.

Pendlebury watched her disappear around the corner at the end of the terrace. She hadn't told him anything especially useful but at least he knew the cover story worked.

He stood on the pavement for a few moments more, considering what to do next. A cup of tea and a sandwich would be a good start. It had been a long time since breakfast. When he had checked out the location on Google maps he noticed there was a busy main road close by, in the direction the young woman was heading. It had shops and cafés on either side, so there would be no shortage of options for grabbing lunch. It was also where he intended to go for the next stage of his investigations.

Bales would use those shops. He would drink in those pubs. He would get to know people. They would get to know him. Maybe he would have said something to them that would give him a lead. People like Bales could never resist opening their big mouths, bragging about what they had done. What they had got away with. Pendlebury needed to find those he had confided in and persuade them to talk. Let them know what kind of a person Bales really was. Somebody would know something and they probably didn't yet realise the significance.

It demanded the type of good old-fashioned legwork policing he used to preach the importance of to junior officers and he was looking forward to it. There was something strangely appealing about getting back to basic coppering.

But it proved a fruitless exercise. One or two behind the counters of shops – the cheaper grocery stores – recognised him as an occasional customer and one or two had exchanged brief pleasantries, but nobody appeared to know him. No one working in any of the four pubs within easy walking distance could recall having served him. None of the drinkers in their pubs gave so much as a flicker of recognition.

It was as if Bales never left his flat.

Pendlebury was footsore and disheartened as he trudged back to the car. He stopped outside the house Bales lived in and gazed up towards the second floor. Was he in there now?

There was still the possibility – likelihood? – that Bales had a job. If he had a job, he had workmates. He might be more inclined to get to know workmates.

That was tomorrow morning's task.

He had to find out where Bales worked.

CHAPTER
FIVE

It was just before seven. Pendlebury drained the last half-mouthful of takeaway coffee and stared through his car windscreen at stubborn skies which still showed no inclination to allow the sun to peep through.

He had been there for ten minutes or so. He wanted to be in position in plenty of time. If Bales had a job and if it demanded an early start, he didn't want to blow an opportunity to find out where he worked for the sake of an extra quarter of an hour in bed. That meant forsaking breakfast, but giving up cereal and brown toast with low-fat spread felt less of a hardship than had it been a full English.

Waking up had not been an issue. The thudding and screeching had made sure of that.

He had seen no warning anywhere that the rooftop of his guest house was the traditional meeting place of the All-North Yorkshire Seagull Clog Dancing team. There was no mention in any of the TripAdvisor reviews. He only found out when they launched enthusiastically into vigorous rehearsals just after dawn.

That set off the day on the wrong footing and his mood was

not helped by the pain. His back had been uncomfortable for a couple of weeks, a constant nagging soreness across both sides just below his ribcage. Bad enough to be hard to ignore but not bad enough to bother the doctor with. When he awoke this morning, it was much worse and was radiating throbbing pain into his groin. He must have slept funny in the strange bed. Pinched a nerve or something.

The discomfort was making him shift almost constantly in the car seat as he peered towards the front door of Bales' block on Regents Crescent, willing him to appear. Cursing him for every minute that he didn't.

Another thirty-five minutes passed. Then five more. Still no sign. Pendlebury's already dimmed enthusiasm was waning even more. Maybe Bales didn't have a job. Maybe he was on benefits.

Movement. He had been staring towards the door so intently that he was not sure, at first, if it was opening or if his mind was playing pain-induced tricks. But it was opening and a shambling figure in a dark grey hooded top emerged through it. His head stooped low but Pendlebury could see he wore a full dark beard. Is that him?

Pendlebury grabbed for his binoculars and focused them on the figure who eased the large heavy door shut behind him and set off down the steps so unwillingly that it appeared only momentum was making him put one foot in front of the next.

It was hard to tell if it was him, with the hood and the beard. This man was a similar height and build but Bales had always been peacock proud of his appearance. This figure seemed to have been dragged through a hedge backwards. But then, at the bottom of the steps, the man raised his head to make sure nothing was advancing along the pavement towards him, just long enough to give Pendlebury a full-face view.

Bales. He was sure of it.

Pendlebury sat poised, waiting to see if the figure would head towards one of the cars in the residents' parking spaces. But then he pulled one arm through the strap of the tatty rucksack he held in his hand and hitched it over his shoulder as he set off walking, up the hill.

It looked like there was no car. Pendlebury snatched his keys from the ignition and opened the door. Swinging his lower body around to climb out was agony and putting weight on his right foot felt as if he was stepping on broken glass but he limped as fast as he could in pursuit, not wanting his quarry to get too far ahead.

Thankfully, Bales was in no hurry and the gap between them began to close to a more manageable yet still discreet distance. With every step, the limp became less pronounced, his progress less painful.

They were heading towards the main road where Pendlebury had focused his previous day's futile investigations, walking past the tall brown stone tower of one church and towards the steeple of another. He guessed the inside of neither was familiar to Bales. At the junction, he turned left, away from the main resort centre, and looked to cross the road. Pendlebury had to hang back as Bales checked the traffic and then followed when he had the opportunity.

They walked on for twenty minutes. Pendlebury began struggling to keep up. The pain that had been easing through movement was building again from the exertion. If it was much further, he might have to give up. But then Bales turned off the road and into the yard of one of a group of small industrial premises.

As he caught up, Pendlebury read the sign, which was fixed to the posts of the forbidding black metal fence that guarded the unit, the words bracketed by a drawn pair of wings.

DYER THE FLYER
Speedy Couriers and Van Hire

Beyond the fence was a small one-storey brick building and a taller, blue-painted corrugated metal warehouse. That must be where the vans were dispatched from, he reckoned.

Pendlebury retreated out of view and found a spot opposite from where he could keep watch of comings and goings. If this was where Bales was working, perhaps he was a driver. If he was there as a customer to hire a van, that would scupper his enquiries but, for now, Pendlebury was grateful for the rest. He found a low brick wall and lowered himself wearily down on to it.

Of all the days to get a bad back. He had been hampered three, maybe four, times in the past by back muscle spasms but they felt nothing like this. He leaned forward from his seat on the wall, trying to stretch it out.

Apart from a few cars and vans on their way to and from other units in the cluster of small businesses, it was quiet on the road and Pendlebury settled as best he could in hope that Bales would soon be on the move again. It would make his next move easier if Bales was not on the premises.

The first of the vans, white with the same logo painted on the side that he had seen on the sign, emerged from the warehouse almost ten minutes later. It was three or four minutes more until another set off and then there were two at once. None of them had Bales at the wheel.

But the next one did. Pendlebury dipped his head as low as he could while still being able to peer from the top of his eyes and make out the face of the man in the driving seat. The hood was down this time and that made the job of identification easier. He watched, to be certain, as Bales stopped the van at the fence to glance both ways before pulling out, then he turned his back in hope of avoiding being recognised. The van drew away, back up the road they had walked down a short time ago.

So far, so good. Pendlebury waited a few minutes more before levering himself upright off the wall with a wince and exhale of air.

'Come on, get on with it,' he chastised himself and set off gingerly to cross the road.

———

The door to the brick building was thick and solid, made to deter any after-hours visitors from thinking they might batter it open. Judging by several large dents by the handle, it looked as if some had tried.

Even in its unlocked state, Pendlebury had to put his shoulder to it to force it free of the frame. It was an effort his back could have done without.

'Sorry, door is really stiff. I tell them many times to fix it,' said the woman in her late twenties behind a desk in the corner of the tiny office. She had bleached blonde hair and an eastern European accent.

'Are you here to collect van?'

Pendlebury stepped inside and let the heavy door swing to jam itself closed against the frame.

'No, I'm…' He hesitated. 'Is the boss around?'

'Sure,' she pointed across the office to a closed burgundy door. 'Knock please.'

He lumbered the few steps needed to cover the distance and rapped his knuckles on the door three times.

'Yeah, come in,' called a cheery voice from inside.

Thankfully, this door offered far less resistance.

This second office was even more compact and considerably more cluttered than the other. Space was restricted by a bank of cupboards and cabinets at the far end of the room, though much of the paperwork appeared to have been filed in large teetering piles on top of the cupboards and cabinets. On a tiny, laminated wood desk were more scattered stacks of sheets that looked as if they had been left to gather dust for a while and an aging computer that was badly in need of both a clean and an upgrade.

A squat man with straggly greying hair and glasses perched on the end of his nose pushed himself back in his wheeled chair to prepare to greet his visitor. He was older and at least a foot and a half shorter than Pendlebury, though almost as wide as he was tall.

He smiled enthusiastically as he thrust out a hand to shake.

'Douggie,' he said. 'What can I do you for?'

'Hi, I'm Jim,' Pendlebury replied, taking the hand. 'I'm hoping you might be able to help me find somebody.'

'Oh, aye.' Douggie took a short step backwards, suddenly slightly less unreservedly friendly. The other fella looked a bit like a copper but he hadn't flashed his card like they usually did.

'His name's David Wilson. I've been told he might work here.' Pendlebury reached for the photo and offered it for inspection.

Douggie did not even glance at it.

'What's he done?'

Pendlebury shot a disarming smile, as if realising he might have given the wrong impression.

'No, he's not in any bother – or at least I hope not. I'm family. We had a big row a few years ago and haven't seen or heard from him since but it's important I find him again. His mother's seriously ill, you see. Somebody he used to be big mates with said the last they heard David was working as a van driver for a courier firm in Scarborough and, well, that's why I'm here.'

The shorter man offered nothing back, still unsure.

'Anything you can tell me would be a huge help.'

Douggie snorted and bustled past to open the door. At first, Pendlebury wondered if he was about to be told to leave but the man stopped and called across the main office.

'Iryna, is David Wilson working today?'

'Yes, I see him,' she confirmed, leafing through a small sheaf of yellow slips held together with a bulldog clip. 'He does Newcastle today. He left half hour ago.'

'It looks like you just missed him,' said Douggie. Pendlebury pulled a frustrated face and uttered 'damn' under his breath, then paused, as if considering his next move.

'Look, I wouldn't expect you to let me have his address because you've no idea who I am, but could you give me an idea what time he finishes his shift? I'd like to come back later to meet him as he leaves and tell him, you know.' He tried to appear solemn, pained. 'The news.'

'Right, of course.' Douggie pondered the suggestion. He could see no harm in it. This fella had showed him nothing to suggest he couldn't be taken at face value. David could decide whether he wanted to talk to him or not.

'He should be back here by four. Might be a bit later if there's traffic.'

'Thanks.' Pendlebury didn't intend to be there at the gates later on. He was maintaining his cover story. What he really needed was to find someone he could tap for information.

'Has David worked for you for long?'

Douggie squinted and gazed to the ceiling, as if the answer to that question was written in small lettering upon it.

'Couple of years. Maybe three,' he said. 'He's a good worker. Reliable. Never any bother. Quiet lad. I don't think I've heard him say more than a dozen words in all the time he's been here. He turns up on time, does his job well and then he's off. I wish more of them were like that.'

Pendlebury winced again and this time not because of his back. It had been the same yesterday. Even those he had asked who recognised the man in the photo knew nothing about him.

'Does he socialise with any of his workmates, do you know?'

'Not that I know of,' Douggie replied. 'I couldn't say what he gets up to out of working hours but I can't remember ever seeing him chatting in a group with the others in the depot or walking off-site with them at the end of the shift. As I said, he turns up, does his job and goes home.'

He leaned forward through the partition door again.

'Do you ever manage to get David Wilson chatting, Iryna?'

She responded without looking up from the green file she was leafing through.

'No. Quiet as mouse,' she confirmed, adding: 'Strange man.'

Pendlebury nodded, trying not to appear too disappointed. 'Yes, he always was a bit of an introvert, our David. Anyway,' he added, sticking out his hand for a parting shake. 'I've taken up enough of your time and thank you very much for your help. I'll look to catch him at the end of his shift but I'd be grateful if you don't mention I've been around before I get the chance to talk to him. I don't want to get him worried until I can explain the situation.'

'Right,' said Douggie, gripping the hand.

Pendlebury turned, muttered 'bye' to the busy Iryna without drawing a response and heaved open the main door to leave.

He paused as he started walking towards the gate and turned his head towards the depot building. Maybe there were one or two people about who might know Bales a little better. Not everybody wants to get chatty with the boss. He could be more at ease talking to his fellow workers. It was worth finding out.

Two men in yellow high-vis vests and hard hats carried cardboard boxes from the back of the warehouse, which was partitioned by long clear plastic sheets like a huge vertical blind, to the loading area. A third man was manoeuvring a forklift truck and lifting pallets into the back of a van. The intermittent shrill beep-beep of its reversing warning pierced the enclosed space as he wheeled the forklift around expertly.

Pendlebury considered that he must be breaking a whole volume of health and safety regulations simply by setting foot in the area but he moved on anyway.

'Excuse me,' he called, trying to make himself heard above the noise of the forklift and attract the attention of one of the men carrying boxes.

A wiry man with sharp eyes and smudged tattoos on his neck

set down his box and looked at the advancing figure limping towards him.

'Don't suppose any of you lads know David Wilson, do you?'

The man cocked his head and crossed his arms. 'Who wants to know?' he challenged. 'Are you police?'

'No, not police,' Pendlebury answered. It was not a lie, but it felt a little like a betrayal to reject the suggestion so emphatically. 'I'm family. I'm trying to get hold of David. We haven't been in touch for a while.'

'He's not here,' said the second of the carriers. He held on to his box, exaggerating the thick muscles of his exposed upper arms.

'I know. I've just been to see the boss. He told me David's off at around four but I'm not going to be able to be back here for that time. Do you know which pubs he goes to?'

'I wouldn't know,' said the scrawnier one.

'Who are his mates, then? Is one of them around so I can ask them?'

The two men in high-vis jackets exchanged a glance.

'Don't think he's got any,' said the one still holding the box. 'He never says a word to any of us. Don't think I've ever said anything to him that wasn't to do with work.'

He turned to the forklift driver, who had come to a halt close by, waiting for the next load.

'You know if David Wilson has got a mate?' he asked.

'Who?' said forklift, taking off the ear defenders that had excluded him from the conversation to that point.

'David Wilson. Beard, dark hair. Never talks.'

'Oh, him,' forklift replied. 'The monk. Nah. I don't think anybody even bothers trying anymore. Miserable bastard.'

Pendlebury realised he was getting nowhere here either. It was becoming too familiar a story. He held up his hand and began to back away.

'OK, thanks lads.'

They watched him leave and returned to their tasks.

At the gates, Pendlebury realised he had a long return walk ahead. He did not feel up to it and so decided to call for a taxi, looking up the number of a firm close by on his phone.

The trip had been a waste of time. Again. He had got nowhere.

He felt dispirited and wearied by discomfort in the back of the cab, which seemed to find every pothole, jarring him every few yards. He decided the best thing he could do when he got back to his car would be to stop off at a pharmacy to buy some ibuprofen, or something stronger if he could, then check out of the guest house and drive home. He could think of nothing more he could do here and nothing more he wanted than to return to the soothing comfort of Kate and his own bed.

Having paid the taxi driver and struggled to get out of the cab, he plodded towards his car and swore.

Five large blobs of seagull shit were splattered in a trail on the bonnet and windscreen. Also plastered to the corner of the windscreen was a yellow parking ticket in a plastic covering.

'Fucking great,' he said, tearing off the ticket.

Can this trip get any better?

Then it started to rain.

CHAPTER
SIX

The rain kept falling, steadily, incessantly. Only dog walkers and their oblivious pets would spend time on the broad, sweeping beaches this day. Families in their colourful waterproof jackets, defiantly still in shorts and light canvas shoes, passed the time traipsing miserably around puddles on the promenade or trading a few minutes' relief from the rain for the assault of loud chimes and flashing lights in the amusement arcades.

Jim Pendlebury was back on Regents Crescent, shifting, occasionally, as much as he dare in the driver's seat of his car, trying to block out the constant throbbing pain in his back. The codeine tablets, the strongest painkillers the pharmacist had been prepared to sell him, had hardly touched it.

He was parked on the other side of the flat this time, so that when Bales returned from work he would have to walk past the car.

The small voice of reason in his head told him it was a stupid idea. He should go home. The plan had not worked. He had got nowhere.

But Pendlebury was not in the mood for reason.

He had returned to the guest house to check out and had suffered even greater torment than before in climbing the three flights of stairs. The stabbing hurt in his back took his breath away. As he sat motionless on the edge of the bed, leaning forward with the flat of his hands on his knees, waiting for the tablets to kick in, he began to feel sorry for himself.

Even in the early weeks following the heart op he had not needed to battle self-pity. The pain was an enemy to be defeated. Step by step, he would prevail and beat it. That was how he got through.

The doctors and nurses didn't need to coax him out of his hospital bed to take his first laboured steps on legs as heavy as lead. He had been the one asking them how quickly he could start the long trek back to a normal life.

But this time he felt miserable and broken. The point of this trip had been to prove he was still a good copper. He wanted to show he was still useful. Finding some small scrap of information that might put right a three-year-old injustice would do that.

He had nothing. Bales, as far as he had been able to tell, had taken no new confidants. There was no small point of weakness he had been able to find with which they would be able to exploit and expose him. Nothing.

That made Pendlebury a failure. Useless.

Maybe it was time to forget about the past and concentrate on making the best he could of the future. Embrace being a former DCI. There was no disgrace in that. It is a time that comes to us all.

He contemplated packing his bag and heading home.

Is this how it ends?

Pendlebury had been proud of his reputation in the force. He was the dog with the bone – the one who refused to quit, even when the odds were against him. He never backed away from a challenge. Was he still that same man?

Is this how you want it to end?

Are you really just going to limp home with your tail between your legs?

As he sat on the edge of the bed, Pendlebury raised his chin off his chest and drew a deep breath. He may not have been able to find anyone else who held information useful to his chances of reviving the case but he knew of one person who definitely did. How could he possibly leave without confronting Bales himself?

Sure, he had promised Clare he wouldn't go anywhere near but she didn't have to know. As long as he kept his temper and resisted the temptation to beat a confession out of the bastard, there would be nothing that could rebound on either of them.

What was Bales going to do? File harassment charges? Good luck finding a local officer sympathetic to that one.

So what if it did get physical? It wouldn't be the first time he had used his imposing physique to scare a suspect into submission. He had never laid hands on anyone, even though he often wanted to.

And he badly wanted to get his hands on Bales.

The one good aspect of not being a serving officer anymore was that he was not bound by their rules. Bales would know that too. He knew how much Pendlebury hated him and he would fear for his safety. Even with a bad back, it was a physical mismatch. Would that fear loosen his tongue?

Pendlebury was well aware that even if he did get Bales to admit to what he had done, a confession in circumstances of duress would be of no use legally. It would be inadmissible.

But at least they would know. At least he could tell that to the Morans.

At least he would be letting Bales know he had not got away with it. That he would never get away with it.

Why not? What have you got to lose?

And so Pendlebury sat in his car, staring through a rain-smeared windscreen at the flat of the man who was about to find out there is no hiding place for a murderer. Waiting.

He had already been there a while but he did not mind. He had nothing better to do. Bales wasn't expected back from his deliveries before four o'clock and it was still not yet three. It was better to be in position two hours too early than two seconds too late.

In the old days, he would have got through the best part of a full packet of cigarettes to pass the time and his fingers still twitched for the want of something to occupy them.

He needed a distraction. He decided to call Kate.

'Hey stranger.' Her voice warmed him. He smiled. They had spent far too much time apart when he was working but he had not fully appreciated how used he had become to them sharing the same space since he had retired. Last night had been the first they had spent apart since he got out of hospital. He missed her.

'How's the cricket?'

'Huh! It's been piddling it down all day. No chance of any play.'

Pendlebury had already decided he would confess to Kate about the deception. He could not extend the lie. He would tell her when he got home. She might be a bit miffed at first and would tell him off for refusing to accept he was no longer a police-man, but she would forgive him. She would understand.

'What a pity. Are you coming home then?'

'In a bit. I've just got to head back to the guest house and pick up my stuff.'

He shuffled in his seat and let out a small involuntary yelp as a sharp jab of pain shot the width of his diaphragm.

Kate picked up on it straight away. She was still hypersensitive to any sign of her husband's little twinges, like she still did not trust he was fully well again.

'Are you all right, Jim?'

'My back's been bad.'

He would normally do everything to hide his maladies, even from Kate. Not this time. He was in need of a little sympathy.

'Is it getting worse, then?' There was concern in her voice.

'Yeah,' he admitted. 'I must have slept funny.'

'You're going to have to see somebody about that when you get home.'

There was no point disagreeing. This was seriously uncomfortable.

'I will. I'll make an appointment.'

'OK.' Kate was appeased, for now. She would remind him of his commitment to her first thing in the morning. 'Just drive safely.'

'Don't worry, I'll be fine. I should be back by seven.'

'All right. I'll make you some tea.'

'Great. See you soon, love.'

'Bye, love.'

They hung up. The thought of being home, being cared for, was so appealing. Just this one last thing to do.

It was almost five before he appeared. The grey of his hooded top was darker, soaked, and so were his jeans. He was even more pathetically bedraggled than he had been when he set out in the morning. Pitiful, almost.

As soon as he spotted him, in the side-view mirror, Pendlebury began the difficult process of trying to prise himself out of the car. Bales had passed him before he was on his feet. As fast as he could, gritting his teeth to mask the agony, Pendlebury half-skipped, half-limped to stay within close distance.

Bales, his hands buried in the pouch on the front of his saturated top, sprung up the half-dozen steps to the front door at the prospect of escaping the deluge at last, but stalled on the top step, fumbling in his jeans pocket to retrieve his keys. By the time he had stopped his cold, wet fingers shaking enough to slip the key into the lock, Pendlebury was at the bottom of the steps, praying there would be no need for his man to turn around.

He did not. Bales pushed open the door, withdrew the key and stepped inside, allowing the large, heavy royal blue door to slowly creak itself closed. Pendlebury set off straight away, almost having to haul his failing body up the steps by grabbing handfuls of the stone rail. He reached the top just before the door could click shut and wedged his foot in the gap between it and the frame as he recovered from the added stress of the burst of activity.

Tentatively, he eased it wider open and peered around the corner, in time to see the soles of Bales' training shoes disappearing from view up the stairs to the first floor. Pendlebury opened the door wide enough to slink through and pushed it closed.

The entrance hall was narrow, with chipped, white-painted panelled walls and checker-board tiles on the floor. There was a white door to the lower-ground flat on his right but Pendlebury knew, from the woman he had quizzed on that first morning, that Bales lived on the second floor. He eyed the stairs warily in prospect of the physical challenge ahead before steeling himself and shuffling towards them.

Pendlebury was really struggling by the time he reached the top of the second flight. Why did the people who designed these buildings make the ceilings so high when it meant extra stairs? Each one was an ordeal.

The short distance from his car to the front door had been enough to wet his hair and the shoulders of his jacket and now his forehead was damp with warm sweat. He could also feel it running down the length of his spine. His heart thumped and he gulped in as much air as he could in shallow breaths through his mouth because every expanded lungful only seemed to antagonise the pain in his back even more. It made him feel dizzy.

This is ridiculous. You're like an old codger.

He forced himself to breathe deeply and through his nose, trying, with every exhalation, to compose himself. The second floor flat door he wanted was right in front of him and, behind it, the man he wanted to bring to justice.

Pull yourself together, man. This might be the last shot you get.

He dragged himself to the door and banged on it, heavily.

A few seconds later, there was the click of a lock on the other side and the door opened.

Bales had stripped off his sodden top but the white tee shirt he wore beneath it was no less soaked and clung to his skinny frame, making ripples over his ribs. He held a tatty beige towel in his left hand and his hair, much longer now than he had worn it three years ago, was ruffled from the first efforts to dry it. There were strands of grey around the chin of a beard that had been allowed to grow out to disguise a face that had been so reviled at the time of the trial. But it could not hide him from the man now opposite, who stared deeply, with loathing, into those dark brown eyes.

At first, Bales couldn't put a name to the face he instantly recognised as familiar. It didn't belong in his new surroundings. It was out of context. It didn't take long for his brain to catch up and his eyes widened with the jolt of realisation. By that time, Pendlebury had barged into the room and had slammed the door behind him.

'What the hell are you doing here? Get out of my flat!'

Horror prickled at every nerve in his short, vulnerable body. For almost a year, this was the man who had badgered, bullied and tried to break him. He was relentless, unwavering. No matter how many times he pleaded his innocence, tried to reason with this man to make him see he could not possibly have been the one, he could not get through. He would not listen. He wouldn't even try to see. As far as Pendlebury was concerned, there was only one suspect and, if it was up to him, they might as well throw him in a stinking hole to rot without the need for a trial.

But there had been a trial. And the jury had believed him.

When he heard later the DCI had collapsed and almost died outside the court, he did feel sorry. The man had been one of his chief tormentors in the nightmare that had overwhelmed his life but he didn't deserve to die. However, there was also relief. The one who had so ruthlessly pursued his persecution had been struck down. It was kind of symbolic.

He didn't expect he would ever have to face that man again. But here he was, physically diminished and stripped of his authority, yet even more terrifying, if anything, for this unexpected reappearance. Like the looming ghost of a vanquished enemy.

'Didn't you hear me? Get out!'

Pendlebury thrust his hands deep into his trouser pockets and stepped slowly around the flat, surveying it like a potential buyer. The main room was divided between lounge and kitchen by a waist-high partition. Through the open internal door to his right, he could see the bedroom with the discarded wet top left where it had been dropped on the laminated flooring. The place had been furnished with thrift in mind, rather than style, but it was bright, clean and tidy. Bales' outward appearance and his employment status might be nothing like it was but he had clearly not let everything in his life go to seed.

'We've got things to talk about first,' he said.

Bales did not take his eyes off his old adversary, as if he needed to be braced to fend off a sudden attack.

'There's nothing to say. We said it all three years ago.'

Pendlebury leaned stiffly and picked up a tatty paperback off the arm of the lone two-seat sofa, inspected the cover and tossed it back down onto the seat. He sensed and revelled in the tension coming from the opposite side of the room.

'Well, not quite. We still didn't get to the truth, did we? You still haven't come clean and shown you were man enough to admit to what you did.'

Bales' head drooped. 'You're unbelievable. The judge and the jury found me innocent and still you can't accept you got it wrong. Why can't you just leave me alone? Why didn't your lot put this much energy into finding out who really killed that poor girl? Why can't you get it into your head? I – did – not – kill –

Abie – Moran. You let the real killer get away and you destroyed my life. There's nothing more I want to say to you. Just leave. Please.'

He raised the damp towel with both hands and buried his face in it. He no longer feared a physical assault. How could it possibly be any worse than the mental torture having this man in his home, twisting new barbs into old wounds, was putting him through again?

Pendlebury could hear the muffled sobs. Bales was cracking. He could finish this here if he could just...

No longer under scrutiny, he allowed his mask to slip for a moment as he flexed his aching back. A wide grimace spread across his face before he slipped back into character. He'd done this a million times.

'You know what, I almost feel sorry for you,' he said. ' It can't be easy living with what you've done. I mean, you can give yourself a new identity, change your appearance, move to a new town, but you must have known, deep down, this day would come because you can never outrun your past. Does that wake you up at night? Does the thought even let you get to sleep at all? I ask because I've come across some real nut jobs in my career. Proper cold-hearted bastards. The type who could take a life as casually as throwing away an old pair of socks and it never bothers them. How can that be? It's like they're not even human. But you're not like that. I bet it really haunts you, knowing what you did. You lured, abused and murdered a young woman. She was eighteen. Had her whole life ahead of her. You were one of the people her parents trusted to prepare her for the journey ahead but you took advantage of that trust, didn't you? You ended that life. How can you live with yourself?'

He took a few short steps and laid his hands on his lower back, letting out a long, silent breath.

'How do you think the other people in this new life of yours would feel if they knew the truth? What about the young woman with the little boy in the flat downstairs? What do you think she would say if she knew what kind of monster was living in the same building?'

He paused again. He knew the words were getting through.

'Don't you think you would be making life so much easier for yourself if you just came clean? Face up to it. There would be no more hiding, no more running. You could come with me right now to the local station and put the record straight, or you could write it all down and take matters into your own hands. It makes no difference to me. But you need to end this, David. Face your responsibilities. Do the right thing. No more hiding. Come on, do us all a favour.'

A convulsive shot of pain almost made him cry out loud but he caught the sound in his throat.

'It's over, David. Just tell me now what really happened. Let me…'

He took his phone out of his jacket pocket, getting ready to record the confession that would surely follow. But the screen was a swimming blur. His fingers were too big, too cumbersome, to make it work.

Pendlebury turned his back and ran his hand over his forehead. It was wet with the sweat which was trickling over his temples and into the corner of his eyes, yet his hand was cold as he wiped it away. Mounting nausea was rumbling in his guts and he had to swallow rapidly to keep down the excess of saliva filling his mouth. The sound of his rapid heartbeat drummed in his ears.

This is not good. His thoughts began to turn from confrontation to exit strategy – trying to get out of there before his dignity was stripped away.

Christ! Of all the times…

'Just tell the truth for once and you… I have to go but… Can't hide forever… Give the parents the…'

Bales noticed the change. He peeped from behind the towel with watery eyes as his large tormentor tried to step towards the door but stumbled, almost tripping over his own feet. He stopped and held his arms to his side, swaying like the floor had turned into moving, undulating mass.

'Are you all right?'

Pendlebury was panicking. *Must get out of here.*

'Yeah, I'm...'

A searing thrust, like a jagged blade being dragged deep across his abdomen, made Pendlebury yell and he doubled up, clutching his arms across his middle as if to stop his guts from spilling out. A low, long anguished moan tore from deep within and he slumped to his knees. As he collapsed forward on to all fours, a surge of vomit poured from his mouth and spread in a pool across the laminated flooring.

'Shit! I'm calling an ambulance.'

Bales glanced frantically from side to side, trying to recall where he had put his phone. The bedroom. He shot towards the open door, having to sidestep the stricken, ailing figure in his way.

Pendlebury did not hear what was said, did not notice the man moving past him. His arms could no longer support him and he fell with a thud, lying face down in a puddle of his own bile.

Each gasping breath became shorter and shorter. He was drowning from the inside.

CHAPTER
SEVEN

It had been well over an hour now. David Bales leaned forward in the plastic bucket seat with his elbows on the table in front of him and sighed again. Why was it taking so long?

He knew the game they were playing. He had been here before.

Make them sweat. Show them to a pokey interview room where there is nothing to look at, never mind do, and leave them there, alone, for as long as you like. Let them think about what they are about to face without distraction and let the magnitude of their situation build higher and higher in their panicked minds. Leave them until the stark grey walls of the room start closing in, squeezing the air out of their chests as their anxiety grows. Leave them until the occasional click and flicker in the stark strip lighting above their heads goes from being barely noticeable to becoming the one thing in the room they cannot ignore. Soften them up. Get them so they will tell you exactly what you want them to.

It was a crude game and Bales had no reason to let it get to him. He had done nothing wrong. That was not enough to make him immune to it. Just being there brought back too many memories. Memories of a nightmare he thought he would not survive.

He knew he had done wrong that time, but he had not done what they accused him of.

Because he had nothing to hide this time, he had agreed to the police officer's request to go with her to the station to answer a few questions. Tell them exactly what happened.

The first person to come to see him in the interview room was an Inspector. He was a grim-faced man with skin the colour of mahogany and forearms as thick as roasted hams straining the edges of his short-sleeved white uniform shirt. He had seen no cause to disguise his hostility. Clearly, he had been briefed – who the casualty was, who the witness was and the nature of their relationship. If it could be called a relationship. Everyone who had talked to Bales about it in the last couple of hours had drawn their conclusions, taken their sides. The Inspector was clearly no different.

He kept it formal. Not even the faintest attempt to put the witness at ease. He read the caution like it was the thousandth time that day he had been asked to say those words and it was starting to really annoy him. He reminded Bales he was not under arrest and that he was free to leave at any time, delivering the words with a deep, challenging glare that added the caveat: 'But don't you fucking dare or we'll soon find a way to make you stay.'

He also pointed out the most important part.

You have the right to free and independent legal advice.

Yes. I would like to have a solicitor present. No, I haven't got my own. I can't afford one. Yes, I would like you to contact the duty solicitor.

I haven't done anything wrong, but I've been here before. I don't trust any of you anymore.

That was where the first part of the interview ended. The Inspector turned off the recording machine and left the room. That was well over an hour ago. Nobody had been in since, not to offer a cup of tea or a bottle of water or anything. Perhaps that was too much to expect.

Bales sighed again and flicked his fingernail at a small fragment of paper he spotted on the edge of the desk. It was the closest he had been to a welcome distraction for well over an hour.

———

The ambulance had arrived pretty quickly but they were too late. Pendlebury was slumped flat out and had stopped breathing in the short time it took to make the emergency call. Bales pressed his first two fingers into the former DCI's neck to check for a pulse but could not find one.

Oh, shit! he thought. *This is not going to look good.*

The paramedics summoned the police as soon as they realised the situation was beyond their influence. A single uniformed officer turned up about a quarter of an hour later. Bales stood in the corner of his small kitchen, taking it all in, like he was watching the opening scenes of a play. Waiting for the cue to take his part in the drama.

He watched the policewoman talk first to the two paramedics, who were already packed and waiting to see if they would be told they could move the body. He could hear their conversation but he was not really listening, so wrapped in himself and what may be about to come his way that he felt detached from it all. The younger of the paramedics gestured towards him and the officer turned, noticing him for the first time. She walked to him.

'Hello, sir. I understand you are the owner of this flat.'

Her tone was gentle at this time, her eyes sympathetic.

'I rent it, but yes.' His mouth was dry and he had to clear his throat.

She flipped to a new page in her notepad.

'Could I ask your name please, sir?'

'David Wilson.' His reply was truthful. He was going to cling to the mask of his new identity for as long as he could.

'And do you know this gentleman, Mr Wilson?' she asked with a flick of her head towards the only dead body in the room.

'I do. His name is Jim Pendlebury.'

'Is Mr Pendlebury a relative?'

'No.'

'Friend?'

'Not exactly.'

She looked up from her pad. He was hard work but she remained patient. He must have been through a very unpleasant experience.

'Could you tell me, then, what your connection to Mr Pendlebury was and what he was doing in your flat?'

They were straying into awkward territory now. There was no escape.

He tried to clear his throat again.

'Do you mind if I get myself a glass of water?'

'Of course not.'

'Do you want one?'

'No thanks.'

He rinsed a glass that was standing on the draining board and filled it almost to the top, swallowing most of the contents in long gulps. He was buying time as much as trying to ease the dryness of his mouth but he knew he could only put it off for a short while.

'Mr Pendlebury was a senior police officer. Former police officer. Retired now, I suppose. Detective Chief Inspector. We knew each other from a few years ago in Sheffield. He was the officer in charge and I was the…' He hesitated. 'Suspect.'

The policewoman stopped writing and stared at Bales, taking in the information. He could not return the eye contact and shuffled uncomfortably.

'I see,' she said. 'So if Mr Pendlebury was a retired DCI, what was he doing here? I presume it wasn't a social call.'

'Ha!' The half-laugh exploded nervously from him much louder than he expected and he blushed. 'I have no idea why he came here. I'd just got home from work. I was drying off because it had been raining. I opened the door and there he was. Believe me, he was about the last person I expected to see. Before I knew it, he'd pushed past me and was in my flat. I don't know why he came. I guess he's the only person who could tell you that and…'

He glanced again towards the lifeless prone body. There was no purpose in finishing the sentence.

'So you didn't expect him to call in on you?'

'Not at all.'

'And he came in uninvited?'

'Yes.'

She wrote down the responses.

'What happened then?'

Bales drew up his hands and rubbed his eyes.

'I told him I wanted him to leave but he said he wanted to talk to me. He started haranguing me. Telling me I should confess to the crime he accused me of four years ago, even though I didn't do it and the jury found me not guilty. He wouldn't let go. Kept going on and on. He was obsessed.'

Bales was pleading. He was desperate for someone to believe him.

'What was it you were accused of?'

This is it. No going back. Bales lifted his eyes to the heavens before his head slumped forward as he said the word.

'Murder.'

'Murder?'

The policewoman was momentarily startled. Her mind then whirred into action, sifting through dormant memories to make everything fall into place.

'DCI Pendlebury was the officer in charge of the Abie Moran murder, wasn't he?'

He did not answer. Did not even move.

'So if you're… But it wasn't David *Wilson* then, was it? It was…'

He sighed. 'Bales.'

'Bales!' she repeated, as if finding the last piece for the puzzle. 'Bales!' She wrote it down with a flourish.

There was a short, awkward silence before she remembered there was still plenty about this strange reunion she did not understand.

'So he burst into your flat, uninvited, and wanted you to confess to a murder you were found not guilty of and then what? Did that make you angry? Was there a fight? Was that how DCI Pendlebury died?'

Bales shook his head.

'Fight him? Have you seen the size of him? Why the hell would I want to pick a fight with him?'

The policewoman stared back impassively.

'I didn't go anywhere near him. He was over on that side of the lounge, close to the bedroom door, and I was over here, just by the partition. I wasn't even looking at him. I was holding a towel to my face. Trying to blank him out, I suppose. I couldn't believe what was happening. You've no idea what I've been through all these years. I only knew something was wrong when I heard his voice change. It was like he had suddenly got all confused and I looked up and he was swaying, like he was about to keel over. There was this look in his eyes as if something really dreadful was happening to him. I asked him if he was OK and he grabbed hold of his guts like there was a sudden intense pain, fell forward on all fours and puked all over the floor. I went into the bedroom for my phone to call the ambulance and when I got back to him he was…'

The officer scribbled notes furiously but said nothing.

'I really have no idea why or how he tracked me down to here.

The last I saw him was in Sheffield Crown Court on the day they declared me not guilty and the last I heard of him was that he had a massive heart attack outside the court. I don't know if that had anything to do with what killed him.'

There was too much about this that was unexplained. It was complicated. The officer realised she would need to call in a superior to make any further judgement but she did know she could not simply release this key witness without taking him in to the station to give a formal statement. Preferably straight away.

Could he have had something directly to do with this sudden death? This might not be natural causes. He had been suspected of murder before, after all.

'I'll need you to come with me to the station, if you wouldn't mind, Mr Wilson. I need you to give us a statement. You're not under arrest but I'd strongly suggest it's in your best interests to come with me voluntarily and go through everything you've just told me again, under caution this time.'

He agreed, reluctantly.

———

The door to the interview room opened and in walked the same surly Inspector, this time with a skinny woman of South Asian heritage bustling in his wake. She clutched a faded red folder to her chest with one arm and balanced a brown leather messenger bag on the shoulder of the other.

Bales watched her as she quickly familiarised herself with the room, like they were strange surroundings.

This can't be the duty solicitor, surely? She looks like one of my A Level students.

The Inspector took up his seat on the opposite side of the desk without a word. No attempt at explaining or excusing the delay.

The woman eagerly reached out her spare hand, trying not to allow the bag to slip off her shoulder.

'Hi, I'm Parveen Razaq. I'm the duty solicitor.'

Bales took the hand and shook it with a half-smile. 'David.'

'Would you like some time to consult with your brief or can we just get on with this?' asked the Inspector, wearily.

'I'm happy to just get this over with,' said Bales, looking to his solicitor as she laid the file on the desk and slid into the seat beside him. She smiled her consent.

'Good.'

The Inspector switched on the recording machine.

'Interview resumed at…' he screwed up his eyes as he checked the clock on the wall to his left, '… eighteen forty-eight with Inspector Clive Evitts present, as is…'

He prompted the solicitor to speak with a nod.

'Parveen Razaq of Paulsen and Brown Solicitors.'

'And…' he looked towards Bales.

'David Wilson.' He and the policeman had an exchange about which surname he should use for the recording when they first spoke. Bales decided he should take a stand. It was his legal name now.

Inspector Evitts rolled his eyes this time but said no more.

'Mr Wilson, I'll remind you that you agreed willingly to attend to provide a statement under caution regarding an incident at a flat rented by you on Regents Crescent in Scarborough earlier today. You have been made aware of your rights regarding the terms of your attendance. Do you agree to proceed with the interview?'

'I do.'

'In that case, could you state, in your own words, the events of this afternoon that led to the sudden death of former Detective Chief Inspector Jim Pendlebury in your flat. From the beginning.'

Bales went through it all again. In the hour or so he had been left alone in the interview room he had at least found plenty of time to establish exactly what he wanted to say.

The Inspector surveyed him with a fixed scowl throughout,

showing every indication that he did not believe a word of the account. When Bales had finished, he allowed his contempt to hang in the silence for a moment before he replied.

'Did you assault former DCI Pendlebury?'

'No!' The suggestion was still ridiculous to Bales' mind.

'Did you give former DCI Pendlebury anything to eat or drink during his time in your flat?'

'What?'

'I said, did you...'

'I heard what you said, I just... No, I didn't give him anything to eat or drink. I wasn't feeling very hospitable.'

'I find it hard to believe that former DCI Pendlebury would just turn up at your flat, out of the blue, to try to get you to confess to an unsolved crime.'

'So do I, as it happens.' At last, they saw eye to eye on something.

'It seems more likely to me that you lured him to your flat under a false pretext. With the intention of taking your revenge against the man who led the prosecution against you, perhaps.'

'That's a ludicrous thing to say. I've spent the last three years trying to get away from all that. Trying to build a new life for myself, away from people who refuse to believe I was innocent of killing that poor young woman, even though the jury found in my favour. Why on earth would I want to stir up all that shit again through some sort of bizarre showdown with an old ex-copper? It makes no sense. You've got my statement. I have no idea what drove him to seek me out and confront me like that. I have no idea what caused him to collapse and die on my lounge floor. And I definitely didn't rustle up a cup of tea and a few nibbles for him when he barged his way into my flat. Are we finished now?'

Bales wanted to get out of there. The small amount of good will he had invested in his voluntary trip to the police station had long since been exhausted.

Inspector Evitts glared back at him.

'For now,' he said. 'Interview terminated at nineteen thirty-two.' He clicked off the recorder and picked it up to take with him. He paused, towering over the two seated figures.

'There will be a post-mortem examination to establish the cause of former DCI Pendlebury's death within the next forty-eight hours. Don't go anywhere. If we have even the slightest cause to believe his death was suspicious and that you had something to do with it, I'll be on you like a ton of bricks. Do you hear me?'

Bales did not respond. He was trying not to show how scared he was. This whole experience was just too, too familiar.

The policeman left the room, though the weight of his warning hung in the air after he had gone. Parveen broke the lingering quiet by opening the red folder and taking out some sheets of paper.

'I have a few things for you to sign please, David, and I need you to give me your contact number. I'll make some calls to find out the results of the PM as soon as they're known and give you a ring to let you know. Hopefully, that'll be the end of it and the police won't have anything to charge you with.'

She offered him a cheap black pen. He took it from her.

'Hopefully,' he said.

CHAPTER
EIGHT

The young solicitor offered him a lift home and he gratefully accepted it. Between a mix-up over delivery notes at his first drop-off, a forty-minute delay due to an accident on the A171 and the sudden death of an old adversary on the lounge floor of his flat, it had been a long day.

Bales saw none of the other residents as he made his way up the two flights of stairs and was grateful for that, too. No more awkward questions.

The flat had been locked after the last of the people called to the scene had finished what they had to do and it was empty now. No dead bodies, though as he stared at the spot where Jim Pendlebury had taken his last breath, in his mind he could still clearly see the large form of the former policeman lying there. His head turned to the right. His unseeing eyes still boring fresh holes in Bales' brittle self-worth.

Before they left, someone had mopped up the worst of the pool of vomit that Pendlebury's head had come to rest in but the shape of the mess was still clearly visible on the floor. Bales rallied himself, resolving to make cleaning that up properly his first task,

and ran a sinkful of hot water, adding a long measure of disin-
fectant.

As he scrubbed at the stain with an old tea towel, he began to
reflect way beyond the misfortunes of this one day. His life had
turned to shit, but it had not always been that way.

It changed one summer day four years earlier, when Abie
Moran arrived at his front door.

————

The final week of summer term was always an odd time. The last
exams had been taken and both we, the tutors, and the students
basked in the huge relief of that. You could feel the stress knots
created by long months of pressured preparation slowly unravel.
All anyone wanted then was for the long six-week holiday to
begin. No student had the slightest appetite for learning new stuff,
which was just as well because none of us had the slightest
appetite for teaching them.

I loved my job. I loved the opportunity to help shape young
lives. I loved encouraging willing pupils of all abilities to make the
most of their aptitude for maths. I even enjoyed the challenge of
coaxing the unwilling to see the value of the subject and apply it
to whatever they wanted to do in the future.

Don't get me wrong. Those six weeks of not having to deal
with the many and varied problems of a disparate mass of eleven-
to-eighteen-year-olds on a daily basis was bliss, but, during term
times, I loved being in the company of young people. I thrived on
their energy.

Yes, if I'm being honest, I also liked being the subject of the
occasional teenage crush. It was good for the ego and my ego,
back then, was a beast that liked to be regularly fed. I wouldn't
encourage young girls to make me the object of their impression-
able desires, but I was aware of the effect I had on some and,
looking back, I didn't exactly discourage them either. I didn't flirt

with them – that would have been utterly irresponsible – but I did indulge them. I'm sure other members of staff didn't like that I appeared to welcome the attention but I didn't care. I was in control and, as I said, I had an ego to feed.

It was all part of growing up, as far as I was concerned. I had the occasional teenage sexual fantasy over some of the more fanciable female teachers when I was at school and I didn't see the harm in that. It's natural. I knew I would never go too far.

I *thought* I would never go too far.

That day was gloriously hot. Tuesday, July the eighteenth. I think that date will be burned into my brain forever.

I had a free afternoon, so I decided I would spend that time at home, rather than slumming around the staff room and taking the risk of being roped into extra duties. The deputy head didn't seem to like seeing staff do nothing. I lived an eight-minute walk from the Brincliffe Edge Academy and so, if summoned, I could easily get back without my absence being noticed.

I made myself a sandwich and opened a cold beer out of the fridge. I took them through to the lounge but it was stuffy in there, so I opened a couple of windows and the patio doors of the conservatory, which led off the lounge, to allow a bit of air to blow through.

It felt really good to loosen the tie, kick off the shoes and stretch out on the sofa with my feet up, enjoying a bit of lunch with a beer and feeling wisps of cooling breeze begin to circulate. No kids, no Gemma, no school politics. No hassle. It was wonderful.

Then the front door bell rang. The spell was broken. I thought about ignoring it. I wish I had.

Whoever I thought it might be – delivery man, neighbour, Jehovah's Witnesses, whatever – I didn't expect it to be Abie Moran. I had no idea she knew where I lived, for a start. I was a bit gobsmacked when I saw her there, to be honest. She was a beautiful young woman, there's no denying that, and a more than capable student, but I'd always thought of her as a bit distant. Maybe that's harsh. She was never unfriendly, but she certainly never had to make an effort to attract her peers. They gravitated to her. If you had no reason to put yourself in Abie's orbit, then you would have little to do with her. As a student, she was very low maintenance. I taught her two years of A Level maths and I don't think I said a word to her outside the classroom.

Her popularity was only partly because she was so physically attractive. She was simply a nice person. She had a way of putting people at ease and never, it appeared to me, gave the impression she thought she was better than them. I guess there must have been a bit of jealousy among her peers because girls that age are very conscious of their outward appearance, giving far too much credence to any slight flaw, and Abie didn't seem to have any. If there was jealousy, she didn't deserve it. Those who liked Abie far outnumbered the petty few who found cause to dislike her.

It was quite amusing watching the boys trying to win her favour. They were like puppies slobbering over a tasty treat that always seemed just beyond the range of how far their leashes would allow them to go. As far as I was aware, she hadn't been out with any of them, though I'm sure she wasn't short of offers. I always kind of assumed she had a boyfriend who didn't go to the Academy. Someone a year or two older, perhaps, but I didn't know. I was never especially interested in teenage relationship intrigue. It always struck me as a particularly complicated business.

Let me say one thing now and you can choose to believe it or not but it's the truth. I never – hand on heart – harboured sexual desires towards Abie, or any of the other students, for that matter. I knew there was a line that should not be crossed. I was old enough to be their father, for Christ's sake. Being the object of young girl crushes was one thing but exploiting them was quite another and I believed I would never do that. I considered it the ultimate betrayal of my profession and yes, I am aware of how that sounds coming from me now.

Abie was just another of my students and, with the exams over, I had no reason to believe I would ever see her again.

And yet there she was. At my door.

She was wearing pink denim shorts and a plain white crop top that rode up just high enough to expose her belly button. Her long, blonde hair fell over her shoulders and she stood there, her head slightly cocked, with her hands behind her back.

'Abie,' I said. I was a little startled. 'What are you doing here?'

She flashed a smile and her blue eyes gave a twinkle as she pulled her hands from behind her back to present a small tub of chocolates. Celebrations, I think they were.

'I brought you these. To thank you for all your help getting ready for the exams.'

I hadn't spent any extra time working with Abie that I could recall. I hadn't needed to. I would have put a fair amount of money on her heading to Uni with straight A-stars across the board.

'That's very kind of you,' I said, accepting the gift. It was not unusual to receive such tokens from students at the end of the school year, provided by parents mostly, but they were not usually delivered to your door.

'You're welcome,' she replied and smiled again.

I didn't know what to say and Abie was showing no sign of being about to leave. What I did say next was about the last thing I should've.

'Would you like to come in for a drink? I've got water, Coke?'

'Thanks,' she said and I opened the door wider to beckon her in. It was wrong and, even at the time, I knew it was wrong but my intentions were entirely innocent. It was unquestionably stupid, though. I've contemplated over and over ever since why I made that choice. I can say that in my head I was not thinking anything other than repaying a small kindness with a small kindness but I'm not certain my head was in full control of my thought processes, to be honest. Though I did have other opportunities to haul myself back from the brink shortly after – opportunities I really should have taken – I regard that offer of a drink, inviting her into my home, as the crucial moment I lost the chance to save myself from everything that followed. Stupid.

'See yourself through to the lounge, it's nice and cool in there,' I said. I watched her as she walked through, ahead of me, as I lingered by the door to the kitchen, guiltily noticing her pert bottom in those shorts.

'What would you like, then? To drink.'

'Water would be great,' she called back, without turning.

I put the chocolates down on the work surface and opened the fridge to get a bottle. As the light came on and the fridge buzzed to retain its temperature, I had what was probably my last moment of clarity that day.

'Shit, David, what the fuck are you doing?' I said, under my breath. I told myself I was going to have to get her out of the house as soon as I could. I had lit a match and then realised I was surrounded by powder kegs.

But I couldn't be discourteous and throw her out straight away. I had asked her if she wanted a drink. It was a hot day. I grabbed the bottle of water.

When I stepped into the lounge Abie was on the sofa, resting against the arm with her tanned legs curled up on the seat like it was the most normal thing in the world for her to be there. She was taking a swig from my beer. It was not a stolen swig, like I wasn't meant to have caught her. She kept hold of the bottle. I put the water down on the table and stood opposite her, using the table as a buffer.

'So, how do you think you did in the exams?' I was trying to maintain the distance in every way.

'OK, I think. The maths papers weren't hard.'

'Even the quadratic equations question in paper one?'

She pulled a face like she didn't want to say it was easy because that might make her appear arrogant and took another swig of beer.

'I interrupted you having your lunch,' she added, diverting her eye to my half-eaten sandwich. 'Don't let me stop you.'

'That's OK,' I replied. 'I wasn't really hungry.'

My appetite had waned. My appetite for food, anyway. I stood there, feeling out of place in my own front room, and tried not to allow my eyes to linger on her too long. Tried not to think about her, sitting on my sofa. Drinking my beer. Then I did another stupid thing. I sat down beside her.

I stayed to the far end of the sofa, which was big enough for three, comfortably, but I should've either sat on the other sofa or stayed standing. I knew I was playing a dangerous game. I couldn't stop myself.

I asked her about what she was planning to do after A Levels and which med school was her number one choice and I burbled on about how living in Edinburgh was expensive but how it was such an exciting city for a young person to live in. I was trying to stay afloat but all the time I was swirling round and round, being drawn deeper and deeper into the whirlpool. I was losing my grip. She was intoxicating. So beautiful, so desirable. I was too weak to stop myself being drawn to her, too arrogant to believe I was not horribly misjudging the situation. She had not come to my home to give me chocolates. She knew what she was doing – the spell she was casting. I wanted her, even though I was still conscious of every single reason why I shouldn't. My head was telling me I should step away. Invent a reason why she had to leave right now. Don't do this.

But, as I said, my head wasn't in full control.

'I'm sorry but I've finished your beer,' she said, shaking the bottle gently from side to side.

'No worries. I'll get you another, if you'd like.'

I shuffled across the sofa. Closer. Too close. I reached out and took hold of the bottle neck, wrapping my fingers around hers. She did not recoil. Did not let go of the bottle. She stared into my eyes and I knew. I knew she was aware of where we were heading. Her lips parted with a small, barely discernible gasp and I knew she was ready. I moved even closer until we could feel each other's breath on our faces and the connection of our eyes tingled in the charged air around us. I kissed her.

There was no way back then. The relationship as tutor and student, right and wrong, society's trust in me, my supposed morals, the career I was running the risk of throwing away – none of that mattered. None of it.

We undressed each other slowly, tenderly, and we made love. It was beautiful. It was so right.

What do you want me to say? It was totally reckless. It was completely, ethically and morally, wrong. I was a fool. I was thinking with my balls and not my brains. I was risking everything for the sake of a shag. I was making a pathetic attempt to recapture my lost youth by seducing a young woman who was half my age. Say what you like and you'd probably be correct on all counts.

It was the greatest mistake of my life. It ruined me. Worse still, it led to the cruel murder of a beautiful, intelligent young woman who possessed the rare quality of enhancing the lives of everyone she met. That was the real tragedy and I've never lost sight of that.

But if you had asked me then if I regretted what I did, I would have told you not one bit. If it was possible to contemplate a different outcome to that afternoon – one where we both got dressed, kissed for one last time and then parted, maybe forever, would I have regretted it later? That's impossible to tell. I suspect not.

Afterwards, as she lay in my arms, her head on my chest, we said nothing. I'm not going to come out with some crap about wishing the moment could last forever or that I could see us spending the rest of our lives together. I knew it would be a one-off. For whatever reason, she wanted me and I wanted her too. We shared something special but fleeting. She was on her way to med school and I would carry on teaching. That was always the way it was going to be, but we would have both remembered that one special afternoon. I knew that was the way it was going to be and it was enough. I didn't feel bad about it, as I suppose I should. It happened and it felt good.

Her head become heavier against me as she drifted to sleep and I started dozing too, but I was jolted awake again by the ring of my phone vibrating on the table. I stretched to reach it. It was Paul, just about my closest friend at the Academy. He taught maths as well.

Shit, Paul, I thought. *It's a good job this isn't on Facetime.* That would have freaked him out.

'Hey,' I said, quietly so as not to disturb Abie.

'David, where the fuck are you?' He was agitated, angry.

'I'm at home. Why?'

'I've fucked up, man. Seriously fucked up.'

CHAPTER
NINE

I t was obvious he needed to talk and I knew I would be letting him down if I tried to put him off. It was also almost certainly not a conversation I should risk Abie overhearing.

'Hang on a sec.'

I put the call on mute and started to slide from beneath Abie's drowsy embrace.

'I'm sorry, I have to take this,' I said and she consented with a low murmur without opening her eyes. I grabbed a large cushion to place under her head and she nuzzled into it. She looked so gorgeous in her unashamed nakedness. So innocent.

I closed the lounge door behind me and stepped into the kitchen to retrieve the call, lowering the blinds to make sure I could not be seen from outside.

'Paul,' I said. 'What's wrong?'

There was a pause and, for a second, I thought he was no longer there.

'I'm in trouble, man. Shit, I could be out for this.'

He was not a guy given to emotional overreaction, so I was

concerned. If Paul was in pieces like this, it must be something serious.

'Just take a breath, mate, and calm down. Tell me what's happened.'

'Fucking Liam Glover, that's what.'

Liam was well known to the staff at Brincliffe Edge Academy. He was trouble. Not a bully, as such, but often disruptive, always treading a fine line between regular suspension and expulsion. He had a complicated home life and that bought him a certain amount of sympathy, but when he officially left at the end of Year Eleven a couple of weeks earlier, no one was sorry to see the back of him.

'What about him? I thought he'd left.'

'He came back this afternoon. I think he must have got bored and just fancied smashing some stuff, for old time's sake. I saw him in one of the empty classrooms, looking around for something to nick or break, and I confronted him. It got out of hand. Fuck, I lost it.'

My heart sank for Paul. Little bastards like Liam Glover knew which buttons to press and would push you to the limit, emboldened by the knowledge there was practically nothing you could do to stop them. You could threaten to exclude him for one week, two weeks, however long you like, and he wouldn't care. He'd come back and be no better anyway. The one thing you couldn't do with kids like Liam Glover was lose it. Any escalation of the situation on the teacher's part and you were in trouble, no matter what the provocation.

'Oh, mate. What did you do?'

'He was giving it all the "what's it to you, you can't stop me, I've left this shithole now, I can do what I like" and I tried to stay calm, telling him to get off the campus. I threatened him with the police and he just laughed. Then he got personal. Really personal. And I went for him.'

Paul was quiet again. I left him to gather his thoughts.

'I got him by the throat against the wall and I wanted to punch him – but I didn't. He was properly choking because I'd really got a grip on him, but it must have only lasted ten seconds, twelve, fifteen at most, until I realised I'd made a big mistake. I let him go and he must've seen the panic in my eyes because he started acting like he knew what I was thinking. He's saying "Oh, you've really blown it now, haven't you? It's me who's going to the police. I'm going to get you sacked for this". I was yelling at him to get off the campus and he left then, but he's right. I'm going to get sacked for this. He could have me in court.'

There was nothing I could say to put him at ease. We both knew there could be serious implications for Paul. We both knew he had gone too far, but I was hardly in a position to judge him right at that moment, was I? All I could do was to listen, try to calm him down and try to get him to think logically about what his options were, who he should inform. That's all I could think to do.

He did start to come down from off the roof, though he still went over and over what had happened, racked by regret and tormenting himself with the ramifications he was certain were going to come crashing down on him. I just had to let him get it all out.

There was a noise at the front door.

It was a key turning in the lock.

That could only be one person.

'Paul, mate, I'm going to have to go. Gemma's here. I've got to go.'

'OK, OK. That's fine. Thanks. See ya.'

He hung up and I turned to see Gemma in the door frame, poised to put her keys back in her handbag but frozen mid-act as she looked me up and down.

I tried to appear casual. As casual as it was possible to be when your wife has come home unexpectedly and you're in the kitchen with no clothes on and there's a naked teenager in the next room.

'What's going on?' she asked.

'Hey,' I said. 'You're early.'

'What the fuck are you up to?' The initial surprise was obviously wearing off and the cogs were beginning to turn. Let me say, at this point, that Gemma and I did not have a rock-solid marriage. There had certainly been others as far as I was concerned and I'm pretty sure there had been for her, too. We hadn't been on good terms for a while but we co-existed on an unspoken mutual understanding that neither of us would look too closely into the personal life of the other. It was a sham existence, really, because we should have had the courage to split up years earlier. Carrying on this way had become too convenient.

'I was just about to have a shower and my phone rang.' I held up my phone as mitigation.

She wasn't going to swallow that. I was doing all I could to stall. I was hoping the sound of voices would wake Abie and that I could buy her enough time to get her clothes and slip out of the back, through the conservatory.

'Where is she?' Gemma had leapt through all the possibilities to what she considered to be the most likely.

'What? There's nobody else here. I told you, I was just about to _'

'Don't bullshit me. I know you too well.'

She stomped off to begin the search. I hoped she would at least head up the stairs to check out the bedrooms first – allow precious seconds more for Abie to make her escape – but she went straight past the stairs and flung open the lounge door.

I saw her come to an abrupt halt a couple of steps into the room and there was a second or two of silence like she was frozen in time. Then all hell broke loose.

I expected shouting. I expected a lot of swearing. I expected violence. I didn't expect the screaming.

Ear-piercing, blood-chilling, heart-stopping screaming, coming from the depths of her soul and almost shaking the house to its foundations. I have never heard a sound like that and I hope to Christ I never do again.

She grabbed handfuls of her dark brown hair as she screamed, screamed, screamed before turning and practically sprinting out of the room, bulldozing into me like I wasn't even there as she tore down the narrow hallway and frantically pulled at the front door to get out. Her eyes – her whole shockingly anguished face – were wild, hysterical. She was terrified. I was terrified seeing her.

I heard her running out into the street yelling: 'Oh, God, help me! Help me!'

I didn't know what to think. I knew that extreme a reaction could not only be because Abie had not managed to get out of the room in time. I was scared to find out but I knew I must. I edged, tentatively, towards the lounge door, my hands out in front of me to protect me from – well, hell knows what I was expecting to have to protect myself from. I hesitated at the door. I couldn't bear to move. I had to will my legs to shuffle me on and finally I did.

I stepped into my nightmare.

According to the timing of the chain of events put forward later by the police, I was on the phone to Paul for twelve minutes and thirty-eight seconds. They took that from the call records. Working by the accounts Gemma and I gave in our statements of what happened after she arrived home, they estimated a gap of around thirteen-and-a-half to fourteen minutes between my answering the phone and Gemma discovering the body.

Thirteen-and-a-half to fourteen minutes. How can that be?

When I left Abie, she was curled on the sofa, serenely asleep. So beautiful. So exquisite.

When I stepped back into the room, her head was tipped limply back, her long hair almost touching the floor, as if she had been dragged backwards, far enough for her shoulders to be beyond the sofa arm. Her right arm was also hanging lifelessly over the edge. I could see her face. Her eyes were wide and her mouth open but her expression was still sort of peaceful, I would say. The room held a strange tranquil grace. Nothing like you would expect from the scene of a brutal murder. Only the ugly red marks around her throat gave away the savagery of what had just happened.

I guess that might have been part of the reason why I was surprisingly calm. It was almost as if I was a visitor to a gallery, studying a great tragic painting like *The Death of Chatterton*. It was like you would imagine an out-of-body experience to feel. Other-worldly, you could say. I just remember being overwhelmed by a profoundly deep sadness. Numbness.

How could such a thing have happened in thirteen-and-a-half to fourteen minutes when I was so close by? I was in the next room. Who on earth could have done it and why would they do it? What could possibly drive someone to take the life of a young, innocent woman? It just made no sense. None of it made sense.

I still ask myself the same questions. I still have no answers.

I don't know how long I stood there, just looking at Abie's body draped over the sofa, but it can't have been that long. I decided I should give her some dignity, so I went upstairs and took a single duvet off the bed in the spare bedroom and used it to cover her. I knew it was important not to move her. The police would want to know exactly how she was found.

After that, I got dressed myself and I folded Abie's clothes neatly, setting them in a pile beside the sofa. Then I sat on the other of our matching three-seat sofas and waited.

It never crossed my mind to run. Why should I have run? I think I realised even then I was in deep, deep trouble but there had been a murder and that made whatever problems I had brought upon myself seem insignificant. So, my career was over and I would be the object of public shaming. So what?

Abie was dead.

———

Bales wrung out the old tea towel and dropped it into the bin before pulling the plug to drain the cloudy water from the sink.

He leaned against the kitchen work surface. The task of cleaning up had diverted him for a while but, having done it, he suddenly felt very alone. Despair gathered like clouds forming out over the North Sea.

He had been so careful. He had protected his new identity so fiercely that he had hardly left the flat, other than to go to work or to buy food. He hardly said a word to anyone. All he wanted was to melt into the background, anonymous, until he could get his head together again. Get his life together again.

Yet his old life had still found him.

Perhaps he would never be able to escape it. Maybe he did not deserve to.

Perhaps he would have to spend the rest of his life running from it but one thing was for sure. He could not stay in Scarborough for much longer.

CHAPTER
TEN

The news of Jim Pendlebury's sudden death filtered back to Sheffield within a couple of hours. It spread quickly around the corridors of South Yorkshire Police headquarters and grim messages were soon dispatched to see that all colleagues, past and present, were made aware.

Clare Larson was at home when she was told, by phone. She burst into tears. She had not cried for a long time.

Jim was a friend, not just a superior officer. Theirs was a true partnership, built on mutual trust, and she had looked up to him from her first day in CID as a raw new Detective Sergeant. He taught her what being a good detective was all about. He taught her who she should get to know and who she should watch out for. He taught her how to appreciate good beer.

If Jim had objected to being paired with the awkwardly big newbie who walked like a weary farmer returning home from a long day labouring in the fields he didn't say. He stood up for her when others made caustic comments about her appearance and made sure she was treated as an equal in what was still, then, a male-dominated department.

They knew what people said behind their backs. The Heavy Mob, others called them. They didn't mind because they got things done. Usually.

So Clare cried for the loss of a friend but when she was told where Jim had been when he died, the tears had a different sting.

Jesus Christ, Jim! You promised!

As she ended the call she was angry, with him and with herself. He said he wouldn't go anywhere near Bales. Low-key. Softly, softly. Nothing daft. He promised.

He knew he could be dropping her right in it if questions were asked about how he got to know where Bales was living and about the new name he had taken. How could he be so selfish? How could she be so idiotic as to give him the information he asked for and so encourage him?

Clare agonised over the news for much of the night, trying to think fondly about her friend but fearing the consequences of his final foolish act.

She thought about coming clean. It would certainly mean disciplinary action, probably demotion. That was the honest course to take but was it necessarily the wisest?

In the end, Clare decided she would only own up to what she had done if the truth was uncovered. That would unquestionably reflect even more badly on her but she had worked so hard to make it to Detective Inspector. She was not inclined to give it up unless she positively had to.

The following morning, she was summoned to the office of the Detective Superintendent and her stomach churned. Was it already so obvious?

'Take a seat, Clare.'

DSU Bob Haley was a thin-faced man in his early fifties with short-cropped hair that had retreated almost as far back as the top of his crown, apart from a few wispy tufts in the middle. His skills were more suited to administration than hands-on criminal investigation but he knew the job and he looked after the people in his department.

'You heard about Jim Pendlebury, I suppose.'

'Yes, sir,' she said, allowing her expression to soften as she spoke. 'Do we have any details yet?'

'Nothing about the cause,' the DSU replied. 'There will be a post-mortem, of course. I suppose the logical conclusion everybody is leaping to is that it was his heart again, but we'll have to wait and see. I called you in to see if you had any idea why he was there. You know he was in David Bales' flat?'

'Yes, sir.'

'You worked with Jim on that case, didn't you?'

'Yes, sir.'

'And had you been in touch with Jim since he took retirement?'

'I had, sir, a few times.'

'When would the last time have been?'

She pondered, but only to make the lie appear more plausible. 'A good few months ago, I would say. Just before Christmas.'

'Did he mention Bales then? Had he mentioned Bales at all on the occasions you saw him since he left the force?'

'Sometimes. It still rankled with him, losing that case, especially with it being his last one. It still made him angry.'

'But did he ever say anything about tracking Bales down for whatever reason?'

'No, sir.'

'Have you any idea how he managed to track Bales to Scarborough?'

'No, sir, but he was a very resourceful detective. He was better than anyone I've ever worked with at digging up information and he knew lots of people. Maybe he called in a favour.'

'Maybe.' Haley held Clare in his scrutiny. She looked straight back at him, trying not to blink.

'I want you to drive over there,' he said, breaking the

exchange. 'I want somebody on the ground working with the North Yorks force so that we can get to the bottom of this. Take DC Short with you. I'll get somebody to sort you out a couple of rooms and I'd like you to stay for a day or two, until we get the results of the PM and perhaps get more of an idea what Jim was doing there.'

Clare nodded. She felt as if she had survived the initial examination.

'This could stir everything up again. If this gets into the press we might be facing calls to reopen the case. That's the last thing we need right now.'

'I'll see what I can find out from the locals, sir. It might even be an idea if I request to talk to Bales myself.'

'Do what you think is right, Clare.' The DSU rose from his seat and Clare took the cue to prepare to leave.

'Christ, Jim. What the hell were you thinking?' he pondered out loud.

Clare forced a half-smile and turned to go. She needed to find DC Short to tell her they were going to spend a couple of days at the seaside together.

CHAPTER
ELEVEN

The flat was no longer his safe haven. David Bales cleaned his teeth and put the kettle on, as had become his usual routine after closing his door on another working day, but he no longer felt able to relax.

In the three years since making the decision to move to Scarborough with hopes of a fresh start, the flat had been the place where he could drop his guard. Out there, he was constantly looking over his shoulder, still not trusting the rest of the world to leave him alone. Once his door was locked behind him, however, they could not touch him. Even the demons inside his head had started to settle into a new spirit of domestic bliss. He was actually beginning to believe he was getting his life back together.

It had still been less than twenty-four hours since Jim Pendlebury ripped through the thin film that had sealed Bales in his sanctuary but he already feared the damage caused was irreparable. The world knew where he was. The demons were restless again.

The phone rang and he jumped. Incoming calls were rare and

usually harmless, though mostly unwanted, but now they were an additional source of anxiety. Potential trouble.

He did not recognise the number. His thumb hovered over the green button before he decided to answer it.

'Hello,' he said, warily.

'David, hi. It's Parveen Razaq. Of Paulsen and Brown Solicitors?'

Her raised inflection at the end of her introduction suggested she did not expect Bales to recognise her and, up to her saying the word 'solicitors', she was right.

'Of course. Hi Parveen.'

'I've just been told the results of the post-mortem and I thought you'd want to know.'

That was quick, he thought. It looked as if people of influence were keen to know the outcome as soon as possible.

'Oh, yes?' he answered, trying to sound as unconcerned as he could. Since the Inspector made his clear threats the previous evening, Bales had been worried. Knowing he had nothing to do with it did not seem to mean he wouldn't get blamed.

'So the verdict is that Mr Pendlebury died of a…' There was a rustling at the other end of the call as the solicitor flicked through her notes. '… ruptured abdominal aortic aneurysm. It was a completely natural event, which is good news. For you, not for Mr Pendlebury, obviously. I probably don't need to tell you what that is, seeing as you're a teacher.'

'I taught maths, so…'

'Oh, right,' she replied and he heard her flick through her notes again.

'So how it was explained to me is that the aorta is the main blood vessel that leads away from the heart and that sometimes, particularly with men, this aorta swells up to twice the size it should be and, sometimes, it bursts. Apparently, it's very hard to spot unless you've been scanned for it but when it bursts it causes massive internal bleeding and can kill you before anybody can do anything about it. That's what I was told.'

'I see.' He had never heard of such a thing but it sounded, as a verdict and a cause of sudden death, pretty conclusive.

'So that should leave you in the clear, as far as the police are concerned. If they do contact you about this again I'd like you to call me straight away.'

Bales nodded. Though he had his doubts when he first saw her, it was reassuring that she genuinely appeared to care. It was not something he had experienced often in recent years.

'Thank you.'

There was a pause before Parveen spoke again.

'Have you seen it?'

He was confused. 'Seen what?'

'The news.'

Bales' heart dropped into his boots. This could not be good.

'No, I've not long since got back from work.'

'Oh!' she said, reluctant to go on. 'The *Scarborough News* are running something on their website about the incident. They know who Mr Pendlebury was and they know he was found dead in the home of the man he investigated several years ago. They mention the Miss Perfect Murder. I thought you'd better know.'

He closed his eyes. He felt sick. This was bad. He remembered how it had become impossible for him to leave the flat he was staying in without being hassled by reporters and cameras after the end of the trial. That was part of the reason why he had to leave Sheffield. It was all going to happen again. How did they find out? These things don't just get out by osmosis. Somebody must have tipped them off.

'I didn't know. Thanks for telling me.'

'Are you going to be all right?' She understood the gravity of the information she had given.

'Yeah, I'll be… Look, I'd better go. Thanks Parveen.'

'OK. Remember, just…'

But he hung up before she could finish the sentence. He needed to think. He needed to see what had been written.

It wasn't hard to find. Top story on the website.

Former detective dies after tracking 'suspect' to Scarborough

He clicked on the link and scrolled down the page on his phone to read the content.

A retired top detective has died after it is understood he confronted a Scarborough man who was once the prime suspect in a high-profile murder case.

An ambulance was called to a South Bay address yesterday evening following the report of an incident. A man in his mid-50s was declared dead at the scene.

The cause of death has yet to be established but North Yorkshire Police have confirmed the dead man was former South Yorkshire Police Detective Chief Inspector Jim Pendlebury.

Mr Pendlebury became a familiar figure in the national news throughout the infamous Miss Perfect murder case four years ago. He led inquiries following the brutal killing in Sheffield of Abie Moran, who was 18, in July 2017.

At the end of the trial, Mr Pendlebury collapsed giving a press briefing and required emergency heart surgery. He later took early retirement on medical grounds.

In a sensational twist, three years after the end of that trial, it is believed Mr Pendlebury died at the home of the man who was accused of committing the Miss Perfect killing.

David Bales, who was then 36 and a teacher at the school where Miss Moran was a sixth form student, was found not guilty to the charge of murder at Sheffield Crown Court on June 21, 2018.

A spokesman for North Yorkshire Police said they had not yet determined the full circumstances of the incident that led to Mr Pendlebury's death and that enquiries were on-going.

. . .

Bales put down his phone and slumped back into the chair. Thank goodness, the report did not include his address or his picture, though it did have a stock image of Pendlebury taken during the early days of the inquiry. They were small mercies. He knew it would only be a matter of time until they found him.

The *Scarborough News* might only be a small-town publication but it was no doubt part of a larger group and the report would soon spread. Once a story like this got into the wind, it could blow far and wide.

Fuck you, Pendlebury, he thought. *Why did you have to die here?*

It would have been much better if he had died outside the court that day.

This development had made the decision for him. He would have to leave – and soon.

But where?

Money was an issue. Bales earned just enough to settle all his bills each month and he had just laid out a large chunk to pay his rent through to the third week of the next month. He barely had enough left this week to buy a one-way train ticket to anywhere and what would he do with his stuff? He could hire a van from work. If they gave him a discount, he could just about afford that but where would he find the money to get a new place to live and where would he go? What would he live on until he landed a new job? Just finding a job would be hard enough. He was lucky Douggie Dyer didn't delve too deeply into his employment history.

Fuck you, Pendlebury.

It was a big problem. He couldn't afford to stay but couldn't afford to go.

He needed to beg a favour but Bales had cut himself off from everyone he knew when he moved away from Sheffield three years ago. That was the whole idea.

It was not as if it had been a huge sacrifice. The only family he had left behind were his mother and his sister, Nikki. His father left them over twenty years ago. Friends and colleagues had long since deserted him.

Nikki did visit him a few times when he was on remand, though not very often. He wanted her to visit more frequently. It was only Doncaster, for God's sake. Hardly the end of the earth. In truth, though, when Nikki did come, it was awkward. She clearly hated being there. She clearly hated being the sister of a man accused of murdering a young woman. She clearly was not convinced of his innocence.

Mum didn't visit at all. Nikki said she had taken it very badly.

But they were family. Who can you rely on, in desperate times, if not family?

He decided to call Nikki.

Hers was one of the few numbers he had programmed into his new phone.

It rang. Her voice when she answered was timid, weary.

'Hi, sis. It's David.'

'David?' It was as if she could not believe he was still alive.

'Are you OK?' he asked.

'Am I…? Jesus, David. We haven't heard from you in years. Where did you go? You never even said. Now you call out of the blue to ask if I'm OK? Jesus, this is… Where have you been?'

'I'm in Scarborough,' he replied. He could feel the strain in her voice. 'I thought it best that I just went. I'm sorry.'

'Sorry? Have you any idea what we've been going through? First the trial and then you just vanish off the face of the earth. How could you be so cruel to mum? This – all this – has crushed her.'

He pictured his mum, as she used to be. Happy, proud. She was always immensely fond of her son, her youngest. When he was accused of such dreadful things she changed.

'I know but after the trial I had to get away. I just figured that

I'd done enough damage to you and mum and that you'd stand a better chance of getting on with your lives if I was out of the picture. I am sorry. There was a lot for me to deal with as well. I really didn't want to hurt either of you anymore, but I want to come home now. I want to try to make it right.'

'Make it right?' she was incredulous. 'How could you possibly make it right?'

'It wasn't my fault, Nikki. I didn't do what they accused me of. The jury found me not guilty.'

'I know what the verdict was.' There was a rising anger now. 'But don't you dare say this was none of your fault. Of course it was your fault. If you'd been able to keep your cock in your trousers for once and hadn't seduced that poor girl – one of your students – none of this would have happened, so don't give me that "it wasn't my fault" crap. You brought disgrace on this family. Mum couldn't handle all the stories and the attention and the gossip and who do you think had to deal with all that? I did. On my own. The pressure cost me my marriage and mum can barely exist now without her meds. It's taken a huge toll on us both. All that is your fault, David. All of it.'

Tears rolled down Bales' cheeks. He was ashamed. He knew he was not the only one devastated by the case but it tore and twisted at his heart to hear his big sister's anguish and to learn how badly mum was still affected.

'I know. I know,' he said. There was no point apologising again. 'Sorry' sounded such an empty word.

'The thing is, I have to get away. They're coming for me again, the press. I need somewhere to go where I can keep my head low, just until it all blows over again.'

'Jesus, not again.' Nikki could well remember what it was like to live in a media spotlight. 'Don't you think if they're looking for you, here is one of the first places they'll look? I can't face that again. I can't expose mum to that again. It'll kill her.'

He hadn't considered that. She was right.

'Yeah, I get that. You're right. I can't do that. But I do have to get away from here. Can you lend me just a bit of money? I haven't got anything. I'm desperate, Nikki.'

She was quiet.

'I haven't got any money for you, David. I'm a full-time carer for mum now. We struggle as it is. A few bits of benefits are all we have. I'm sorry, David, but you're going to have to get out of this new mess on your own. We can't help you. You lost your right to expect anything from us when you left us to fend for ourselves three years ago. Good luck, David. Don't call us anymore.'

Nikki hung up. The tears were unstoppable now. He was a wretched, weak, toxic man.

He sat for hours, wallowing silently in his misery as the gathering dark of night began to close in and hide him away. He willed it to devour him and give him release from his hopelessness. He had nowhere else to turn.

Unless.

Nikki had not been the only person to visit him in Doncaster Prison. There was Jane.

Jane Featherby was the head of sixth form at Brincliffe Edge Academy. He hadn't expected to see her, so he was surprised the first time she showed up. They hadn't been particularly close as colleagues, but, from then on, she came to see him every two weeks, without fail.

Something in his plight had struck a chord with Jane. Maybe she was one of those people who were irresistibly attracted to an underdog cause and Bales was unquestionably an underdog. She believed in him when no one else would. She championed his case, writing to editors and programmers to lambast what she saw as breaches of impartiality in their reporting and filing official complaints with the regulatory authorities. Not that it did much good, but she did it anyway.

Jane Featherby even resigned her position at Brincliffe Edge because she said she could no longer tolerate the endless sniping and condemnation from other staff and pupils. That's how committed to the cause she was.

Jane was, in many ways, his only lifeline. His trial solicitor made all the right noises but Bales knew it was only a job to him. Gemma, his wife, had disowned him. Nikki grew increasingly distant as her support waned. Only Jane was unwavering.

She had been there when the jury gave their verdict and had redoubled her campaign to balance the media coverage in the weeks afterwards. She had even tried to hide him away by letting him crash on the sofa in the small flat she shared with her partner. Hers remained the only friendly face he could trust.

Bales realised he had not so much as thought of Jane since he decided to leave Sheffield without telling a soul. Until now.

What must she have thought of him when she returned home that day and found he and his few belongings were gone? How did she feel when she discovered the phone number she had called so often was now dead?

It felt like the only way then. The kindest way, almost. He saw how heartless it was now.

How could he even consider asking Jane for another favour when he had acted so abominably to her three years ago?

Did he even have her number anymore?

Bales recalled he had written it in the back of the journal he kept in prison. He sat still. The room was in almost total darkness now. Dare he call her? Wouldn't it be just one more act of extraordinary selfishness?

But he was desperate. He could see no other way out than this one pinpoint of light in the gloom. Jane might be his only chance of escape.

He jumped to his feet and went to the bedroom to retrieve the journal from the bottom of the drawer where it had sat for three years.

There it was, written on the inside back cover in pencil next to the words 'Jane F'. He keyed in the number, apprehensively.

'Hello?'

It was almost too much for him to speak to her. He almost hung up.

'Jane, hello. It's David Bales.'

The words had to be allowed to seep through. She was shocked.

'David. Thank goodness. I've been so worried.'

Instant forgiveness. He did not deserve that. He wept again.

'Jane, I'm so sorry for running away like I did, after everything you did for me. I can't tell you how bad that makes me feel, but I didn't think I had a choice. I was still in prison in Sheffield. I had to break free.'

'I understand,' she replied, her voice cracking too. 'I'm so glad to hear from you at last. Are you all right?'

'I'm fine,' he said. He hadn't felt so happy, so relieved, in years. All the while he had been suffering in his solitude and there was a comforting voice out there all the time, remaining unheard. 'How are you?'

'Oh, I'm doing OK. Where are you?'

'Scarborough.'

'Scarborough! Wow! I was there myself only a few weeks ago, at half-term. I could've... Never mind. It's just good to hear from you again.'

Bales wiped away the tears that were blurring his vision.

'Jane, I'm in trouble again,' he said and she fell silent at the other end of the phone. 'Pendlebury found me here and, well, Jane – he's dead. He just keeled over and died on my lounge floor.'

'Oh, my God,' she gasped.

'The thing is, it's blown my cover. It's on the local paper's website and they've named me. It didn't give my address but they'll find me, no doubt about that. I've got to leave but I've no money and nowhere to go.'

'You can stay with me,' she blurted.

'It would only be until I can find another place and get a job.'

'However long it takes. You'd be welcome here. It's only me now. I split up with Mel.'

'I'm sorry to hear that.'

'We were… It was… Never mind. Do you want me to come to get you?'

'Could you? I haven't got a car and I haven't got much stuff but…'

'I'll come tomorrow. Text me your address. When would you like me to get there?'

'I work until four. I'll have to let them know I'm quitting. I think they'll be OK about that but I can't leave them completely short without doing the jobs that need doing tomorrow and I could do with another day's pay.'

'That's fine. I'll be there around five. Will you be all right before then?'

'I think so. I don't think they'll figure out where I live so soon. I've taken a different surname since I moved here.'

'That's smart,' she added.

Bales felt as if he had been swept up in a tornado and was floating in the utter peace in the eye of the storm. He did not know where it was carrying him but he had faith that the outside forces could not hurt him anymore.

'Jane, I don't know what to say.'

'It's OK. Just text me that address and I'll be there. Around five. Stay safe, David.'

'I will and thanks. I'm beyond grateful. You might just have saved my life. Again.'

'Yes, well.' She was discomfited. 'I'll see you tomorrow. We've got a lot to catch up on.'

They ended the call.

Bales had sat on the end of his bed as he talked to Jane but allowed his whole body to relax, flopping back on to the mattress. His sense of relief was overpowering.

After laying there a while, he jumped to his feet again. He was ready to make something to eat, then he needed to pack.

He had a friend. He had hope.

CHAPTER
TWELVE

David Bales stood at his second floor window for almost quarter of an hour, peeking in all directions through gaps in the drawn curtains, before convincing himself there was nothing unusual out there. Nobody waiting to ambush him. No lurking camera crews.

He looked all ways again when he timidly eased open the large front door, until he was sure it was safe to set out. Everyday life on Regents Crescent was going on as normal. Bales skipped down the stairs, hunched under his hooded top, and set off up the hill with much more urgency than usual, hoping his turn of pace would catch out any dozing stalker.

No one approached him and, as he turned the corner to head towards the landmark steeple of St Andrew's Church, he slowed.

The miserable rain of earlier in the week had chased through and the July sun was already warming the early-risers setting about their new day tasks. It was Friday. Not only the end of a working week this time, but also the last day of his time in this town.

Bales flicked back the hood off his head and ran his fingers through his dark hair, raising his head high to meet the sunshine. He felt on the cusp of a new start – a better new start – and a rare visitor had entered his heart.

Optimism.

Jane Featherby. Loyal, generous, forgiving Jane Featherby. She was coming that evening to rescue him before the world collapsed in on him again and her unconditional acceptance had restored his faith. He knew he would never be free of his past. Like the stump of a severed limb, he would have a constant reminder, but the thought of not facing it alone any more made it possible to contemplate a time when he could adapt and live with it.

He had thought a lot about Jane since their conversation the previous night. Strangely, he could hardly recall a thing about her before the day everything changed. She was maybe six or seven years older than him and had been at the school for much longer, going back to the days when it was plain old Brincliffe Edge Comprehensive. They had worked together for eight years, since Bales joined the Academy as its new deputy head of mathematics, but they did not socialise and hardly spoke in school. He always regarded her as quirky, difficult to read. Outwardly, she was unnoticeable, like she preferred to blend into her surroundings. Mousy, almost.

He had no idea of the depths of strength she possessed. When he was most in need, how that mouse roared!

Bales passed through the gates of the black metal fence and headed straight for the small office building. He wanted to see Douggie Dyer before the start of his shift, to let him know that this would be his final day on the job. He would be OK with that, he reckoned. He was a decent guy. Working as a courier driver had never been anything other than the means to bring in a wage but as he entered the office with the customary hard shove against the outer door, he reflected on his time there with something close to affection.

Iryna was at her desk, as usual, sour-faced and efficient. Before

Bales could say a word, she shot him a glance and barked: 'Boss wants to see you.'

He nodded and turned towards the burgundy door without breaking stride. He hadn't expected to be pre-empted.

'Come in, come in,' said Dyer, beckoning him through with a wave of the hand. He waved in the other direction as Bales stepped through, indicating he preferred the door to be shut. Bales did as requested and stood, uncertain of what to expect.

'Sit down David.' The next gesture pointed him towards the scruffy plastic chair on the other side of the desk. Bales had to move a pile of files to be able to sit on it. Dyer was shuffling papers on his side of the desk as if trying to locate something important. He stopped abruptly and made eye contact for the first time.

'I expect you're the talk of the yard this morning.'

'I've only just arrived. I don't...' This was worrying and confusing. He could think of no reason why Dyer would have made the leap to link him with the man in the news article on the local paper website. Surely, there must be some other reason for him saying that.

'I wondered what was going on when he came looking for you.'

Bales was startled. *Pendlebury came here?*

'I'm sorry, who?' It was best to stay playing dumb.

'You know who,' Dyer was annoyed. He was no fool. 'That copper came looking for you on Wednesday, asking questions. Some bollocks about a long-lost son and a family crisis. I thought he was bogus and then when I saw his picture on *Look North*...'

Shit! It was on TV as well?

'...I started to put it all together. The false name threw me for a bit.'

'That's my real name,' Bales needed to defend himself. 'I changed it legally.'

'Whatever,' Dyer replied, dismissively. 'It was obvious from the pictures on the internet it was you. Look, I can understand how you might not advertise who you really are but it was a bit disappointing to find out like this.'

'I'm sorry but what would you have thought if I'd told you at the start? I needed the job. I didn't lie to you.'

Dyer considered that. 'Fair point,' he conceded and leaned back in his chair. 'I'm not judging you, David. Christ knows I've done things in the past that I'd rather nobody knew about, stuff I'm not proud of, but this? This is different league. I get that you're an innocent man in the eyes of the law, but we both know it's not that straightforward sometimes. You attracted a lot of attention last time and once everybody cottons on to what happened the other day, you're going to attract a lot of attention again. I don't want a load of journalists hanging around my yard, looking for you. I don't want to risk anybody prying too deeply into my business, if you get what I'm saying.'

Bales understood. He had become accustomed to being the pariah. Family, friends, his wife – all of them had scattered to a safe distance as if they feared they might be infected by staying too close. Almost all of them.

'I don't want to make it awkward for you, Mr Dyer,' he said. 'You've been good to me and I appreciate that. I came in to tell you I'm leaving Scarborough, just in case things get complicated again, but of course I'll do whatever jobs you've got lined up for me today. I feel bad about not being able to give you proper notice.'

Dyer stood to his full unimpressive height. 'I think it's perhaps best if you go straight away.' He stepped around his desk and Bales rose to him.

'I'll pay you for today, I'll sort that with Iryna. I'll also happily do you a reference when you start looking for a job wherever you're heading next. You've been a good worker and I've no reservations about telling anybody that. I'm sorry it worked out like this, David.'

He offered his hand. 'Good luck to you. I hope the future is kind.'

Bales grimaced and shook his hand, then turned to go.

So that was it. Perhaps Dyer was right. Maybe it was for the best that it ended this way and he had been very good about it. The extra day's pay for nothing was a bonus and would come in very useful.

He thought about calling Jane to see if she would be able to head over sooner. It would not take long to load all his stuff into her car. Packing last night, it had been sobering to be reminded how little he possessed. There were only a few phone calls to make: to the landlord and the council and such. It could all be done in the time it took her to drive over.

'Bales!'

The call made him jump but he tried not to show it. Tried not to look towards where it had come from. That would be to acknowledge he knew they were calling him. Though it was obvious they were and so had put two and two together in the same way as Dyer had, he didn't want to give them the satisfaction of letting them know he realised that.

It came from beside the gates. He could see four of them, all looking over at him. Waiting for him. There was no way of avoiding them. He would have to brazen it out.

'Bales! I'm talking to you.'

The one who was shouting was the scrawny one with the cheap tattoos who always looked as if he was up to no good. He reeked of prisons. There had been so many like him in Doncaster. Sneaky little rodents who kept well clear of the big dogs but suddenly got brave in a crowd of other rats.

Bales tried to do as prison had taught him. Head down, go about your business as if they were not there. Don't let them intimidate you. Don't let them smell weakness.

But as he strode towards the exit, two of the others stepped into his path, blocking his way.

'I always knew there was something not right about you,' said Scrawny.

Bales attempted to sidestep the pair in front of him but they countered his move.

'Just get out of the way, will you? I've no argument with you.'

They showed no sign of letting him through. It was pointless trying to make a run for it. The chances were at least one of these four were quicker than him.

'I never had you down for a murderer and a paedo, though,' Scrawny spat out.

'I'm neither.' Bales stared into the narrow eyes of his accuser. Don't back down.

'We know what you did. Everybody knows what you did. Little Miss Perfect. You raped her and strangled her. How did you get away with that, eh? Raping and killing a little schoolgirl, that's really sick shit. Like 'em young, do you Bales? Is that why you wanted to be a teacher? Did you make them keep their uniforms on?'

The others smirked at his words. They were all enjoying this. It was planned. Bales had seen enough of this type of confrontation in prison to know that it didn't usually end well.

'Look, I'm leaving. I've quit my job. Just let me get on my way and you'll never see me again, if my being here offends your sensibilities that much.'

It was a bold riposte but he didn't want them to know they were scaring him. He had to keep that inside.

'You're not going anywhere.' Scrawny put both hands on the centre of Bales' chest and pushed, firmly enough to send him staggering back two steps.

'You really think you're better than us, don't you? Smarter. Too good to talk to any of us. But you're not. You're a murderer and a paedo. You're the lowest of the low. Cop killer as well now, I see. I suppose we should give him some credit for that at least, eh lads?'

That amused the others. Scrawny was feeding off them, becoming more and more empowered. This was dangerous.

'You don't know what you're talking about,' Bales muttered. 'Just let me go.' He tried to step past them again but the one on the end, the biggest of them, one of the forklift drivers, grabbed hold of his arm and shoved him, hard.

'We don't like you, Bales,' said Scrawny. 'We're going to show you what we think of kiddy-fiddlers around here.'

The biggest one took hold of Bales again, this time wrapping his large hands around both upper arms from behind. There was no breaking the grip. He frog-marched Bales towards the gates.

On the road was a battered blue Vauxhall Astra with one of the others from the loading bay behind the wheel, peering through the windscreen at the approaching party. Bales tried to wriggle free but his captor was strong and squeezed his thick fingers deeper into flesh.

He could not let them get him into the car. He didn't like his chances of escaping unharmed if they did. He tried to dig in his heels but kept being shoved forward. Scrawny opened the back door and went around the rear of the car to the other side to get in.

Bales resisted all he could but he could not stop Forklift bundling him in and shuffling in beside him. The door slammed shut. He was trapped.

They drove off the industrial estate and were soon heading on the main road north out of the town. It was a familiar route. No one spoke. Bales could see nothing to gain from trying to reason with these people. They were clearly intent on doing him damage and stoking their fires was not going to make them go easier on him. If there was an opportunity, wherever they were taking him, to get away or attract the attention of someone who might help, he would go for it. If not, he was just going to have to take his lumps. Soon, he would be away from here for good. He tried to use that thought to fortify himself.

Just past the hospital, they turned towards the North York Moors, soon leaving the built-up outskirts behind. They drove beyond a lake and the road began to get narrower, the cover on either side of them denser. They clearly had somewhere secluded in mind.

Thick woods dominated the view on both sides. The road that twisted through it was not much wider than a single car but there was a passing place on the left and the driver pulled into it, turning off the ignition.

So this was it.

Scrawny got out of the car first and Forklift grabbed Bales' arm again, to discourage any attempt to make a break for it. He opened the door with his spare hand and dragged Bales with him.

'Move it!' snapped Forklift.

There was no option. Before Bales had the chance to find his feet, he was in the unbudgeable grip of Forklift's great hands again and all four of them were moving deeper under the suffocating heavy cover of the trees.

They walked him in for no more than a hundred yards before Forklift barged powerfully with such force that Bales' head snapped back. He tumbled into the dirt of a small clearing, breaking his fall only partly with his now-free arms. By the time he was able to spin around onto his backside and face his attackers, they had him surrounded.

They stood over the helpless, vulnerable creature who scrabbled among the dead twigs and tufts of grass of the woods floor. He was completely at their mercy and they did not appear likely to show him any.

'You don't have to do this. Just think about it. You don't have to do it.'

It was a desperate final plea. He knew it wouldn't do him any good.

'Sure,' snarled Scrawny. 'But we want to.'

After the first however many it was – six, eight, twelve – it became impossible for Bales to distinguish between the kicks as they sank into the soft flesh under his ribs, cracked against his spine or splintered the bones in his hands as he attempted pathetically to shield his face. After a while, it was almost as if they could not hurt him further, as if he had reached an upper threshold of pain, beyond which it was pointless trying to inflict more because the human body was too limited in its capacity to register it. That did not stop them trying. Bales no longer reeled from their kicks and was capable only of passively absorbing them. Blow after blow after blow. If not for the weight of every boot as it sank into its target, he would not have moved at all.

Inside that battered shape, he was almost detached from his body. It was overwhelmed, useless. Inside, he was clinging on to an increasingly fragile consciousness, trying to stop the remaining wisps of his spirit from seeping out and vanishing into the air.

Finally, they stopped, all three of them breathing heavily from the burst of exertion. Their anger and their limbs were exhausted and they panted, attempting to soothe the swimming tiredness behind their eyes as if they had just sprinted, full pelt, beyond their limits.

'Come on, let's go,' wheezed Forklift at last. The other two nodded but did not have the strength to leave yet.

'Let's go. Before somebody comes,' Forklift added.

He began to stumble wearily away. The driver followed. Scrawny bent forward, his hands on his knees, and inspected their handiwork.

They had done what they set out to do. Maybe more. They had taught the paedo a lesson.

'Come on!' yelled Forklift, turning back.

Scrawny stood straight and breathed deeply through his nose.

They had taught him.

He raised his boot one more time and stamped it down on Bales' head.

CHAPTER
THIRTEEN

'Are you sure I can't get you another cup of tea?'

It was the third time the constable had been over to them to see if she could do anything to make their wait a little easier. She was not quite giving it the full simpering Mrs Doyle but was close to shaping up as a much younger version. At least she had the good grace to be embarrassed that they had been there, in the out-of-the-way corner of the office usually reserved for visiting members of the public and pushy solicitors, for almost fifty minutes. Waiting to see the Inspector.

'We're fine, thank you,' replied Clare Larson with a strained smile that made it plain the situation was not entirely fine. She was distinctly irritated now. They had gone way beyond discourteous to the point where it was downright rude.

'I hope Inspector Evitts will be with you soon,' offered the constable, sympathetically.

Clare managed another faint twitch of the corners of her mouth. There was nothing to be gained by giving her a blast. It wasn't her fault.

DC Hannah Short sat alongside Clare. They had driven over to

Scarborough that morning. It was Friday, the day after DS Haley had suggested they make the trip and two days after the shock sudden death of former DCI Jim Pendlebury. They were there to help with the investigation into his death. So much about it remained unexplained – officially. Clare would have to tread a fine line because of what she already knew about Pendlebury's purpose.

Hannah was silent. She was far too junior to qualify for the right to express a strong opinion about being kept waiting. The DI was doing enough huffing and muttering for both of them anyway. Hannah's more pressing priority was that she needed the loo but was too frightened of being in the toilet when they were, eventually, called through to see the Inspector. That would annoy the DI even more.

A phone rang on a desk close by. The longer ring of an internal call. The officer catching up with paperwork at the desk answered it and, after a brief 'Yes sir,' hung up again.

'The Inspector says could you go through now, please ma'am,' he said, turning to face Clare.

She was quickly to her feet, stomping towards the Inspector's office door with Hannah in tow.

'About bloody time,' she mumbled crossly and opened the door without knocking.

The Inspector did not even look up as she stood, filling the frame of the doorway. He continued poring over the document on the desk in front of him for just a few unnecessary moments more before rising and offering a handshake.

'Clive Evitts,' he said.

'Clare Larson.' She accepted the handshake. It was cursory rather than welcoming.

'And this is DC Hannah Short.'

'Sir,' responded Hannah, timidly. He did not acknowledge her.

'Sorry to keep you,' said Evitts, out of obligation. No explanation. 'Have a seat will you.'

Before they had fully lowered themselves into the chairs, he added, pointedly: 'So they've sent you to make sure we're doing our jobs properly, have they?'

There we have it, thought Clare. *It's a territory thing. Alpha male. Pathetic.*

'Not at all,' she responded, managing to keep her tone light. 'Detective Superintendent Haley thought it would help get to the bottom of this quickly if we came over to assist. I was Jim Pendlebury's DS through the Bales case and so I know all the background. We thought that might save some time.'

Evitts was conceding no ground. 'Yes, well, I don't think we'll be keeping you long. We had the PM report through last night.' He sifted through a small pile of papers to his left and slid a thin stapled document across the desk so that Clare had to get up to collect it.

'Natural causes. He had an aneurysm. Nothing suspicious.'

Clare scanned the official papers. 'I see.' She would need to read them more closely but it sounded like the kind of thing that could have happened at any time. That was good. The least cause to look into his death in more detail, the better.

'We still didn't know what former DCI Pendlebury was doing here and especially why he approached Bales. I understand you conducted the interview with Bales,' she said. 'Did he give you anything?'

Evitts eased back in his seat and pulled a face.

'Not much. Maintained Pendlebury turned up out of the blue, forced his way into the flat, started accusing Bales of being responsible for the Moran murder again, tried to make him see the error of his ways and confess. Then he took a turn for the worse, collapsed and died. No struggle, he said. The PM seems in line with that part, at least.'

Clare was trying to remain patient. She'd had more co-operative suspects.

'So that's all he told you about why Jim turned up? Have you no other information on that yet?'

'We did talk to Pendlebury's widow,' Evitts added. 'She came over with her daughters to do the formal identification yesterday. She said her husband was here for the cricket.'

Poor Kate.

Clare made a mental note to go to visit soon. The first sight of Kate's anguished face, drained of colour, in the initial hours after Jim's cardiac arrest leapt to the front of her mind again. Though Clare took her hand in an attempt to offer some small comfort it would not stop trembling. She was in pieces then, how must she feel now?

'The cricket?' she said.

'The annual festival at North Marine Road. It brings in a lot of visitors every year,' said Evitts, matter-of-factly. 'Wednesday's play was called off because it rained. Maybe Pendlebury was wandering around to pass the time, saw Bales, recognised him and followed him back to the flat to have a go at him?'

'I can see that,' Clare answered. She liked the way this version of the sequence of events was heading. It was in a different direction to the one where anyone might want to point fingers at those they suspected of feeding Jim the information he needed about Bales' location.

'I do know that Jim held on to a great deal of bitterness about this case. It was his last one before he had to retire and he took the failure to convict very personally.'

Evitts mulled this information. 'It's a good thing to care so deeply, I suppose,' he suggested at last. 'All of us get involved when we're handling the big cases but we all suffer setbacks and we all have to learn to let go.'

His arrogance annoyed Clare.

'What about you, DI Larson? You were his DS. Have you got over it yet?'

Prick.

'I moved on. You have to, as you said. The big difference was that DCI Pendlebury didn't have the chance to turn his attention to the next case. He had too much spare time to let it eat away at him.'

'Hmm,' said Evitts, knitting his fingers together across his belly and pulling an expression like a cheap psychoanalyst. 'And what is your opinion now, DI Larson? Is Bales still our chief suspect? I must say he didn't come across as a cold-blooded killer.'

Clare considered her response. She was never utterly convinced of his guilt at the time, even though she did all she could to secure the conviction. She wasn't going to bad-mouth her former boss for the satisfaction of this bloke, all the same.

'There was enough about the case that didn't sit right and I think that was why the jury declared him not guilty. Having said that, there was no reason to suspect anyone else specifically and the main flaw in the case was a piece of missing evidence, so it was reasonable to believe Bales was our man and I thought we put together a strong enough argument. In the end, I guess we didn't. If you're asking me now, three years on, if I'm totally convinced Bales is guilty, I'd have to say no,' she conceded. 'DCI Pendlebury was always far more adamant in that respect than I was.'

'Interesting,' Evitts nodded. He eased upright again and leaned on the desk. 'But as I said, I don't think we need detain you very much longer. The PM report gives us no reason to charge Bales with anything in connection with former DCI Pendlebury's death and I would suggest that's the end of it. I'm sorry you've had a bit of a wasted trip.'

It looked as if he was right but Clare did not want to let him fob them off quite so easily. She still wanted to be seen to be doing a thorough job.

'I'd still like to talk to Bales myself, while we're here. I'll be expected to submit a full report when I get back.'

'Be my guest,' said the Inspector, raising both hands to show his palms, like he was surrendering. 'I'll get someone to give you his contact details.'

He rose to his feet and so did Clare. They shook hands again before she and DC Short turned to leave.

Clare was still bristling over Evitts' attitude towards them but she decided not to share her feelings with her junior. It would be inappropriate. She headed straight for the constable who had taken the call to summon them to the Inspector's office. She was not going to wait for Evitts to get round to giving them what they needed.

'Can you get me a number for David Bales, also known as David Wilson, who was interviewed on Wednesday in connection with the death of DCI Pendlebury?' she demanded, looming over him.

'Er, yes ma'am,' he answered and tapped on the keyboard of his computer. He scribbled a mobile phone number and an address on a pad and tore off the sheet to hand to her.

'Thank you,' she said, taking it from him. 'Is there a spare desk and a phone we can use?'

'Of course,' said the officer, a little flustered. Clare could be an intimidating figure when she put her mind to it. He cast his eye around the office. 'Would that one be all right?' he added, pointing to a spare desk.

She approved by making straight for it, with DC Short following dutifully, feeling in the way. They sat down.

'The Inspector was a bit curt, wasn't he?' suggested the younger woman, searching for the words to be as diplomatic as she could.

'Hmph!' grunted Clare, not saying anything but saying it all. She smoothed out the piece of paper in front of her and picked up the phone to call the number.

It rang five times before it was answered, by a woman. Her voice was timid, shaken. 'Hello?'

Clare shot an icy glare towards the male constable, obliviously getting on with his work at his desk. *If he's given me the wrong number, he's going to get a roasting.*

'Is this the right number for David Wilson? I'm trying to get hold of David Wilson.'

'Err, I don't…'

Whoever this was at the other end of the line seemed genuinely shaken.

'Who is this please?' Clare asked, attempting to take control.

'My name's Alice. We were out walking in Raincliffe Woods. He was just lying there. He's in a bad way.'

Clare went cold.

'Listen, Alice. My name's Detective Inspector Clare Larson and I'm going to help you. Are you saying you've found a man in the woods and he's injured?'

Bales. It had to be. This is his phone.

'Yes. We've called for an ambulance. We said we'd wait with him until they arrived. He's not moving. He's unconscious.'

'Is he breathing, Alice?'

The voice at the other end went quiet for a few seconds, as if she was checking.

'I think so. I told the ambulance people he was. They got me to check his pulse and I could feel one but it wasn't very strong.'

This was serious. Had there been an accident? Has he been attacked? Has he tried to kill himself?

'You've done the right thing, Alice. If you could stay with him until the paramedics can get there and keep an eye on him, that would be great. Any obvious change in his condition, you call 999 again and they'll talk you through what to do next.'

'My friend's still on the line to them, like they asked us to,' she replied. She sounded so frightened.

'That's great. It sounds like you've got everything under control. I'm going to ring off now, Alice, because I need to alert people to what's going on at this end, is that all right?'

'Fine, yeah.'

'Please just tell me the name of those woods again.' Clare scrambled among the files on the desk trying to locate a pen.

'It's Raincliffe Woods.'

She found a pen and wrote down the words underneath Bales' address.

'Good to talk to you, Alice. Thank you for your help. I'm sure they'll be with you very soon.'

DC Short stared at Clare throughout the conversation, her face full of concern.

'That doesn't sound good, ma'am.'

Clare shook her head.

Not good at all.

'Come on, Hannah. It looks like we're going to have to disturb the Inspector again.'

CHAPTER
FOURTEEN

It was late evening and they were heading home. The trip to Scarborough had not gone as anticipated but at least they had been able to make themselves useful. Even Inspector Evitts appeared to appreciate their contributions.

When it became clear David Bales had been the victim of a serious assault, rather than being left unconscious by accident or by an attempted suicide, DI Clare Larson had volunteered herself and DC Hannah Short to visit his workplace. They needed to see if they could shed any light on how Bales had come to be in the woods in the first place.

The owner of the courier business confirmed Bales had been in that morning, to say he was quitting his job and leaving town. The owner said they had agreed it was best Bales left straight away and they had parted on amicable terms. That was around seven-fifty a.m., he reckoned.

The walkers in Raincliffe Woods had discovered Bales lying seriously injured at around ten forty-five, which allowed ample time for him to get to the woods by foot, though it seemed unlikely he had. They also established he had no car. He must have been taken there by whoever assaulted him.

Before they left the courier business, Clare had asked to see any CCTV footage, to confirm if Bales had left the premises alone. A camera had been trained on the main entrance, to monitor all comings and goings.

It did not take long for them to strike gold. The footage clearly showed Bales being intercepted by four men at the gate. There appeared to be quite a heated verbal exchange between him and one of the four and they physically barred his attempts to get past them to leave. One of the men then took hold of Bales by the arms before he and the one who had been doing all the talking forcibly escorted Bales towards a waiting car outside the main entrance. The three of them got into the car and it was driven off.

Their initial guess was that the car was a dark-coloured Vauxhall. Another man had been behind the wheel throughout the exchange. They had watched him drive out of the main gate and park up before Bales reappeared in the footage, intending to leave after going to the office to see the boss.

Mr Dyer, the owner, co-operated fully and was able to identify the four men at the gate as employees. He was not sure who the driver was but they were able to get a clear read on the number plate of the car as it drove towards the gate.

Dyer was angry, especially when he was told what had happened to Bales. He said he was quiet, a good worker, no trouble.

Clare called through for back-up and they made five arrests, four on the spot and one later. Two of their co-workers had given statements to confirm that the five conspirators had been talking about seeing Bales on the TV news the previous night and had decided to take matters into their own hands.

Once they had interviewed all five suspects and had gathered forensic evidence from their clothing and the car, the police were confident they would have more than enough to charge all five. It appeared they had quickly wrapped it up.

The only unknown was whether the main charge would be attempted murder, or murder.

When she called Scarborough General Hospital later that afternoon, Clare was told Bales had arrived in a critical condition and was in surgery. They suspected severe internal injuries and a fractured skull. They were not certain he was going to make it off the operating table alive.

After ending the call to the hospital, Clare carefully placed her phone on the desk in front of her and rubbed her eyes with her left hand.

'What did they say?' asked Hannah, concern etched on her face.

'He's in surgery,' she answered and sighed heavily. A sombre silence fell between them.

'Look, I'm going to nip out,' Clare suddenly added. Hannah sat up, ready to go too, like an obedient puppy.

'No need for you to come as well. I'll be back in a couple of minutes.'

She rose quickly and headed for the exit, leaving Hannah looking abandoned.

The elation of being a part of a job done efficiently, with the five arrests, evaporated as swiftly as a teardrop hitting a hot surface. All the while they had been reacting to the news of the assault and moving to establish who was responsible she had not truly thought about Bales and his condition. It was not her priority. With the job done, the call to the hospital left her completely deflated.

Who was responsible for Bales fighting for his life on an operating table? *Really* responsible?

She was.

There was nothing she could have done to prevent Jim Pendlebury's death. From what she had learned, the main blood vessel leading from his damaged heart could have been swelling dangerously for weeks, undetected, before it burst and flooded his chest cavity. It could have happened anywhere, at any time. As it turned out, that time came while he was in Scarborough.

She felt sad for Jim's death but not guilty.

However, if she had not agreed to supply him with the information he had asked her for – about Bales' new identity and whereabouts – Bales would now be going about his normal routine in the new life he had constructed for himself. Not teetering on the brink of death because she had exposed him to his past.

Unintended or not, that was on her.

Did it make her feel any better that such an horrific fate had befallen a man she had previously worked so hard to convict of murder? Not at all.

If David Bales had killed Abie Moran, he deserved justice. Not this.

No one deserved this.

Clare was away from the police station for much longer than the couple of minutes she had promised.

During that time, she contemplated coming clean about her involvement in Jim Pendlebury's trip to Scarborough but decided against.

What difference would it make? What good would it do? It would only ruin one more life. Hers.

Clare's natural pragmatism was winning the debate inside her head. Facing her misjudgement had seriously undermined her self-belief but she decided the most sensible course would be to learn from her mistake and continue to do her duty to the best of her ability. Try to move on.

She also decided they should wrap up at the station and get out of Scarborough as soon as they could.

But first, there was one more call she had to make.

'Are you sure you don't want to come in with me?'

Clare pulled into the hospital car park space, tugged on the handbrake and turned off the engine.

'Nah, you're all right, ma'am. I'll wait here.' Hannah was not a fan of hospitals. They brought back too many unhappy memories.

'OK. I really won't be long this time.'

Hannah said nothing, though she hadn't been impressed by the DI's estimation of what being left for a short time had entailed earlier that afternoon.

Clare was not going to argue with the DC's choice and opened the car door to get out.

'If somebody comes snooping around wondering why we haven't paid for parking, just flash your warrant card and say I'm interviewing a suspect.'

She made straight for the accident and emergency department. That was where they would have brought Bales and it was the best starting point for trying to find out where he was now.

The signs directed her towards a gold-coloured canopy in front of a stark red-brick building. Spending too much time going in and out of emergency departments was an unfortunate but inevitable circumstance of being a police officer, it seemed. At least this was a change from the Northern General.

It was quiet inside the building. Reasonably quiet, anyway. Far too early for the Friday night loonies. The calm before the storm.

Clare walked towards the reception desk, all pastel colour paint and light-stained wood panels, and took out her identification to show the nurse sitting behind a computer monitor.

'Hi. I'm here to ask about a patient called David Wilson who was brought in this morning. I believe he was in a pretty bad way.'

The nurse tapped at her keyboard and looked at the screen.

'I have a David Wilson who was admitted today at eleven-forty and has now been moved to Critical Care.'

Inwardly, Clare breathed a sigh of relief. At least he was still alive.

'He's out of surgery then,' she said. 'That's good. Any indication yet on his condition?'

The nurse checked the screen again.

'Not yet. He was only taken up to ICU less than half an hour ago, so they'll still be making their assessments.'

'Would I be able to pop in to talk to someone on ICU to see if they can tell me more? I'm on my way back to Sheffield, you see, and I'd like to have some sort of idea of how he is before I set off.'

'You could try,' said the nurse. If she had been dealing with anyone other than immediate family, the answer would have been different but the police usually knew how to conduct themselves in a hospital environment. They knew not to get in the way.

'If you turn to the left here,' she added, indicating the corridor to the right of the reception area, 'there are lifts and stairs to the first floor and you'll be able to pick up the signs from there.'

Clare smiled her thanks and strode in the direction she had been told. She took the stairs, happy for the few extra seconds to prepare herself for what lay ahead.

The overhead signs told her she had arrived at the Critical Care Unit. Being admitted here was never good news but Clare knew Bales was on Intensive Care, rather than High Dependency, and that was a notch or two up the seriousness scale.

It could have been worse. Clare half-expected her only option might have been to head to the mortuary.

A male nurse, in a white top with blue epaulettes, was at the station. He appeared to be searching for something and didn't seem to be having a great deal of success finding it.

She took out her warrant card again and presented it for when the nurse broke off from his search and noticed her presence.

'Oh, hello,' he said. 'Sorry to keep you waiting. I was just... I'm Billy, how can I help?'

He flashed the friendliest of smiles, like he was behind the counter of a book shop. Clare was constantly amazed by how un-intense the staff usually were who looked after the sickest of the sick patients in intensive care. Calm when all around was turbulence.

'I wonder if I could just grab a minute to talk to someone about David Wilson,' Clare asked.

'David Wilson,' he replied, peering towards a closed door at the end of a corridor. 'He's not been with us long and the doctor is still in with him. I'm afraid I can't let you in to see him yet but I could ask the doctor to come to see you when he's finished.'

'That would be great, thanks,' said Clare, gratefully.

'If you'd like to take a seat for a few minutes over there,' the nurse indicated with his eyes the area behind Clare's back. 'The lady there is waiting to see about Mr Wilson as well, actually.'

She was puzzled. As far as she knew, Bales had nobody. Who else would be here for him, such a relatively short time after the assault? Clare spun around to find out.

The other woman was gazing so fixedly from behind large round-rimmed glasses it was a wonder she had not bored holes in the back of Clare's head as she stood at the station. It was an uncompromising face; the expression of one who had been building up to a confrontation and was now completely ready to let rip. Her long frizzy hair was parted in the centre and streaked with grey. She sat, leaning slightly forward, with her hands cupped together on her lap and her knees tightly drawn in, and was wearing a yellow raincoat over a plain grey sweatshirt and jeans.

Clare needed a moment to recognise her but soon did.

Jane Featherby. Unwavering David Bales champion and general pain in the arse, through the investigation, through the trial and, especially, after the verdict.

'Jane,' she said, coldly. 'What are you doing here?'

'I might ask the same,' came the reply through lips so tightly pursed they barely moved.

'I'm the police. I'm *meant* to be here.'

The implication was clear but the impact was deflected straight back.

'Huh!' Jane snorted. 'Have you come to see if he's still alive so you can wrongfully arrest him again?'

Cow!

Clare did not bite. She was not in the mood for a fight. She picked out a seat as far from Jane as she could and sat, then took out her phone to appear distracted.

An uneasy calm fell between them but it could not last. The bubbling fury within Jane would not be contained.

'Really, you've got some sort of bloody nerve to be here. How dare you show up when David is a few feet away, surrounded by machines and hooked up to all sorts of wires and tubes, fighting for his life – and it's all down to one of your lot.'

Clare was momentarily stunned by the outburst. 'Excuse me? I think you should calm down a bit.'

'I will not calm down. I'm bloody angry. If your ex-boss hadn't shown up like he did, raking up the past, victimising David just like he did four years ago, none of this would have happened. You want to know what I'm doing here? It's because David phoned me last night fearing for his safety. He had no one else to turn to. He wanted me to collect him and take him away from this place before something bad happened. Well, guess what? He was right. Something bad did happen and I'm too late to help him. Why did it happen? Jim bloody Pendlebury and his stupid vendetta. All this is his fault. It would have been better if he'd died three years ago. I hope he burns in hell for what he's done to this innocent man.'

The spite in the words left Clare reeling. Too many of them found their mark and tore at the wound that was opened that afternoon. She was vulnerable but she wasn't going to let that woman know it. She wasn't going to let her get away with saying those things.

'You sanctimonious bitch!' she growled. 'You have no right to talk that way. Jim Pendlebury gave thirty-odd years of his life to serving the public and was responsible for getting countless dangerous criminals off the streets and behind bars to keep people like you safe – not that he ever expected you to appreciate that. Jim Pendlebury never pursued vendettas. He stood for truth and justice. He was the most hard-working, straight up and honest copper I ever had the privilege of working alongside and only two days ago he collapsed and died. He has a family who'll be bereft without him and hundreds of former colleagues who held him in the highest esteem and will miss him terribly. Don't you ever talk ill of him like that again. You should learn some respect.'

The battle lines were drawn. There was no retreating.

'I'm sorry for his family, of course I am, but what respect did he show David by bursting into his home and stirring up all this poison that should have been allowed to settle and drain away years ago? He did it purely out of spite. He was a bitter ex-copper who couldn't admit he got it wrong – and now look. Why should I respect a man like that?'

'You accuse him of not being able to accept the truth?' Clare countered. 'All along, you refused to see the weight of evidence piled against David Bales. Even if he'd been caught holding a knife still dripping with her blood you'd have still said he was being framed because you're so wrapped up in your liberal perse-cution complex to recognise the complex process of an investiga-tion such as this. You think you've got it all worked out, but you have no idea how the real world works.'

'Any fool could see David was incapable of murder.'

'And yet you were the only one who could? That must make you feel so superior.'

There was real venom in Clare's words. Jane drew a deep breath.

'If you mean was I the only one not carried away by the law of the mob in baying for a head – any head – to mount on a stake then yes, I'm proud to say I was. But what about the twelve men and women of the jury? They heard all your so-called evidence. Did they get it wrong too?'

'A failure to convict doesn't always mean the accused isn't guilty, believe me.'

'Nonsense,' Jane retorted. 'The only thing David was guilty of was being a man – weak, like so many of them are when a pretty girl gives them the eye. I taught Abie Moran since she was eleven years old. She was bright, personable and charming, but she was not all sweet and innocent like everybody made out. She knew what she was doing when she went to his home that day. David's big mistake was that he fell for it and he deserved to pay for that with his job, not with his liberty or the rest of his life.'

'Oh, so now this is all Abie Moran's fault?'

'I didn't say that. I simply said –'

'You really are a nasty piece of work, aren't you? Blame anyone as long as you don't have to admit that everyone else might be right and you could be wrong.'

'I did get it right! The jury –'

'Ladies, please!'

The words silenced them both. They turned simultaneously to face a tall, thin older man in green scrubs who was glaring at them from close to the nurses' station.

'Could I remind you that this is the Critical Care Unit of a hospital, not the tap room of the Red Lion. We have some exceptionally sick patients here.'

Jane's cheeks reddened. 'Yes, of course,' she muttered.

Clare was also suitably contrite. 'Sorry.'

He allowed their naughty child shame to hang in the air a little longer.

'That's better. Now, my name is Dr Lewis Dews and I'm the lead consultant in critical care. I understand you are waiting to find out about David Wilson.'

Clare stood to greet him properly. 'Detective Inspector Clare

Larson of South Yorkshire CID. I've been part of the investigation into Mr Wilson's assault earlier today.'

'Jane Featherby.' She also stood. 'I'm a good friend.'

'Not of DI Larson's, I gather,' added the doctor, unable to resist.

The two women shrank into their embarrassment again.

'Sorry for that disturbance,' Clare said, her head slightly bowed. 'How is he please, doctor?'

He sighed.

'Not very well at all, I'm afraid. He suffered puncture wounds to both lungs caused by rib fractures and a fair bit of internal organ damage. He must have taken quite a beating. But it's what's going on with his brain that is giving us most concern. He suffered trauma from a skull fracture and there was swelling and some bleeding in his brain. We have him stabilised and heavily sedated at the moment but it does not look promising, I must warn you. We'll know more in the next few days but, in the mean-time, if you have faith, I suggest you concentrate your energies on praying Mr Wilson pulls through because he is going to need all the help he can get.'

It was a sobering diagnosis for the women. The news weighed heavily on them and they were silenced.

'I can allow you in to see him in a short while, if you would like, but he is not responsive.'

Jane nodded.

'Thank you doctor,' said Clare.

'Yes, thank you.' Jane tried to clear the tightness in her throat.

The doctor raised his eyebrows and turned to leave them. The women sat again, absorbing the dismal prognosis for a minute or more.

'We made arrests this afternoon, by the way,' said Clare at last. A peace offering.

'Sorry?'

'Five of them. They all worked at the same place as David. We have them on CCTV bundling him into a car and driving away. They're working on the forensic evidence right now but it's pretty much nailed on they are the ones responsible for assaulting him. We've got them. Keep it to yourself but I thought you'd want to know.'

Jane was surprised by the speed of the development.

'I see. That's quick. Good news. Thank you.'

'You're welcome.'

The hostility had dissipated. Instead of having so much to say to each other they were awkwardly aware neither knew what to say next.

'So how did you come to know about this, you know, the assault, so soon?' asked Clare, as non-aggressively as she could.

'I was driving over. I was on my way to pick David up, as I said. He was going to stay at my place for a few days until he could find a job, get on his feet. Until the heat died down. I called his phone to say I was only twenty minutes away and the call was answered by a nurse. She told me he'd… I suppose my name must have come up on the screen when it rang and they realised I was a friend or family or whatever.'

'That was very good of you,' added Clare. 'To help him out like that.'

Jane shrugged. 'I couldn't just leave him. He sounded desperate.'

'You worked together, didn't you?'

'At Brincliffe Edge Academy, yes. For about eight years.'

'And were you close?' The words came out before Clare could stop herself. She had unwittingly gone into interview mode. She realised too late she was raising an implication that was none of her business.

'We became good friends,' said Jane, bristling a little. 'In the build-up to the trial, especially. If you're asking if we were in a relationship, the answer is no. It wasn't anything like that.'

'I'm sorry, I didn't mean…'

Jane softened. 'That's OK. It's just that I had to deal with people insinuating all sorts and making lewd comments all the time. Some people don't seem to understand how two members of the opposite sex can become close friends without wanting to jump into bed with each other.'

'I can imagine.' Clare had also been at the centre of wild sweeping assumptions over her relationship with male colleagues, even Jim. She had to admit to herself, however, that she had occasionally wondered what exactly was going on between Jane and David Bales.

She checked her watch. It was time to go. She had left Hannah Short alone too long.

'I really should be off. We're going back to Sheffield. Are you heading back tonight as well?'

'I might stay for a few days,' said Jane. 'When David wakes up, I want there to be a familiar face to greet him.'

When he wakes. Clare noted the optimism.

'I'll leave you then.' She rose to go but then hesitated.

'Look, Jane, I know we've had our differences, but I wouldn't be surprised if there was a move to reopen the case soon, because of what has happened to David. Maybe it's time the evidence was re-examined to see if there was anything we overlooked.'

'I see.' Jane looked down at her knees. 'That would be good.'

'We're not infallible. We're human, but we always operate with the best of intentions. There's never an agenda other than to see that justice is served. We prosecuted David because we honestly believed, on the weight of evidence, he was responsible; but you're right, if we got it wrong we have to big enough to admit that. If there's a killer still out there, we need to find him and make him pay for what he's done – for Abie, her family and for David. We want to get to the truth as well. We're not so different in that respect.'

'Yes, I see that.' Jane nodded. 'Good luck.'

Clare forced a smile. 'Thanks. You too.'

She turned to go.

A long and sombre drive lay ahead. If they found somewhere to stop on the way home, she owed it to Hannah to buy the coffees.

CHAPTER
FIFTEEN

'Well this is turning into a proper shitstorm, isn't it?'

It was Monday morning. Detective Inspector Clare Larson had worked over the weekend on her report from the trip to Scarborough to make sure it was on Detective Superintendent Bob Haley's desk first thing. He was a stickler that way. He called her through to his office almost straight away.

The first thing that struck Clare about his terse assessment was that she had never heard DSU Haley swear before. She hoped it was not a bad sign but, all in all, agreed with the sentiment.

'I mean, not only are we no closer to finding out what the hell Jim Pendlebury was doing there in the first place, we now have this business with David Bales on top. What a mess!'

He shook his head mournfully as he flicked through the four stapled pages of the report again like he had been issued with an eviction notice.

Clare remained quiet. She got the impression DSU Haley was not seeking her opinion anyway.

'So what we are saying is that Jim took it upon himself to reopen a cold case, even though he'd been retired for three years, and that not even his wife was aware what he was up to. Then, having forced his way into the flat of the former chief suspect of that cold case, he keeled over because of this, this…'

He rapidly scanned the pages, trying to find the information he needed to complete the sentence.

'Ruptured abdominal aortic aneurysm, sir,' interjected Clare.

'Exactly so,' said Haley. 'Just keeled over and died. Could have happened on the street, in bed, in the supermarket – but no. It was in the flat of a man we tried for murder in a high-profile case and now the press are all over it. And just to make it worse, a bunch of vigilantes have nabbed our former suspect and have beaten him to within an inch of his life. We're getting all sorts of grief over this already. Have you seen what's been in the media?'

Again, Clare did not believe she was required to provide a response but, this time, she gave one anyway.

'Some of it, sir.'

The reason she had not viewed more than a small slice of the coverage was deliberate. What she had seen did not make her feel better.

It had gone national. From the low-key report on the local Scarborough newspaper's website, the news had spread rapidly. Even though Pendlebury had not been on official police duty because he was not, in fact, a police officer anymore, the police force in general was bearing the brunt of the media's ire.

At first, the story was treated as a bit of a curiosity. Ex-policeman who led one of the most high-profile murder cases of the last few years hunts down ex-suspect in said case with the intention of doing heaven knows what – and dies.

Wow! Who wouldn't want to read all about that?

But when it became known there had been repercussions for the ex-suspect – serious, life-threatening repercussions – the story took on an altogether more sinister aspect.

Jim Pendlebury, from being painted an obsessed former police-man, suddenly became representative of the police in general. It was as if the whole force was complicit in his irrational pursuit of David Bales and, by implication, the attack that had put Bales in the Intensive Care Unit.

Bales, universally reviled in the media from the day he was arrested until they started to lose interest in the whole story following the verdict, was now the victim.

Held to blame was not so much the gang of thugs who decided to exact justice with their boots and fists but the police. It was because of Pendlebury's intervention that Bales was attacked. Pendlebury represented law and order and, therefore, the police were responsible.

The media feasted on that line over the weekend and so a fresh approach was needed on Monday. The focus broadened to re-examining how the police had got it so badly wrong in the original case. If they hadn't been so incompetent in the investigation into Abie Moran's murder, none of this would have happened.

If it was accepted Bales was innocent – and many commentators appeared far more comfortable with that possibility than they had, even at the end of the trial – then Abie's murderer had still not been made to pay for their crime.

Social media had quickly fastened on to this affront to natural justice. Action was demanded. The headline of one newspaper, placed beside a familiar picture of the beautiful, smiling Abie, spoke for so many.

SO WHO DID MURDER MISS PERFECT?

The demand was for the police to re-open the case. DS Haley's problem was that it had been heard by his superiors.

'I had a call from Detective Chief Superintendent Valentine,' Haley said ominously. 'He wants us to take another look at the Moran case. I suppose he wants us to have something to throw to the wolves to keep them at bay. I see from your report you're of the same mind, Clare.'

She had thought about this plenty over the weekend. Though she had been a little wary she might be overstepping the boundaries by putting in the report that she felt it was time to have a fresh look, she decided it was too important a point to leave out. She was personally invested in the case again.

'I am, sir. I know it wasn't a popular view at the time – and I was among those who believed we were prosecuting the right man – but there's too much doubt over Bales' role in the murder now, in my opinion. I think it demands re-examination.'

'I see,' nodded Haley. 'And what is your feeling on your involvement if we re-open the investigation? Is it time to look at this through new eyes?'

Clare was not sure if she was being challenged or trusted. She needed to stick to her guns.

'I think it would be wise for me to lead it, sir,' she said. 'It certainly wouldn't do any harm to have officers on board who were not involved in the original investigation, but I'm familiar with the background and the characters involved. I think that would be useful. It could save us a lot of time that might otherwise be wasted going over old ground when we should be looking for new leads.'

Haley smiled. 'I agree. I'd like you to be senior investigating officer on this, Clare. I can't give you a big team but I'd like you to choose two to begin with and we can look at allocating more resources if we turn up something worth pursuing.'

Only two? Clare wondered if what the DSU had in mind was no more than a gesture – a token effort to be made for as long as it took for the press' attention to move on to something else. He seemed to read her mind.

'It's not much, I know, but it's all I can spare for now and you will have my backing, believe me. I want you to be thorough, Clare. No stone unturned. There may have been something we missed first time around and I want you to find it. It's time we put this case to bed. The person who murdered that poor girl may still be at large.'

'Understood, sir.' That was reassuring. Clare was already thinking about who she wanted to have on her team.

'What about the business with Jim Pendlebury, sir?' This, too, had been weighing heavily on Clare's mind over the weekend.

Haley exhaled slowly.

'There will be an investigation, in case questions are asked, but I think all the signs are Jim went rogue on this. His wife thought he was in Scarborough for the cricket, you said? For all we know, maybe he was. Maybe his encounter with Bales was simply by chance, as you suggested in your report. Only two people might know the real answer to that and one of them is dead and the other is in a coma.'

He picked up the report and flicked through its pages again.

'We'll look into it, but we'll do all we can to preserve Jim's reputation. He was a good man and an excellent detective. I've no desire to see his name dragged through the mud. That reminds me, we must keep an eye out for when the funeral is. I'd like to go.'

Clare gave a half-smile. 'I'll make sure you're kept informed, sir.'

'It's a very unfortunate way to go and, God knows, I wish it had happened anywhere but where it did if it was going to happen at all, but we don't get to choose these things, do we? It shouldn't tarnish our memory of a dedicated policeman and, who knows? Maybe some good will come of it. Jim could have inadvertently provided the opening that leads us to the real killer. Let's hope so, eh?'

'Definitely, sir.' Clare stood to leave. She was ready for the challenge.

CHAPTER
SIXTEEN

Unfortunately, there were no rooms available at Owlerton Heights, Jane's usual guest house of choice, with its sweeping views across Scarborough North Bay to the castle. Having enquired at such late notice, that was no great surprise.

Thankfully, Mrs Keats was able to recommend a place a few doors further along Blenheim Terrace where she thought there was a vacancy, and this had worked out just fine. The Westlake was run by a couple who were not only gay but were of different racial heritages and it gave Jane particular joy to know that by supporting their business she was demonstrating her full acceptance of their lifestyle.

However, it also created a dilemma. When she next decided to visit the resort, should she return to Mrs Keats and risk being open to the implication she was not completely comfortable with staying under the same roof as a gay couple of different racial heritages? Or should she book in again at the new place and risk upsetting Mrs Keats?

The likelihood that no one else, most likely including Mrs Keats and the gay couple, cared at all about this dilemma was immaterial. It mattered to Jane and wrestling with it troubled her when she was not with David in hospital.

When she was with David in hospital, she had other, more pressing, concerns.

It was three days on now and David was still on the Intensive Care Unit. He had shown no signs of improvement.

But Jane spent as many hours as she could at his bedside every day, trying not to give in to negativity in the face of a bleak outlook. David may have been utterly dependent on the machines that performed the functions his body was no longer capable of providing for itself and on the steady drip of medication being fed into his veins, but he was helpless, not hopeless.

The doctors and nurses had not sugar-coated it for her. She knew the odds were tipped against him pulling through and that they were even longer against him coming out of the coma without having suffered debilitating long-term damage. They had prepared her to expect that, at best, David might never be the same again. At worst, they told her he might remain the shell of a man that lay unresponsive on the bed before them. Existing, not living.

But Jane stayed strong to her faith that David was still in there, struggling to find a way back to the surface, refusing to allow his predicament to inundate him. That was why she talked to him all the time and when she ran short of news to tell, she read to him. Her voice had to be the pinpoint of light through the dark; the life-line he could aim for and scramble towards. She wanted to believe she could help pull David through.

She needed to.

———

That day was burned into the memory of everyone who had been part of the Brincliffe Edge Academy community. Hearing that one of their brightest stars had been extinguished so suddenly and so cruelly was unfathomable to comprehend. Finding out that another of their own, one of the most popular teachers, was suspected of being responsible amplified their shock even more. How could such a thing happen in their ordinary, happy school?

It was so close to the end of term, the time when everyone was set to disperse for the summer, but they needed to draw close again to get through it. Jane had been head of sixth form and did all she could to help counsel stunned students who struggled to make sense of what was so senseless. Everyone did all they could, but specialists also had to be drafted in to help the helpers. Parents' reactions ranged from embracing a share of the grief to lashing out in rage as if a deep fault in the way the school was managed had been exposed. The media descended to capture scenes from the heart of the impact for the benefit of a wider public who had also been rocked by the shockwaves and their scrutiny added to the unreal discord of it all. They were hard days.

At first, everyone was consumed by their mutual pain. Abie was gone and her loss was deeply mourned, but soon the mood changed. When David Bales was charged with her murder, the focus turned on the cause, rather than the symptom. Bales was the monster, a depraved beast who lured an innocent young woman to his home for sex and killed her in cold blood because – well, there was no shortage of possible explanations offered as to why he killed her. The one thing almost everyone agreed on was that he surely was the killer. Didn't the fact that the police had arrested and charged him so quickly confirm that? His guilt was unquestionable.

When the summer holidays were over, a new school year began at Brincliffe Edge Academy. It wasn't back to normal straight away. Numbness lingered in the corners of classrooms that had stood empty for six long weeks but when the bustle of the everyday returned, that feeling gradually dissipated. The school did not forget the tragedy that struck so close to home but it learned to adapt. Life had to go on.

What upset Jane was that opinion against Bales remained firmly entrenched. Even in the staff room, among colleagues who had counted themselves as his friends not so long ago, the mood of condemnation was absolute. No one appeared willing to doubt that David was capable of such a cruel deed and Jane could not understand that. Sure, none of them could say they truly knew him, knew every facet of his character, but what they did know should surely have left room to doubt he had done what he was accused of. Jane knew him less well than many, yet hers was the only voice willing to speak up in his defence.

That was why she decided to leave. She could not stand working alongside people like that anymore.

She decided to visit David in Doncaster Prison, where he was on remand. She wanted him to know he was not alone and it was a short step from there to making him her new cause.

Jane came alive when she had a cause to rally behind. She was fascinated by stories of the great urban rebellions of the twentieth century – from the Suffragettes through to the miners' strike – and had defied her parents to catch a coach to London with her friend Carol to take part in the big Poll Tax protest in Trafalgar Square when they were only sixteen. Carol had her lip split by a stray elbow in a fracas and Jane was grounded for two months, but it was worth it. Her appetite for the underdog cause was ignited.

Her idealism led her to teaching. She chose it as a profession because she wanted to connect with and guide young people. They, she reasoned, are the future and by helping to shape them into more responsible, caring adults, she was doing her bit to make the world a better place. Increasingly, however, the connection had become strained.

Each generation was becoming more alien, with their gadgets and their sets of problems she didn't really understand. Sometimes, it was as if they were talking a different language. The simple truth was that while her students were always in the eleven-to-eighteen age bracket, Jane continued to get older. She was forty-five – no longer the age where she could be their big sister, more like old enough to be their mother. Hell, she had taught some of their mothers!

She was turning into a person she never thought she would become, and not because her attitudes had changed but because the young people had decided she was no longer relevant to them. She could just about hold their attention in a history lesson when she was doling out the information they needed to get through the exams, but when she tried to encourage them to think in broader terms about the world around them, they too often stared blankly back as if she was some sort of relic.

Jane considered doing something to try to update her image but decided that would be vain and probably counter-productive. Dyeing her hair or dressing more fashionably would just make her look ridiculous. She could never be comfortable with that. How on earth could she reconcile it with her favourite 'be proud to be who you are' message to the students?

And so Jane became stuck in a slow, downward spiral of disillusionment and detachment. She needed a cause to reignite her fire. She needed to feel at the cutting edge again.

David Bales' predicament and the response to it of those around her appealed to her sense of indignation. It presented an opportunity to take on the establishment again. Stand up for the downtrodden again. Swim against the popular tide again.

Better yet, the jury proved to be of like mind. She was vindicated. It was her greatest triumph.

When David left that day, without warning and without so much as a note of explanation, it hit her hard. She was lost. She split up with her partner shortly after and not only because the case had put such a great strain on their relationship. Mel was not enough for her anymore. He had to go.

And then, after almost three years in the doldrums, David had phoned her, out of the blue. There was no room for bitterness on her part. He had reached out to her and of course she was willing to help him. He was in trouble again and she could protect him again. For however long it took him to get back on his feet, she would take care of him.

The attack was another savage blow but there was no doubt in her mind David was going to pull through. He would wake soon and when he was able to leave hospital, she would take him back to Sheffield and nurse him back to full health.

It was meant to be.

––––––––

The morning was so beautiful, with puffs of cloud drifting lazily across a bright blue sky and gulls gliding in the gentle breeze off the North Sea, that Jane decided to take a walk after breakfast. She took the meandering path down from the clifftop terrace to the North Bay promenade and strolled to the headland beneath the castle, standing for a while alongside a small crowd that had gathered to watch a pod of dolphins playfully breaking the surface of the water in the near distance. She then headed back along the promenade past the Freddie Gilroy sculpture, up to the beach and through Peasholm Park. Even though she had taken the route so many times, it lifted her the same as it had when she first took it, many years ago.

She set off to the hospital in high spirits. She should have realised. How many times before had life built her up only to knock her down again?

Yet she only suspected what might be heading her way when she saw Billy's face on the Intensive Care Unit. It went momentarily serious and his shoulders sagged for only the briefest time, but then he went from there to his normal cheerful self far too quickly for it to have been normal.

Something was wrong.

'Hi, Jane. How are you?'

She wasn't fooled.

'What is it, Billy? What's happened?'

He smiled again but this time it was in resignation. He wasn't trying to hide anything. He only wanted to break the news as gently as he could. Being the one to pass on bad news went with the territory.

'Come and sit with me for a second.'

Jane did not need to sit. She did not want him to think she could only face what she soon had to face if she was sitting down, but she wasn't going to make a big thing of it. They sat.

'I'm afraid we lost David this morning.'

She nodded, instinctively, as if accepting that it was all right. But it wasn't all right. She didn't think it was going to end this way. David was very poorly but he was stable. If there was to be a change in his condition, she had expected it to be a small step in the right direction. A first small step to getting out of hospital and being able to go home, with her. She was going to help him get better.

Jane tried to swallow down the sudden tightness in her throat.

'How did it…?' That was as much as she could get out. Despite her natural revulsion for showing weakness in front of relative strangers, the tears welled anyway.

'There was nothing else we could have done. His body and his brain had taken a lot of punishment.' The nurse took her hand to offer what comfort he could.

'Why didn't you call me?' The words were desperate, rather than accusing.

'It literally just happened in the last hour and it was very quick,' he explained. 'We were expecting you in, as usual, and thought it was better to break the news face to face.'

Jane acknowledged the sense of that with a nod.

In the last hour? That will have been when she was on her walk. If she hadn't decided to head out for a walk after breakfast, if she had gone straight to the hospital instead, she could have been there. At the end.

That made it so much worse. She had let David down.

'Is there anything I can get you?' Billy asked.

She looked at him. He had been so kind over the last few days. They all had. At least David died surrounded by people who cared. That was something.

She shook her head and he rose slowly from the chair with a stiff consolatory smile.

Jane sat, unmoving, and allowed the tears to flow. David was gone. Her plans were in ruins again.

What now?

CHAPTER
SEVENTEEN

Three officers was hardly much of a team and so Detective Inspector Clare Larson needed little time to decide who she wanted on it.

Detective Sergeant Phil White was a straightforward choice. They had worked together a lot in the last couple of years, especially since Clare made DI, and got on well both personally and professionally. He was in his late twenties, wore an unfashionable moustache without a hint of self-consciousness, could take on the largest pile of donkey work with unfailing patience and had a neat pot belly that looked as if he was concealing a mixing bowl under his shirt. Phil had been around at the time of the Moran murder investigation without being closely involved, which Clare reckoned made him perfect for their fresh look at the facts.

The other officer she asked to join the team was DC Hannah Short, who Clare had taken quite a shine to in their eventful little trip to the seaside. Hannah had been quiet at first but, as she grew more comfortable in the DI's company, Clare came to realise she was not only taking in the new experiences but had been formulating pertinent and pretty astute observations. With an opportunity such as this and as part of a close-knit team, Clare was confident the young officer would really come into her own.

The three of them threw themselves into the task straight away. Even if it did turn out their superiors had only decided to reopen the investigation as a token gesture to placate the reinvigo- rated public interest, Clare had decided they were going to give it maximum effort.

'Well this doesn't add up,' said DS White.

Clare had opened their investigation by running through in detail the time line of the day of the murder and they were now independently reviewing all the interview statements to check for discrepancies that didn't match the sequence of events as they understood it. Dozens of statements had been taken, including from students and staff at the school. If they were open to the possibility that someone other than David Bales committed the murder, there might be a clue in one of these statements which pointed to the real culprit.

'What's that, Phil?' Clare and Hannah both looked up from their screens.

'The wife,' he said. 'Both she and Bales said she arrived back at the family home at approximately two twenty-five, discovered the body, went berserk etc, but there's a time gap in her account.'

He checked the statement again, just to be sure.

'Yeah, here it is. Gemma Bales says she worked as an estate agent on Chesterfield Road in Woodseats and left work at around twelve, twelve-fifteen, saying she had a migraine coming on. She said she had to call in on a landlord near Hunters Bar to pick up keys before going home but that can't have been far out of her way. If she left at twelve-fifteen, drove to Hunters Bar – that's what? Quarter of an hour, allowing for traffic? It can't take that long to park up and pick up some keys, then it's only another five minutes, ten if we're being generous, to the family home. That leaves quite a lot of time unaccounted for, as far as I can see.'

———

Clare did not like Gemma Bales.

It was natural to allow a fair amount of leeway to a person who had discovered a dead body in her front room and had seen her husband accused of murder, but Gemma was not an easy person to feel sympathy for.

The first time they met was a couple of hours after the alarm was raised. David Bales had been taken to the station by the time Clare and Jim Pendlebury arrived at the house and Gemma was at a neighbour's; being comforted, they assumed. After being briefed by the officers who were first on the scene and conducting their own initial observations, Pendlebury suggested they talk to Gemma. They would have to tread carefully, they realised. She had, after all, just had a tremendous shock.

No two people react to extreme situations exactly the same, Clare knew that, but Gemma had gone from deeply traumatised – running out of the house tearing at her own hair and screaming – to bitterly vindictive particularly quickly. That surprised both of them.

The neighbour appeared much more disturbed by it all than Gemma, who sat perched on a stool at the breakfast bar with a glass of iced water in front of her when they arrived. She was happy to talk and did not hold back. If she had been wildly irrational in what she said about her husband – demanding instant castration or stringing him up from the nearest lamppost – Clare could have understood that reaction better. But Gemma was measured, cool almost.

She explained to them what happened after she arrived home, earlier than usual, and left the impression she had expected something like this from her husband for quite a while. She demonstrated not an ounce of doubt that David had killed Abie. There was no suggestion the foundations of her being had been rocked by finding the man she was married to had committed such a foul act. There was no cry of self-pity – how could he do this to me?

None of that. Gemma appeared completely in control of her emotions and entirely clear-headed.

'It's a good job I came home when I did,' Clare recalled her saying as she raised her glass with a steady hand and took another sip of water. 'Who knows what else he would have done to that poor girl's body if I hadn't caught him?'

It was a grisly thought but only the neighbour, her face turning a little paler, was shaken by it.

'David was always a self-obsessed bastard who didn't know how to keep his cock in his pocket,' Gemma added, casually wiping away the ring of condensation left by her glass on the surface when she had picked it up. 'Nothing could stop him when he'd set his sights on another conquest and he's finally gone too far this time. He's sick. I should have left him years ago. I thought for as long as I stayed around he might keep a lid on it but I should have known better. It could have been me he strangled to death.'

Did she say strangled? How could she have known that then?

'We'll need you to come to the station to give us a full state-ment, Mrs Bales,' Pendlebury said to her. 'As soon as you feel up to it.'

Gemma checked her watch as if considering whether it was practical to go straight away and still be back in time for her favourite TV show.

'I can do it now, if you like.'

Pendlebury decided he would drive her there and take the statement himself. He said he thought it would help him get a better understanding of the background to the case. He had not been appointed senior investigating officer at that time but it was a fair bet he would. Clare stayed at the scene.

Looking back, Clare remembered how angry this case made Jim. He mentioned several times the fact that Abie Moran was the same age as his youngest daughter, Natalie. That made it kind of personal for him. Did it also cloud his judgement? Was he too quick to assume Bales' guilt and too hasty in dismissing the possibility another hand might have done the deed?

Clare reviewed Gemma Bales' statement. There were gaps, as DS White had highlighted. Jim should not have let her go without explaining exactly what happened in the approximately two hours and ten minutes between her leaving work and arriving home. The Jim she knew was usually more conscientious than that.

———

'You're right, Phil,' said Clare after scanning through the original document. 'We need to find out where Gemma Bales went in that intervening period. I'll arrange to go to see her. I was planning to make her one of the first people I reinterviewed anyway.'

'Did you ever have reason to suspect the wife at the time?' asked Hannah.

Clare considered her response. She didn't want to prejudice the thinking of her colleagues with her personal feelings but she wanted them to be alive to the possibility that someone – anyone – might be their real murderer.

'She was never regarded as a suspect, as far as I can remember – but then the focus of the case was very much fixed on the one suspect we had. Maybe the focus was too firmly fixed on David Bales. I can't recall anybody at the time suggesting we should broaden our scope and treat others with suspicion. It all seemed so cut and dried. We have to keep an open mind this time.'

'What did you make of her, boss?' said Phil, leaning back in his chair.

Clare sighed. She had to speak honestly. 'She struck me as a queen bitch, to be honest. I thought it was odd how cool she was only a couple of hours after walking in on a murder scene but I thought that might have been the way she responded to the shock of it. I expected there might be some sort of reaction when the magnitude of what had happened sunk in but that never happened, as far as I'm aware. Every dealing I had with her, she was bold as you like, combative, completely unbending in her hatred for her husband – and I never thought that was just because he was under arrest for murder. I got the impression she hated him for much longer than that. I could never figure out why she didn't get out of such a poisonous marriage a lot sooner. How could she be so well aware of her husband's affairs and still live under the same roof as him? I could never get my head around that. It wasn't as if she was a shrinking violet who didn't have the self-belief to stand on her own two feet. Whatever her flaws, lack of self-confidence was never one of them, as far as I saw. Like I said. Odd.'

'What did that make her capable of, though, ma'am?' Hannah added. 'What's that old saying? Hell hath no fury like a woman scorned?'

'I'm not certain quite what Gemma Bales is capable of, to be honest,' answered Clare. 'I'm not sure, practically speaking, how she could have committed this murder, though. That was one of the main reasons why David Bales was regarded as such a nailed-on strong suspect, because it was such a stretch to see who and how anybody else could have done it – but that's not to say it wasn't possible. I guess a good way to start establishing whether or not Gemma should be eliminated as a potential suspect would be to get her to explain where she was in that time between leaving the office and arriving at the scene. I'll set up when we can go to talk to her and see if we can find out.'

CHAPTER
EIGHTEEN

There was a number for Gemma Bales on file. Clare Larson hesitated before dialling it. Any time she needed to have a conversation with that woman in the past felt like she was walking into a fist fight and those old sensations rose again. They were never pleasant exchanges. Clare raised her hackles in preparation. She was not one to back down from a scrap.

'Hello.' The delivery from the other end of the line was snipped, abrupt, like it was meant to warn whoever was calling they had better have good reason to disturb her. There was no way she could have this number programmed into her phone to recognise the caller. She probably wouldn't have answered at all if she had.

'Gemma, it's Detective Inspector Clare Larson from South Yorkshire CID.' There was no emotional giveaway in her voice. She knew those words alone would be as if to toss a live grenade into an adjoining room. She was braced for the explosion.

'Detective *Inspector*?' Here it comes. 'That's how your lot reward incompetence, is it? Promotion.'

'Still not let you back into charm school, then?' Clare expected no less. The mocking tone, the wearying use of sarcasm as a default setting. It was so familiar.

'No point. I was thinking of joining the police and they told me I didn't need any.'

The sparring had begun. The probing for soft vulnerable flesh under the guard.

'Just as well you decided to stick with flogging doss houses for a fifth-rate estate agent, I suppose.'

'Fuck you.'

Round one to Clare. Gemma was not floored.

'I see your old boss finally found a way of making sure that worthless bastard ex-husband of mine got what he deserved. Bit of an extreme method, mind. Still, two birds with one stone, eh?'

Clare bit her tongue this time. She knew she would not be dealing with a grieving widow. She also knew there might be reference to Jim Pendlebury.

That bitch had better not say any more about Jim, that's all. If she went too far, Clare could not be sure of keeping her temper. They still needed to talk to Gemma for the purposes of the investigation. It was time to cut out the jousting and stick to business.

'Look, I need to speak to you again. We've reopened the investigation and there are aspects of your statement we need to clarify with you.'

'No chance.' Gemma let out a hollow laugh. 'You had your chance and you blew it. You should have got it right first time. I have nothing more to say to you.'

'I wasn't asking you to do it as a favour,' Clare replied, sternly. 'We are going to interview you again. We can either do it at your place or I can have you brought in. That bit's up to you.'

'I haven't got time. Call me back next week.'

'Tomorrow. We are going to do it tomorrow.' Clare was not in the mood to give any ground. 'At home or at the station? You choose.'

Gemma went quiet. Her seething irritation was practically crackling down the line.

'For fuck's sake,' she cursed. This bout was lost. 'I'm not going to waste any more of my time than I need to driving all that way. You can come here, if you must.'

Clare clicked down the top of her ballpoint pen. 'I can be there late afternoon. Let's say half four.' This was a bit of a compromise. She was inclined to make Gemma have to get out of work earlier, out of devilment, but decided against.

'Fine.'

'What's the address?'

'You've got the address.'

The reply took Clare aback. Surely she didn't mean…

'You're still at Stamford Road?'

Not unreasonably, Clare had assumed Gemma must have sold the marital home and moved on. Who would want to carry on living there after what happened, for God's sake? From what she knew of her fractious relationship with David, it had hardly been a happy home before the murder, but to add the oppressive burden of knowing it was the scene of a violent death to the atmosphere of memory – why on earth would any human being *not* want to sell up and get away?

'Of course. It's my home.' Gemma replied, nonchalantly.

Wow!

'OK. I'll see you tomorrow at four-thirty.'

———

After another full day of trawling through past statements and old evidence, Clare decided Hannah Short probably needed the change of scenery, so she decided to take the young DC with her to see Gemma Bales. Both of them were nearing the stage where they had read so much they might not be able to spot a missed clue if it was highlighted in bold type and circled with marker pen. DS Phil White was a different animal. He was in his element, so they happily left him to it.

Clare pulled up outside the house on Stamford Road and turned off the engine. Hannah moved to unfasten her seat belt, but Clare stalled her with a hand on her arm.

'Don't be afraid to speak up if you have a question to ask or a point to make, but be aware of the kind of person you are dealing with here. She'll try to intimidate you, get under your skin. Don't let her. You have to rise above it.'

Hannah nodded, warily. They got out of the car.

Clare had not been to the house since the early days of the investigation. It was so calm, so ordinary now. The first time she was there, four years earlier, she and Jim had to nudge their way through the blue-flashing chaos of a tangle of police vehicles cluttering the street and the bustle of officers seeking to establish the security of the scene. The activity, outside and in, diminished with every subsequent visit. Soon, this unexceptional suburban home which had been thrust unwillingly into the spotlight was allowed to shrink back and blend into the row of other forty-odd-year-old undistinguished brick and tile buildings.

They edged past the black Audi on the paved driveway to the front door and Clare knocked. They were bang on time but they were made to wait at the door for almost a minute until the knock was answered. Of course they were. Another petty point was being scored.

Eventually, the door was opened by a tall, slim, dark-haired woman wearing the scowl she saved for people she held in particular contempt. She was in a smart dark blue skirt suit, as if she had arrived home from work only moments before, and had on black heels that some might have considered too impractical for everyday wear. Her figure, fake tan and generously-applied make-up betrayed a person who refused to accept that trying to appear in your early thirties should be the exclusive domain of those who were actually in their early thirties.

She cocked her head and disdainfully scanned the woman in front of her from head to foot.

'You've put some weight on,' she sneered and spun on her toes to meander, cat-like, back into the house, leaving the door open as a tacit invitation to enter.

The two police officers exchanged a look. Hannah arched her eyebrows, as if to say, '*I see what you mean*'.

They followed Gemma through to the front room. *That* room.

Clare led the way but she stopped a couple of paces beyond the door. In her mind, she could see the half-dozen figures in white disposable forensic suits, as the room was when she and Jim first arrived. The body had not yet been moved. Abie was as she had been found, partly dragged over the arm of the sofa by the far wall of the room, close to the door that led to the conservatory. She had been covered over with a duvet, with only a limp trailing hand and her golden blonde hair, fluttering wistfully in the gentle breeze, exposed outside it. The activity going on all around, as officers dusted, checked and bagged, gathering all evidence they could before any disturbance could occur, made her appear almost incidental. The ignored centrepiece.

This was the first time Clare had been introduced to the room as a normal, everyday living space, but it could never really be normal. Once it was a murder scene, it would always be a murder scene for her. She had been to far more gruesome crime scenes than this and had, at times, revisited them, long after the event. They never reverted to the innocent location they once were. They would always bear a stain that no amount of industrial-strength chemical cleaning fluid could ever shift. That was an inevitable consequence of being a detective who deals with homicide cases. Others might be aware of what had happened at a certain location and feel a slight shiver down the spine at the thought. Once you had seen it and picked through it in all its gory detail, that lives with you forever.

That was why it was so extraordinary to conceive how Gemma Bales could still live in this house. After seeing what she did.

Had she even redecorated? Clare had not paid much attention to colour schemes and soft furnishings at the time, but it did not appear so.

And those sofas. Could they really be the same sofas? They seemed to be.

What kind of person could tolerate that?

One thing Clare was certain of was that the two three-seaters were in the same places. It was as if the room had been preserved, as a film studio recreation or a tourist trail feature.

That sofa on the far wall. That was where poor Abie was killed. Look closely and you might still find some of her lovely blonde hair on the chair arm.

It was strange at best. Sick at worst.

Then another possibility occurred. Had Gemma deliberately set up the room this way for their visit? Was she trying to get inside Clare's head? The notion could not be dismissed.

Gemma had positioned herself, cross-legged and faux-elegant, on the other of the sofas. She gestured the two police officers towards the one by the far wall.

'Do come in,' she purred, with an exaggerated tone of welcome and a barely concealed half-smirk. 'Make yourselves at home, please.'

She knew what she was doing.

Hannah waited for her boss to move first. Clare walked unwaveringly across the room but then delayed and turned to Gemma before sitting. She wanted to let her know she knew what she was up to.

'What's the matter, Detective Inspector? Not afraid of ghosts, are you?' Gemma was loving this. Clare snorted and shook her head, as if to suggest it would take much more than this to unnerve her, and sat at the end of the sofa closest to where her hostess was draped.

Hannah took her cue to move towards the further end.

'That was where I found her, you know,' Gemma interjected before Hannah could sit. 'She was dead, brutally murdered. She was kind of lying at that side of the sofa, over that chair arm. Pretty little thing. Not much younger than you, I'd guess.'

Clare silently chastised herself for leaving Hannah open to that opportunity for Gemma to get at her. She should have taken the far seat.

The young officer stalled for only a second. 'Oh!' she said with a shrug of the shoulders and sat down.

'*Good lass,*' thought Clare.

'So you're reopening the investigation?' asked Gemma, undeterred.

'That's right.'

'And you've thought about the practicalities of putting a dead body on trial for a second time and decided you'll look for somebody else to blame instead.'

Clare smiled. *She's put a lot of thought into how to make herself this obnoxious.*

'Is that your way of telling us you want to confess?' she countered.

Gemma ignored that. 'I don't know what else you think I can tell you. I told you everything I saw four years ago. That should have been enough.'

'Not exactly everything,' said Clare, taking out a notepad. 'Before we start, I will point out this is an informal interview but that anything you say could be used in evidence as part of a police investigation. Do you understand that?'

Gemma shrugged.

'You also understand you have the right to legal representation at any time.'

No reaction. She was certainly playing it cool.

'Then do you mind if we record this conversation?'

Hannah took her phone from her bag in readiness.

'Help yourselves.'

'OK.' Clare shuffled in her seat. 'I'd like you to explain in more detail your movements *before* you arrived home on the afternoon of Tuesday, July the eighteenth, 2017.'

'I've been through that already,' snapped Gemma, suddenly annoyed.

Clare fixed her a stare. 'Again then, please.'

With a petulant sigh, Gemma conceded.

'I was at work all morning, as usual. We were quiet, as I recall. It was a hot day and the office could get stuffy. The air con was useless – still is. I think that was what brought on one of my migraines. I could feel it coming on. I suffer a lot from migraines.'

Clare was tempted to say something about having heard migraines were a symptom of using too much Botox, but she resisted.

'Because we were quiet, I said I thought I needed to go home before it got too bad. The boss said that was all right but he asked me to pick up some keys from a landlord on the way home. I said I would.'

'What time would that be?'

Gemma threw her head back as if it was taking a huge effort to find the answer.

'I don't know. Lunchtime. Twelve-thirty? One o'clock?'

'You said in your original statement that it was twelve to twelve-fifteen,' Clare corrected.

'Fine then. Twelve to twelve-fifteen. What did you ask me for if you knew what I'd already told you?'

The question was allowed to hang in the air, unanswered. 'Go on,' prompted Clare.

'I left the office – at twelve to twelve-fifteen, apparently – to drive to a rented property we had just leased out near to Hunters Bar. The boss had arranged for me to meet the landlord there. He handed over the keys, we had a brief conversation about something or other – some aspect of the lease or trying to screw more money out of it, probably.'

'Was there much traffic about?'

'Not that I can recall.'

'And you were at the property for how long?'

Gemma screwed up her nose. 'Ten minutes? I don't remember exactly.'

'And what then?'

'Then I went home and found that my husband had murdered one of his students in my front room after having sex with her.'

Clare flicked through the pages of her notepad, more for effect than anything. She had no need to check really.

'You told us in your statement four years ago that you arrived home at around two twenty-five yet, by my reckoning, according to what you've just told us, you left the rented property at around twelve forty-five. Which way did you drive home, Gemma? Was it via Barnsley?'

Her back straightened. Gemma was aware the timings did not add up.

'No. That's right. I remember now. I didn't drive straight home. I could feel the migraine coming on and I knew I'd run out of co-codamol tablets at home, so I left my car parked outside the rented property and walked down to the shops at Hunters Bar to find a chemist.'

'I see. Did you find one?'

'Yes.'

'And what then?'

She shuffled uncomfortably. 'I bought a bottle of water to take a couple. Then I decided, as it was such a nice day, that I'd cross the road and have a bit of a walk through Endcliffe Park. I followed the path next to the river. It's a nice walk. Good exercise. You should try some of that sometime.'

Clare did not bite. 'Did anybody see you there? Anybody who would recognise you and would be able to verify your story?'

Gemma rolled her eyes, conducting a mental check. 'Not that I'm aware of.'

Of course not.

'My auntie suffers a lot from migraines,' interjected Hannah. 'When she feels one coming on, she'll take herself off to the bedroom and close the curtains until the medication kicks in because she says bright light makes it so much worse. That day was really warm and sunny, wasn't it? Why did you go for a walk in the park when it was so bright outside? Surely you just wanted to be in the shade.'

Clare smiled inwardly. Fair point.

'I was wearing sunglasses,' scoffed Gemma, like she was pointing out the obvious to a foolish child. 'Beside, the tablets started working quickly. The pills and the fresh air did the job.'

'And then you went home?' asked Clare.

'Then I went home. Is that it? Are there any more stupid questions you want to ask me?' She delivered the second part of the sentence directly at Hannah, who did not flinch.

Clare attracted the attention back to herself. 'Why didn't you mention anything about the park when you made your original statement?'

'I suppose because nobody asked me.'

'It didn't occur to you that accounting for your movements for an hour and twenty minutes just before the time a murder took place might be relevant?'

Fury flashed into Gemma's eyes. 'It was a deeply traumatic day. I stuck to the facts I knew were relevant. Clearly, your boss was thinking on the same lines.'

Why didn't Jim make her spell it out? Why didn't the defence lawyers pick up on it when Gemma was in the witness box, for that matter? The lapse didn't seem to have occurred to anyone at the time. The focus was all on David Bales. Was his wife given an easier ride than she should have?

'You wouldn't just be making this up as you're going along, would you Gemma?'

'You'd better be careful what you say, Detective Inspector.' Gemma was full-blown angry now. That was just the reaction Clare wanted. Angry people sometimes say things they come to regret.

'Then tell us what really happened in that missing hour and twenty minutes.'

'I've already told you.' She shot to her feet. 'Are you seriously suggesting I had something to do with this murder? I think this conversation is over.'

Clare eased back in the seat, calmly. 'I wasn't suggesting anything of the sort. I just don't think you're telling us the truth.'

A noise from outside the room distracted them both and snapped the growing tension between them. Someone was coming in through the front door.

Seconds later, a man entered the lounge. He was over-average but not exceptionally tall, in his early thirties, with dark hair stylishly ruffled on top and fading on the sides into a shaped, close-stubble beard. He was wearing shorts and carrying a sports bag.

'Hey Gem,' he said, turning his attention straight away to the two strangers on the sofa. 'I didn't realise we were expecting company.'

He dropped the sports bag on the laminated wooden floor and sauntered straight to Hannah. The younger and prettier one.

'Hi,' he breathed through a crooked smile, extending his hand.

Clare rose and held out her hand. The man recognised the cue but took the handshake reluctantly.

'Detective Inspector Clare Larson from South Yorkshire CID,' she said, making sure to grip him especially firmly. 'And you are?'

'Err, Paul Shirley,' he answered, glancing uncertainly towards Gemma.

'The police are trying to make out that I had more to do with the murder than I'm letting on,' she explained, laconically.

'Really?' he said and withdrew his hand. 'How on earth could…?'

The man stood still, awkward in the gaze of the three women.

'I need a shower,' he said, suddenly. 'Nice to have met you.'

He snatched up his bag and headed out of the room far more quickly than he entered.

'That your new fella?' asked Clare. It was obvious the information was not going to be volunteered.

'What's that got to do with you?' bit Gemma.

'Just making polite conversation.' She smiled sweetly back and left it there for a few long seconds. 'Anyway, we should probably head off now. Thank you for your time.'

The two officers rose from the sofa almost in unison and started to head to the door.

'Just one other thing,' said Clare, as if suddenly prompted by remembering a point. 'When we saw you the first time, a couple of hours after you raised the alarm, you said that in the light of what had happened, you wondered if it might just as easily have been you David strangled one day.'

Gemma stared blankly back. 'Did I?'

'Yes you did. How did you know at that stage Abie Moran had been strangled? I mean, you saw her dead for only a few moments before you ran screaming out of the room and you can't really have worked out in that short time how she died, unless she had something obvious, like a bullet wound, that is. So how did you know she was strangled?'

'There were marks. Around her neck.'

'True, but could you really have noticed that from the opposite side of the room, in only a few seconds, in a state of panic as you were?'

'Somebody must have mentioned it, then. One of your lot.'

'So one of our officers came to you, in your neighbour's kitchen, specifically to tell you the cause of death? None of our officers would say such a thing. That just doesn't happen.'

Gemma began walking, circling the sofa.

'I don't know. I can't even remember saying that. Maybe it was just a figure of speech.'

'Figure of speech,' repeated Clare, considering the point. She broke off suddenly and turned for the door again.

'We'll be going. Thanks again, Gemma. I look forward to seeing you again. Soon.'

Gemma watched as they exited through the lounge door, not even considering the courtesy of seeing them out.

CHAPTER
NINETEEN

'I warned you,' said Clare, tugging at the car seat belt so hard that it locked, reluctant to release any more material until it was treated more gently.

Hannah stared back at her, wide-eyed. 'What a nasty bitch! Is she always like that?'

'Pretty much,' Clare replied, finally coaxing the seat belt to click into place and starting the car engine.

'She was a nightmare in the build-up to the trial, constantly bad-mouthing the police to anybody who'd listen, saying we weren't doing enough to put her husband away for life. Then every time we had to get in touch with her to ask for further information or clarification about whatever, you'd have thought we were asking her to cut a vein and bleed into a cup. Honestly, bearing in mind we were supposedly on the same side, wanting the same thing, Gemma Bales is the worst I've ever had to deal with.'

Clare stopped the car at the end of Stamford Road, flicking her head from side to side as she waited for her chance to turn right on to the busy main road.

'You should have seen some of the stuff she put on social media,' she continued after completing the manoeuvre.

'Yeah?' Hannah prompted.

'Serious malice. I mean, you can understand how any woman would react if they walked into the situation she said she walked into that day but you wouldn't put it all out there on social media for the world to see, would you? You'd think an experience like that would send you into your shell a bit, make you want to shut it all out. It would me, anyway. Not her, though.'

'What kind of stuff was she posting?'

'Some of it was blatant self-pity; pretty thinly-disguised invitations for her friends to reply "aww hun!" and send virtual hugs, you know the type of thing. Mostly they were rants. Stuff that made Donald Trump look rational. She used to have a go at us, as I said, but then as it got closer to the trial she started posting stuff that could have caused real issues. I remember she put out an instruction to anybody who might be on jury duty at the trial, telling them to find her husband guilty because it was definitely him who committed the murder. Once we got wind of that one, we had to tell her to take it down and stop using social media to talk about the trial. We tried to tell her she was prejudicing her husband's right to a fair trial, which I don't think she could have cared less about, not even when we pointed out she might be causing the prosecution case more harm than good. She was a key witness, for Christ's sake, and all she was doing was trashing her own credibility. She actually refused to take the posts down. It was only when we said she might be prosecuted for contempt and end up in jail herself that she gave in. Gemma's a proper loose cannon.'

They drove on, heading back to the police station, in silence for a while.

'What did you make of her story about the missing hour, then?' asked Hannah.

Clare snorted. 'I'm not sure I believe a word that comes out of her mouth, to be honest. I think there's something she's not telling us. Something she did in that hour she doesn't want us to know about.'

'Like what, though?'

'I don't know yet,' Clare admitted. 'She's hiding something.'

'Is your instinct telling you we ought to be treating her as a potential suspect yet?' Hannah was comfortable speaking honestly to the DI but wondered if she was pushing the point too far.

'Possibly,' said Clare, an edge of hesitation in her voice. 'We haven't really got reason to think that way for now. Did she have the opportunity? Maybe, if you don't go for her story about taking a walk in the park. Did she have the motive? I'm not sure suggesting jealousy is enough because it seems pretty plain to me their marriage was a car wreck. Is she capable? Gemma's a mad cow but that doesn't make her a murderer. I don't know. It doesn't add up yet, but something's missing. I don't think we're seeing the whole picture yet.'

Clare was trying hard to keep the cork in her personal dislike of Gemma and not let it sway her judgement. Hadn't Jim Pendlebury made a similar mistake?

'I thought you handled her very well, by the way,' she said, more cheerily. Hannah smiled. 'Especially when she tried to spook you about the sofa.'

'That was a bit creepy,' the younger officer admitted, her face falling at the memory. 'But I wasn't going to let her see I thought it was. I knew she was trying to get at me.'

'Undoubtedly, she was. I wouldn't be surprised if she rearranged the whole room to look like it did on the day of the murder, just for our benefit. It was all part of her trying to get one up by unsettling us. That's the way her mind works. What I can't get over is she's still living there at all. I mean, who'd want to, knowing what happened there?'

'Perhaps she hasn't got a choice,' suggested Hannah. 'Like you said, the house has a history now. Perhaps she's tried to sell up and she can't find anybody who wants to buy it, because they know what happened there as well.'

'I suppose,' Clare had to drag the words grudgingly from her throat. 'We might have to give her the benefit of the doubt for that, but I still think she's lying to us about what happened between leaving work and arriving back home. It's too long after the event to draw on CCTV to track her movements, but I'd love to know what she really got up to.'

———

DS Phil White was still at the same seat in the same pokey office, still hunched forward studying the same computer screen, when the rest of the team arrived back bearing coffees and cakes.

'Treats for the workers,' declared Clare. It had been her suggestion to stop off at the café on the way back to the station. She rarely needed persuasion to call there but reckoned they had especially deserved it this time.

'Ahh! Marvellous!' Their return broke the spell that had bonded Phil to the screen for practically every second since his two colleagues left to speak to Gemma Bales and he celebrated his freedom by arching his back and reaching up his arms in a long, slow stretch.

Hannah set down the cardboard cup carrier she had clutched all the way back from the café and ran through the mental inventory to make sure she allocated the right takeaway cup to the right person. Cappuccino with chocolate sprinkles for the DS, mocha for the DI and skinny flat white for herself.

Clare had taken personal charge of ensuring the cakes were safely transported and, her mission complete, she triumphantly opened the box on the desk where Phil had been at work. She had chosen all three cakes herself. In theory, it was one each, but she had a pretty good guess their youngest member, being at the age where she still cared a great deal about maintaining a slim figure, would eat only a half of one, at most. That would leave another half which would have to be dealt with by, in all likelihood, the senior member of the team. Such is the responsibility of leadership.

'Take your pick,' she told Phil. 'You're the one who's been hard at it.'

'Ooo!' He surveyed the options with eyes sparkling like a kid's at Christmas. It was only really a choice of two. He knew not to pick the cream-filled doughnut covered in caramel because that was Clare's favourite. He carefully plucked out the billionaire shortbread between thumb and forefinger. 'Thank you!'

Clare snatched up the cream-filled doughnut covered in caramel and Hannah stared at the thick slab of rocky road, then glanced around the office for a knife to cut it in half.

'So,' said Clare between chewing her first bite of the doughnut. 'Did you come up with anything else?'

Phil tore out a blank page from the notepad he had been scribbling on all afternoon and scanned the desk for a space to lay it so he could use it to protect his cake from the scruffy surface.

'Not a huge amount,' he said, sucking crumbs and caramel off the ends of his fingers. 'There are one or two I think we should reinterview, just to be sure there wasn't anything we missed first time around, but I haven't spotted any glaring holes. How did you get on with the wife?'

'Mmm!' mumbled Clare, caught out by having too much of a mouthful to be able to talk this time. 'We asked her where she got to between leaving the office and getting home and she gave us some tale about taking a long walk in the park to get rid of her headache.'

'And you don't believe her?' asked Phil.

A derisory curl of the lip gave him her answer. 'We've no reason not to, at the minute,' she conceded. 'But I don't trust her. She's hiding something. Oh! Here's another thing,' Clare recalled the thought with such urgency that she had to put what remained of her cake down on the desk.

'She had the room set up just as it was on the day of the murder. She even had the same sofa Abie Moran's body was found on in the same place. How weird is that?'

'Sick, I'd call it,' he said with a sorrowful shake of the head. 'She sounds a right oddball.'

'It's all part of Gemma's little game. She made it so that we would have to sit there while we interviewed her. That's her way of trying to let you know who's in charge. Didn't work though. Hannah was excellent. Shrugged it straight off.'

'Good for you,' said Phil to the young DC.

'There's a new bloke on the scene I think we should look into as well,' Clare continued. 'It looked to me like he lived there. I'd like to know who he is and how long they've been an item. Have they been seeing each other since before the murder or after?'

'Right,' Phil picked up a pen, ready to add a new name to the list on his pad. 'What's he called?'

'Paul. Paul something.' Clare reached for her notes.

'Paul Shirley,' Hannah intervened.

'That's the one. Younger than her. Early thirties maybe. Struck me as a bit of a dick. Needs his head seeing to if he's shagging her.'

Phil's brow was furrowed as he processed the information. 'I know that name,' he said. 'I've come across him in the statements. I remember because it made me think of that *Airplane* joke.'

Clare was stilled. 'You know what? I think you're right. I didn't make the connection when we met him, but I think you are right.'

The DS was already scrolling up and down the computer screen, searching for the note that rang the bell, and Clare rolled her chair beside him to look too. Hannah, sensing they might be on to something, moved to watch over their shoulders.

'I'll find it,' he said with resolve after a short burst of searching. 'I've definitely seen that name.'

'He was with the school,' said Clare, suddenly, the connections from four years ago clicking into place. 'I'll tell you who he is!'

She sprang to her feet. 'He was the one who called David Bales. He was on the phone to Bales when Gemma arrived home and caught him naked in the kitchen!'

Phil quickly narrowed down his search and found the statement they were after, sitting back with a satisfied 'There he is!'

All three of them scanned the statement.

'So he was one of David Bales' big mates at the Academy and now he's shacked up with Gemma. Doesn't that strike you as a bit... cosy?' suggested Clare.

'Interesting,' agreed Phil. Hannah nodded.

'So think about Bales' version of events. According to him, when he began his phone conversation with Paul Shirley, Abie Moran was alive, and when he cut it short because Gemma stormed through the door, we know Abie was definitely dead. If we are to believe Bales' account, somebody sneaked into the house, strangled Abie and sneaked out again in the time it took to have that phone conversation with Paul Shirley. And who do we know was in the vicinity at the time? Who was first on the scene?'

'The woman now living with Paul Shirley,' added Hannah.

'Very interesting,' added Phil.

Clare sat again. 'Especially if it turns out Gemma and Shirley were in a relationship at the time of the murder. We need to find that out.'

'He was pretty keen to get out of the room when we were there a bit earlier, when he realised why we were there to see Gemma,' said Hannah. 'He was definitely flustered.'

'Yeah, you're right.' Their minds were now spinning with possibilities. 'How long was that phone call, Phil?' Clare asked.

He searched the screen again. 'Twelve minutes and thirty-eight seconds.'

'You know what?' Clare tried to put the timing into context. She used to be able to swim eight hundred metres freestyle in under ten minutes and that used to feel like an age in the water. 'That could be long enough – if you've got it all worked out. If, for example, you tell your lover to keep your husband talking on the phone for long enough for you to do the deed and sneak back around the side of the house then burst through the front door.'

'What are we saying, then?' Phil was also trying to straighten it out in his thought processes. 'Gemma comes home and realises somehow her husband is having sex with another woman on the sofa…'

'Perhaps she arrived back earlier than she said and saw Abie going in, then spied on them,' Clare suggested.

'OK. And she's so infuriated by this she calls her lover…'

'Perhaps he was already with her. Perhaps they were going back to her place for a quickie.'

'Fair enough. She tells her lover to get on the phone to the husband and get him out of the room so she can sneak in through the conservatory and take her revenge. Through the back, strangles Abie, round the side, through the front door, runs out screaming, everybody thinks the husband has killed her.'

'Is that more or less plausible than our only other current theory? The one where Bales panics and strangles the young woman he's just had sex with?'

The three of them took a moment to contemplate.

'It certainly deserves us taking a closer look,' said Phil. 'It's the best alternative theory we have right now, but until we dig a little deeper to see if it stands up, I don't think we ought to concentrate only on Gemma Bales and Paul Shirley.'

'I agree,' Clare nodded. 'We'll go through that list of people we need to interview again and sort out the priorities, then we can work our way through it between us, but I know there's more to this Gemma thing than we understand so far.'

She reached forward and grabbed the rest of the doughnut, popping it into her mouth and chewing in silent reflection.

She wiped at a smudge of cream she had left on the desk and swallowed.

'I'd love to catch that bitch out.'

CHAPTER
TWENTY

It surprised Clare how sorry she felt when she heard, two days earlier, that David Bales had died of his injuries in hospital without regaining consciousness.

This time, her own part in his unhappy fate, having provided Jim Pendlebury with the information that led to the shattering of Bales' secluded anonymity in Scarborough, was not at the front of her mind. She felt properly sorry for a life lost. If they had got it wrong four years ago and Bales was not responsible for the murder of Abie Moran, it had been a life lost long before those thugs took him to the woods to dispense their own version of justice, if the truth be told, and that was even sadder.

It also surprised Clare that she thought about Jane Featherby and how devastated she must be. Jane's feelings for Bales ran deeper than those of an ex-colleague taking the side of the underdog. That was obvious.

Jane had been a complete pain in the past but their mutual hostility had melted a little that evening at the hospital, on the day Bales was attacked. Clare had, for the first time, seen the person behind the protest banner. They had both let their defences down. She thought about phoning Jane when she heard Bales had died, solely to offer support to a woman who would be hurting. She could relate to that. Her own feeling of loss was still raw.

She hadn't called, though, and she wished she had now. Clare needed to see if Jane would be able to help her with information and it stung her to realise that their next contact would be seen as motivated mostly by professional needs, not human kindness.

The phone rang for a long time and Clare was waiting for it to be diverted to the answering service when a croaky voice answered 'Hello.'

'Jane, it's Clare Larson.'

The bedroom was dim, made lighter only by the glimpse of sun that peeked through the gap at the top of the curtains and shot a narrow line of brightness across the foot of the bed. Jane fumbled for her round-rimmed glasses on the bedside cabinet and strained to focus on the hands of her alarm clock. Just after half past ten.

Sleep had come only in fitful bursts for the last two days and her growing, clinging fatigue was feeding her overwhelming apathy. The ringing of the phone had infiltrated the jumbled mess of her latest confused dream and it had taken her a few seconds to realise the noise was coming from outside, rather than within, her tormented mind.

This was the first time she had spoken to anyone since she left the hospital.

'Oh!' she said, still stirring from her half-asleep fug. 'You.'

Clare winced. Jane sounded rough.

'I wanted to call to see how you are. I know this must be really hitting you hard.'

Jane turned onto her back and attempted to muster the strength to haul herself up to a sitting position on her elbows but gave up and allowed her head to sink back into the pillow.

'I'm OK. I was just... I haven't been sleeping well.'

'You sound awful, Jane. Do you want me to send anyone to help you?'

Awful was a fair assessment. She felt awful. But she didn't want help. She just wanted to be left alone.

'No, I'm fine. I'm just so tired. What do you want?'

Clare considered cutting the call short right there, repeating the claim that her only concern was for Jane's welfare and saying she would leave her in peace. She thought about it. But she still needed to know if Jane could assist their investigation.

'I wanted to know you're all right and tell you that I'm here if you need me, but I also wondered if you'd heard that the men who attacked David have been charged.'

'Really?' said Jane. She hadn't thought about them. She didn't care about them.

'Three have been charged with murder and the other two with being accessories to murder. All five of them will be going away for a long time.'

'I see.' Jane could not work out if she was meant to take comfort from that but she did not feel any.

'The other thing is to tell you we've reopened the investigation into the Abie Moran murder. If we can find the evidence we need to clear David's name, we will.'

Jane blinked, her eyes opening beyond the barely-conscious narrow slits they had been set at through the exchange so far.

'Good. That's good, isn't it? You said it might be reopened.'

'Yes. I pushed for it when I got back to Sheffield and they put me in charge of it, which is what I wanted. Look, I can't really reveal any detail but we're setting out by reinterviewing a few key figures from the original investigation…'

Panic suddenly gripped Jane. 'I can't. Not now. I just can't…'

'No, no, no!' Clare realised the misinterpretation. 'I wasn't suggesting we need to talk to you. I was just wondering if you could help us with one thing.'

The panic subsided. 'I don't understand.'

'It's about Gemma Bales,' said Clare.

The name gave Jane a shudder. That woman had been obnoxious to her, spreading rumours on social media about her and David having an affair and openly haranguing her for having the audacity to stand up for him every unfortunate time their paths collided through the trial. Gemma even spat in her face once, right outside the court – still inside the court building. Plenty of people saw it. She should have had that bitch arrested.

'Dreadful woman.'

'I completely agree,' said Clare. 'As I said, I can't go into details but we found something out the other day that I wanted to run by you. Were you aware, when you were still at Brincliffe Edge Academy, that Paul Shirley was having an affair?'

'With Gemma Bales?' Jane was incredulous.

'With anyone,' added Clare. It was obvious where she was heading but she didn't want to limit the scope of the question.

Jane tried to gather her thoughts. She remembered Paul Shirley well enough. Smug, arrogant, fake. Completely full of himself. She never warmed to him but he and David appeared quite close.

'Not that I knew of. He was in a relationship with Alexis Roper. She was one of the geography teachers, but she left to take up another job the year before I left. As far as I was aware, they were still together. I never heard otherwise, but –'

'Alexis Roper, you say,' Clare wrote down the name. 'Do you know which school she moved on to?'

'Shiregreen Park Comp, I think it was.' Her mind had been sent buzzing by the latest revelation. 'Was he really having an affair with Gemma Bales?'

Clare hesitated. She shouldn't really say but she wanted to earn Jane's trust.

'They're certainly together now. What we don't know is how long it's been going on. I think I might need to talk to this Alexis to see what she can tell us. So relationship troubles weren't the reason why Alexis moved on, as far as you're aware?'

'Not that I –' Jane was still dumbfounded. 'Well I never! Paul Shirley and Gemma Bales.'

She mulled on the thought a moment or two longer.

'They deserve each other.'

Clare smiled.

Ideally, Jane would have been able to confirm something had been going on with Gemma and Shirley, but they had a new name, a new lead. They would have to get in touch with Alexis Roper.

'Thanks for your help, Jane,' she said. 'I'm sorry to have gone on a bit at a difficult time but it's been most helpful and I meant it, if there's any way I can help you, don't hesitate to ask. You've got my number. It will get easier for you, I know. It still hurts but you do start to come to terms with it. I know how it hit me when Jim died.'

Raising the subject of Jim Pendlebury was a risky move but she reckoned the show of empathy was worth it.

'Yes, of course,' Jane replied. 'When's the funeral?'

Could she be contemplating going to the funeral? Clare quickly dismissed the suggestion.

'Monday morning.'

Jane nodded solemnly.

'I hope it goes – you know.'

'Thanks.' It almost sounded like they were growing close, thought Clare. It was weird.

'I'm going to leave you to it now. I hope you get some sleep and I hope you're on your feet soon. I'll be back in touch before long and you can always call me.'

They exchanged goodbyes and ended the call. Jane placed the phone and her glasses on the bedside cabinet and reflected on what she had just been told. She no longer felt so dog tired. She lay still for another quarter of an hour and decided she would shower and get dressed for the first time in two days.

CHAPTER
TWENTY-ONE

'Right,' announced Clare, laying her phone on the desk. The other two members of the investigative team in their small office carried on with what they were doing. 'We've got a name for Shirley's ex-girlfriend. Jane Featherby said she wasn't aware of something going on between him and Gemma Bales, but we need to talk to the girlfriend to find out what she knew, when they split up and, hopefully, get a better idea of what Shirley is like. This is one for you, Hannah.'

DC Short stopped tapping at the computer keyboard to pick up a pen, ready to take down the details that were coming her way.

'Her name is Alexis Roper and the last we know she was teaching at Shiregreen Park Comprehensive. That was nearly four years ago, mind, but that's your starting point for trying to track her down.'

'Got that, ma'am.'

'I'm going to arrange to see Gemma Bales and Paul Shirley again. I'll ask them up front how long they've been seeing each other but I doubt I'd get an honest answer – if I get one at all. I'll knock on one or two of the neighbours' doors while I'm up there to see if any of them noticed when he moved in. I also need to talk to him about that phone call with David Bales on the day of the murder. You were going to put together everything we know about that, Phil.'

'Just – a – second,' said DS White with a flurry of keyboard activity followed by the flourish of a click on the mouse.

'I've just sent you both the three references we have to the phone call from the original investigation. The first is from Shirley's statement. He says the reason for the call was because he had an issue with a former pupil who had come back to school that morning, looking to cause trouble. He said he phoned Bales in a panic because he'd had to lay hands on the boy to get him to leave and he was concerned he had gone too far. He said the boy was threatening to call the police and that spooked him. I haven't been able to find any reference in our records to a complaint having been made.'

'Have we anything to corroborate this story about the returning pupil?' asked Clare.

'No ma'am.'

'Does he give us a name for this boy?'

'He doesn't, ma'am, but Bales does, in his statement. Bales talks in much more detail about the incident, as Shirley told it to him on the day.'

The other two clicked on the email attachment to see the statement for themselves.

'As you can see, he names the boy as Liam Glover, apparently well known as a disruptive influence through his time at the school. Bales says Shirley was in a state when he phoned and it was obvious something was seriously wrong. He said that was why he felt it necessary to slip out of the room he had been in with Abie and take the call in the kitchen, where he had more privacy.'

'Either preventing him from preparing to dispose of the body or presenting an opportunity for someone else to carry out the murder,' Clare interrupted.

'That's right. Bales says Shirley confessed he'd had Liam Glover by the throat up against the wall and threatened to punch him. Shirley told him he thought he was going to get sacked and end up in court.'

'Neither of which happened, as far as we know.'

'No.'

Clare eased back in her chair in contemplation.

'What's the third reference you found?'

DS White clicked the tab on his screen to bring up what he wanted.

'That was from the court records. When Bales took the stand he was questioned about his version of the sequence of events and, when it come to the part about the phone call, he refers to, quotes, "a panicky call from one of the other teachers who had to physically restrain a former pupil who had come back to school to cause trouble", end quotes, but he doesn't name the pupil. He does name, when asked, Paul Shirley as the teacher. Shirley was called to court to give evidence by the defence. He corroborated Bales' story and was asked about Bales' demeanour through the call. He said Bales was calm, which the defence suggested was evidence their man knew nothing about what was going on in the other room. Would a man who had just committed murder be so composed?'

'Hmm, I remember that at the time,' said Clare. 'The prosecution argued that Bales took the call to give himself an alibi, not expecting Gemma to come home and scupper his plans to get rid of the body, but it felt like the defence had the better of that little exchange. If Shirley did only make the call at Gemma's request, with the intention of setting Bales up for murder, his testimony might have been a bit of an own goal.'

She stood and circled to the back of the chair, leaning against the backrest.

'So what we know for sure is that the phone call happened. We know the time it was made and how long it took. We also know from the accounts of the two men involved in the call what was said, but what hasn't yet been verified is whether or not Shirley was telling the truth about this supposed confrontation with the former pupil. Who is this Liam Glover and did the incident take place – or was it just a lie spun by Shirley at his girlfriend's request to get Bales out of the room where Abie Moran was sleeping? There was no reason for anyone to question whether or not the confrontation happened at the time of the original investigation because the only relevant details then were the fact that there was a call and the length of time it took. It's only because we can now make a connection between Gemma Bales and Paul Shirley that it takes on extra significance. We need to establish if the incident referred to in the phone call took place or if it was a cover story cooked up to give Gemma the chance to sneak into the house through the conservatory and strangle Abie. I'll question Shirley and Bales about it and you'll have to do some digging around, Phil.'

'Righto.'

'Double-check the police records to see if a complaint was made and check with the school as well. Were they made aware of it at the time and did they need to discipline Shirley as a result? We also need to find Liam Glover. Get him to tell us what happened – if, indeed, it happened at all. If he's the type of character we're led to believe he is, it's quite possible he's got a record and might even be serving time right now. Whatever way, we need to find him.'

CHAPTER
TWENTY-TWO

Two lines of police officers stood on either side of the narrow road leading to the chapel at City Road crematorium, forming a guard of honour for the hearse carrying former Detective Chief Inspector Jim Pendlebury.

They all wore dress uniform and white gloves. DI Clare Larson made the mistake of not having taken hers out from where it had hung in the wardrobe until the day of the funeral. It had been there, unworn, for at least two years. Maybe more. To her horror, the trousers were far too tight and the jacket pulled across her bosom. It was time to think seriously about losing a little weight.

Her self-consciousness and hope that the safety pins would hold out were forgotten as the cortege drew close. The officers dipped their heads as the lead car bearing the coffin drove by and came to a slow, reverent halt beneath the canopy of the old stone chapel.

Clare raised her eyes again to watch the funeral directors moving in their synchronised efficient bustle, as if they were on castors. They were preparing to take the coffin from the back of the hearse and carry it through to the chapel.

Good luck with that, lads, she thought.

He may have lost a few stone after his heart surgery but he was still quite a size.

It was a good turn-out. That had been guaranteed. So many former colleagues had wanted to be there to say goodbye to an old friend. Jim had been popular in every department he had worked and moving up through the ranks had not changed him. He remained the same top bloke.

The Chief Constable was there, service medals pinned to the chest of her tunic. She had passed on the task of 'saying a few words' to Detective Superintendent Haley but that was fair enough. It was a real show of respect for her to be there at all, especially as Jim was three years retired and had not died on active duty. Not officially, anyway.

The coffin, topped with a wreath of white roses and Jim's peaked police cap, was pulled along the rollers towards the door of the hearse where the six pallbearers waited to take him on the last leg of his final journey.

The most unobtrusive of smiles tugged at the corners of Clare's mouth for a moment as she imagined a very much alive Jim clambering out of the back of the hearse, like he'd just gone for a quick lie-down. She thought about his reaction to seeing her in a uniform she was making look like one of Norman Wisdom's cast-offs. He would have had something sharp to say, for sure. But that fleeting happy thought was wiped away when she noticed Kate.

Jim's beloved Kate. Even in jest Clare had never heard Jim say a bad word about his wife. The job meant so much to him but without Kate he would have had nothing. So many other officers' relationships perished to the demands of the role but not Jim's. It was so special.

Their two daughters stood on either side of their mother, arms linked in mutual support, all three of them consumed by sorrow as the coffin was carried on six shoulders into the chapel. All three of them crushed. Clare did not easily become over-emotional but she could not bear the sight. She looked away and only when she could no longer put it off did she blot the tears that swam across her vision with the back of her white-gloved hand. She hoped no one had noticed. She glanced around and saw she had no need to worry. She was not the only one.

Clare had not been able to face going to see Kate, giving herself the excuse that demands on her time did not allow it. That was only partly true. She was still unsure how she could sit opposite Kate and tell her how sorry she was when she was part of the reason Jim had been in Scarborough at the time of his death.

The aneurysm would have taken him anyway. Clare tried to console herself with that knowledge. But Jim should have been with his Kate when it did, not with some chasing evidence in a case he should have let drop years ago. That was on her, in part at least.

She made herself promise to seek out Kate after the service and not take the easy option of convincing herself she could not because she had to get back to work. Back to the case. She must do that duty first.

The two lines of officers turned, ready to troop in time into the chapel and take their places on the pews. Clare risked popping the stretched buttons of her tunic by drawing in a deep, deep breath.

It was time to say that final, difficult goodbye.

———

Across the city, in the chapel of Hutcliffe Wood crematorium, an awkward, empty silence crept into the spaces which opened when the blandly gentle choral music came to a sudden stop. An ancient CD player, worn to the point of despair by too much exposure to Robbie Williams' Angels and the theme from Titanic, had finally lost the will to go on. No one appeared in any great hurry to try to revive it. Such a move would surely have been cruel.

It was almost time for the start of the service anyway. In truth, the minister could have got on with it ten minutes ago. No one else was going to show up now.

Seven mourners was a pitiful gathering.

David Bales' mother and sister sat, straight-backed and stony-faced, on the second row, looking for all the world like they were only there at all because it was expected of them. The white-haired mother appeared so frail that she might crumble into dust if the gentlest wind slipped into the chapel through an open window. She must have only been in her late sixties. She had aged twenty years in the last four.

The sister, Nikki, was pinch-lipped and tense, constantly fiddling with the paper tissue she held between her fingers on her lap. On the next row behind them was an elderly couple, well turned out and grim. An aunt and uncle, maybe? She was the only one in the chapel wearing a hat and she constantly reached under its short black netted veil to dab at the corner of her eyes with a neatly folded white handkerchief.

Two other women sat separately, almost as far back as they could in the rows of wooden pews, out of the way. The ex-wife was not there, of course. That was no surprise. No one from the Academy had bothered either. That was a shame.

Jane Featherby, with one side of the chapel to herself, had not hoped to see some of her ex-colleagues there out of a desire to catch up. It was purely a matter of respect. But they had burned their relationships with David long since and clearly had no wish to acknowledge they might have been wrong in their cruel condemnations. That was for their consciences to deal with.

Jane had no time for the others anymore anyway.

She was in the simple black trouser suit she had worn so often during the trial that there was a shiny trail on the right thigh where she had rubbed her hand nervously to wipe away the perspiration.

The days since David died had been her lowest. She had never felt so desolate, so without purpose. The times immediately after

David left her without saying goodbye or where he was going were bad enough, but at least she knew he was still out there. Somewhere. This was so final.

If it hadn't have been for her efforts to track down David's sister, Jane doubted she would have learned about the funeral plans. She hadn't expected it to be so soon. The date had been set with unseemly haste, she thought, as if the driving motivation was to get it out of the way as quickly as they could, attracting as little attention as possible. That was probably not far from the truth. Nikki had been reluctant to pass on the date, time and place but Jane had prised it out of her in the end. They hadn't so much as exchanged a nodded greeting at each other since they arrived at the chapel.

The plain light brown coffin was set on a platform draped in blue material in a discreet alcove to the right of a wooden pulpit. Long curtains in the same blue material hung on a circular rail around the back of the alcove, awaiting the press of a button that would complete the curtained circle and signal it was time for the coffin to be taken through to where the fires were stoked and ready.

Jane's eyes were fixed on it. A simple bunch of flowers wrapped in cellophane, looking as if they had been bought as an afterthought from a supermarket on the way to the crematorium, rested upon it.

She had decided not to take up the offer to see David for one last time before she left the hospital that day. There was no point, she told herself. He had gone. But all she could visualise now, as she stared at the blank wooden box, was David lying inside it. He wasn't as he had been in the hospital – battered and helpless. He was as she remembered him from their days together teaching at Brincliffe Edge Academy. Before it happened. Immaculately dressed. Confidence shining in those dark eyes. Handsome.

It was much better that way.

She barely heard a word of the short service. She mumbled her way through the two hymns and mouthed the word 'Amen' after the prayers, just as she had become used to automatically doing in so many school assemblies. She had no time for religion, but it was not considered acceptable for a member of staff to openly show dissent on such matters. She had been functioning purely out of habit for days. On auto-pilot.

When the service was over, that was when it all really hit home. Jane scuttled towards the exit, overcome by the irrational thought that she might otherwise hear the sound of the coffin being taken away, and was unable to cope with that possibility. She wanted to get out while David's family gave their thanks to the minister, avoiding any awkward confrontation with them herself. Her head was spinning and her heart racing. She had to get away before she broke down and embarrassed herself. The whole morning had passed by like it was happening to someone else and now she needed to escape the nightmare.

She practically broke into a trot in her rush to get to the car park and, at first, she did not hear the voice calling behind her.

'Miss! Miss!'

Turning, Jane saw a young woman running to catch up. Through the wash of tears she did not recognise who it was at first, able to make out only the flaming flow of the figure's long ginger hair as she clattered noisily on short heels down the path from the crematorium.

The woman soon made up the ground between them and only when they were no more than feet apart did Jane, blinking her vision clear, realise who it was.

Megan Owen was a part of that last group Jane had taken through as head of sixth form at Brincliffe Edge Academy. The same year as Abie Moran. She had been at the school all the way from year seven and was never any trouble but, in her own way, she was hard work.

Megan was a bundle of irrepressible energy, like a puppy but without the relief of times when she would crash to a halt. If she ever approached you, as a member of staff, she would bombard you with questions and give the impression she was constantly forming the next question in her thoughts rather than listening to the answer to the last. She was a nice enough girl but more than ten minutes in her company could be exhausting.

'I thought it was you.' She beamed at Jane with a broad, generous smile and sparkling green eyes. 'I was at the back of the chapel and I thought to myself "that's Miss Featherby" but I wasn't certain until you got up to go.'

'Yes, I –'

'How are you, Miss? I asked about you when I went back to see everybody at Brincliffe but they told me you'd left.'

'I did. I –'

'Are you still teaching? I hope you're still teaching because I used to love your history classes. It was because of you that I wanted to do history at uni. I did Modern History and Politics at Southampton.'

'That's good. Did you –'

'I left a year ago with a two-one but I haven't been able to find the job I want yet. I've been working at Waterstones in Meadowhall. You know, just until –'

'Megan. Take a breath.' Jane held up the flat of her palm in the space between them. It was a tactic she had deployed successfully for years with Megan and students like her. The most effective way to get them to stop babbling. Puppy training.

'It's lovely to see you again but why...? What are you doing here?'

'Mr B,' said Megan. 'I wanted to pay my respects. He was always nice to me. It might not be the sort of thing I should say now after, you know, but I always had a bit of a crush on Mr B. I think most of the girls in school did.'

'Well, I don't know about that,' Jane muttered.

'I was really sorry when I heard he'd died, especially in the way it happened, so I thought it was only right that I came to the funeral. I had to ring around loads of funeral directors to find out when it was. There wasn't anything in the paper. I'm glad I came.'

'I'm sure he would have appreciated that, Megan.'

The younger woman appeared overcome by a sudden melancholy. For once, her natural effervescence had fallen flat.

'It's really sad, isn't it Miss? I mean, that's three now. Three people who were part of my life when I was at sixth form and now all three of them are gone. First there was Abie, then Brandon, and now Mr B. All in the space of four years. It makes you think, doesn't it?'

Jane instinctively reached to touch Megan's hand and suddenly, unexpectedly, found herself wrapped in a hug instead. She was not generally the hugging type but decided to go with it on this occasion.

'Sorry,' she said, attempting to draw herself free. 'Brandon?'

'Brandon Carr, Miss. You remember him, don't you?'

Jane didn't, at first, but then a face flashed across her memory and she chided herself for the delay in placing him. Of course she remembered Brandon Carr. How could she not?

Brandon was exceptionally bright, academically, but socially totally inadequate and so painfully intense that he had withdrawn inside a shield of self-isolation which wrapped him like a suit of armour. He came to Brincliffe midway through his A Levels, which was far from ideal, having spent the first year at one of the bigger city sixth form colleges. The story was he had been bullied. That experience and the disruption of moving did nothing to increase Brandon's self-confidence. Jane, having been made aware of his issues, tried all she knew to coax him out but she could not reach him.

'I remember,' she said. 'I didn't know he had…'

'Mmm,' confirmed Megan by pulling an especially sad expression. 'It wasn't long after we all left. A couple of months maybe. Paige Fiora told me about it. Killed himself, Paige said.'

'Oh, Lord!' Jane was genuinely shocked by the news. 'I had no idea.'

She would never have said Brandon was a prime candidate to go on to have a happy and fulfilled adult life but it never crossed her mind it might end like that. How tragic!

'The story was he took Abie's death really hard. She was always so nice to him. You know what Abie was like. She used to ask him stuff about the maths course. Ask him to explain things to her, like she didn't understand, but you know she did understand because she was so smart. She'd listen to him explaining it to her and he used to talk so quietly that I bet she couldn't even hear him most of the time, but she'd listen like she could and then be so grateful when he'd finished, like it all made sense to her all of a sudden. She was only doing it to try to make Brandon feel good but she did it in such a nice way and I think she did get through to him. He doted on her. Sometimes, he used to follow her about the school, you know, trying to keep a distance so she wouldn't notice. We noticed. We thought he was properly in love with Abie.'

Jane rolled her eyes to the skies. The sad fate of Brandon Carr, David's funeral – it was all too much. Her state of mind had been left fragile enough in the wake of everything that had happened in the last couple of weeks without having to deal with an older, previously unlearned, calamity on top. She needed to get away. Retreat home and try to heal.

'I'm sorry, Megan, I really have to go now,' she said, beginning to move away. 'Lovely to see you again, but… Goodbye.'

She turned and scooted towards the car park. A call of 'Bye, Miss' tailed away and floated off into the wind behind her.

CHAPTER
TWENTY-THREE

The black Audi was on the same side of the driveway as when they arrived last time and the red Mazda MX-5 she had noticed as they left was beside it.

Somebody has issues with his penis size, thought Clare, ungenerously.

She was in a spikey mood. The last time she called to interview Gemma Bales at home she had been too defensive, too wary of straying into striking range and her foe's poisonous bite. Clare was ready to be the aggressive one this time. She knew things they did not want her to know and that put her firmly in control. She was going to enjoy this.

Clare wanted to interview them both, together. She wanted to revel in their shared discomfort.

Gemma answered the door, eventually, wearing skin-tight black leggings, trainers and a lilac hoodie over a black top that exposed her tanned waistline. Her dark hair was dragged back into a ponytail which flicked as she haughtily turned to head back to the lounge without saying a word. Clare had not expected a warm welcome. She followed her through.

Paul Shirley was waiting on the sofa, leaning forward and gripping a large lime green water bottle between his hands. He was wearing a grey vest to show off his muscle definition and the extensive indistinguishable tattoos which almost covered both arms.

Clare headed straight to the other sofa. The murder sofa. The room was still set up the way it had been that day. Perhaps Gemma hadn't made a such a special effort last time.

She sat and smiled disconcertingly towards them, opposite her.

'Well, don't you look the athletic couple? You could have stepped straight out of the *Sports Direct* catalogue.'

'Get on with it,' said Gemma. 'We've got a class booked at the gym. You do know what a gym is, don't you?'

Clare nodded. 'Sure I do. They're everywhere these days, aren't they? They have them in prisons as well, you'll be glad to hear.'

Was that a momentary flicker of concern that cracked Gemma's hardened façade?

'Is that where you two met, then? At the gym?'

Shirley stared intently at his water bottle. Gemma crossed her legs.

'I don't see what business that is of yours. Get to the point,' she said.

'Oh, but it is my business and it is a very important point.' Clare stared back, fiercely. 'You see, when I got back to the station after the last time we met, the penny dropped about who you are, Paul Shirley, and the part you played in the original murder investigation. Then it became very much my business. The embittered ex-wife and the treacherous best friend, eh? Who would have thought it?'

Neither of them moved a muscle. Clare allowed them a moment to absorb the fact that their secret was not a secret anymore.

'So, how long has it been going on with you two? Were you having an affair before the murder or did love blossom in the courtroom?'

'That's nothing to do with you. It's not illegal.' Gemma was clearly rattled.

'Don't get me wrong,' Clare added. 'I normally wouldn't care at all about your squalid love life but it's relevant this time. You see, if I find out you two were having an affair before the time of the murder it raises a few new questions. Like was the reason you sneaked off early from work that day because you were meeting your lover for a bit of elicit shagging? Like did you two concoct a story between you for Paul to phone David and get him out of the room, away from Abie?'

'That's just ridiculous –'

'Like was the person who sneaked in through the conservatory to strangle Abie, as David alleged, none other than his own wife?'

'Now you're just being –'

'Like was that poor girl sacrificed just because you wanted your husband out of the way, at whatever cost, so your lover could move in instead?'

Shirley said nothing. He had gone pale, like he was about to be sick. Gemma's perma-tan was also a few shades lighter than when it was originally applied but she had deeper reserves of audacity to draw from.

'I think I'd like to hear you say that again with our solicitor present. You've gone fucking mental, woman. This is stupid. I've never heard such –'

'We can do this formally, if you'd like,' Clare said calmly. 'Or you can prove to me right now I've got it wrong. Let's start by you telling me how long you two have been seeing each other.'

'I'm not telling you anything,' snapped Gemma.

'Then we'll find out by other means,' Clare replied. 'What will Alexis tell us, Paul? One of our officers was due to visit her this afternoon.'

Shirley shot her a look, alarmed.

'I thought so.' She smiled. 'In the meantime, how about you tell me a bit more about the phone call you made to David that day. Did you make that story up?'

'Of course I didn't.' Shirley stared back at his water bottle.

'I believe you admitted you pinned this boy, Liam Glover, against the wall with your hand to his throat and threatened to punch him. That's a serious assault. If that actually happened, how come he didn't go to the police, like he threatened to? I'm assuming he's not the type to forgive and forget. Write it off as a bit of fun that got out of hand. Why didn't he use what happened to get you into trouble, Paul? Or did you just make the story up? Did none of that happen?'

'It did happen,' Shirley had to squeeze the words out. 'I sorted it, that's all.'

'You sorted it?' Clare repeated incredulously. 'Sorted it how? Did you kiss and make up? Did you have him bumped off? What do you mean sorted it?'

Shirley stalled. 'That's all I'm saying.'

'No matter. We're tracking Liam Glover down as well. We'll see if he's aware of his part in your little story and, if it's true, I'm sure he'll be able to enlighten us as to how you sorted it so that he didn't have you arrested, or fired, or both.'

Gemma stood.

'This has gone on long enough. We've nothing more to say. If you want to make any other wild accusations you can say them in front of our solicitor. You need to go. Now.'

Clare appeared to consider if she really wanted to leave yet but then rose to her feet. She had introduced enough chaos into their cosy little world for now. Their lies were collapsing in on them. She had been interested to see how they reacted.

'Sure,' she said. 'I'll see myself out. Have a good workout.'

———

There is something hauntingly quiet about a school building with no pupils. It's like a vast stadium after a major sporting event. The last discarded evidence of the huge swell of activity is yet to be swept away and the crushing noise still echoes around the memory, but the peaceful silence which follows is amplified somehow. The slightest sound or movement, normally lost in the regular hubbub, echoes like raised voices in a parish church.

DS Phil White pulled into the Brincliffe Edge Academy car park beside the only other car there. He had arranged to see the principal and hoped the car was his. Term ended a week earlier but the principal had still suggested this was the best place for them to meet.

When Phil had last been here, to play in an inter-school football match a decade or so ago, it had been plain old Brincliffe Edge Comprehensive and had a headmaster, rather than a principal. He headed towards the main entrance, his eyes drawn to the teaching block that hadn't been there the last time he visited. Clearly, a lot of money had been spent on modernising the place to reflect its upgrade to academy status.

He pressed the intercom button beside the heavy glass and steel electronically-controlled main doors and it responded with an angry buzz. No one answered for long enough for Phil to contemplate pressing it again but then a voice came through, terse and clipped.

'Yes?'

'DS White from South Yorkshire CID. I've an appointment to see Mr Allott.'

The doors clicked and twitched into life to beckon him in. Phil wandered through into the large empty atrium and looked around, waiting for direction and taking in his surroundings. The reception desk, the banner posters of happy, smiling, immaculately-dressed students, the framed artwork on the walls – it was all so corporate. So different to the days he was still a school pupil, not so long ago.

A man emerged, walking briskly, from a corridor to the left, his smile already set and hand outstretched.

'Hi. Scott Allott. Sorry to have kept you waiting.'

He was in his mid-forties and well turned out, as if he was so used to feeling he needed to look his best that he was unable to drop his standards even on the occasions he had no reason to maintain them. As his small concession to casual, he wore crisp dark blue chinos and a pink polo shirt with a designer logo but it was all too neat to suggest something he had just pulled on to nip into work. In his normal crumpled dark grey work suit, Phil felt scruffy by comparison, like he could be in for a telling-off and told to straighten his tie.

He accepted the handshake. 'Phil White. Thanks for agreeing to see me.'

'Not at all,' the principal gushed. 'Shall we go through?'

He led Phil back down the corridor he had recently appeared from and swiped them through a door to the administration offices using his security pass.

'This place has changed a bit since the last time I was here,' said Phil.

'Oh yes? When would that have been?'

The principal directed him with a gesture of the hand to a seat and moved to take his place on the opposite side of a large, polished light oak desk.

'I'd have been fifteen, sixteen, so at least twelve years ago. It was for a football match. We won, as I remember.'

'Ha!' Allott was happy to allow the moment of reflected triumph. 'We have an excellent sports programme now. Our mixed year tens were national lacrosse champions last year.'

'Really?' Phil attempted to sound impressed. He wasn't completely sure what lacrosse was.

'Can I get you a drink at all? Coffee? Water?'

Phil held up his hand to decline the offer. 'I'm fine, thanks. I don't want to take up too much of your time. You're probably busy.'

'It never stops! Even when the term ends,' he laughed.

'We're looking again into the Abie Moran murder case. You've probably seen there have been a couple of incidents regarding the case recently.'

Allott's fixed air of confident assurance sagged at the mention of the case. So tragic, so unfortunate, so damaging.

'Yes, I did see that.'

'Well, one of your members of staff, Paul Shirley, was one of the people we took evidence from. Paul made a phone call to David Bales at a key time in the murder timeline and it was the reason for that phone call I wanted to ask you about. You did work here at the academy at that time, didn't you?'

'I did,' he nodded, mournfully. 'I was vice-principal then. It was a dreadful time for everyone at the academy. How can I help you in this matter, though?'

'Well,' Phil shuffled in his seat. 'You may recall from the evidence given in court that Paul Shirley rang David Bales about an incident he alleged had happened at school, on the day of the murder. Shirley said he'd been involved in a confrontation with a former pupil, Liam Glover.'

'I was aware of that, yes.'

'Was disciplinary action taken against Paul Shirley as a result of that confrontation?'

Allott stroked his chin, contemplating. 'Not to my recollection.'

'It was a potentially serious allegation. Bales said in his statement that Shirley told him he grabbed Glover around the neck, pushed him against a wall and threatened to punch him. An incident like that would have serious ramifications, surely?'

'We have a zero-tolerance policy regarding unnecessary physical interventions by staff against students, yes,' said the principal. 'If we received a complaint regarding an incident of that nature, we would certainly have looked into it.'

'Are you saying there was no official reporting of the incident? No one lodged a complaint, not even Glover?'

'I'm pretty sure not. I'm certain I would have known about it if a disciplinary procedure had been launched against Paul.'

'And he still teaches at the academy?'

'Paul's our head of maths, yes.'

Bales' old job. Phil nodded to himself.

'Could I ask you to double-check your records to make sure there was no complaint made and no disciplinary procedure against Paul Shirley in regard to this incident? It's important we know for certain.'

Allott shrugged. 'Sure. I'll go through the records and get back to you. But I'm pretty certain.'

Phil took out a business card from his inside jacket pocket and slid it across the desk. 'That would be appreciated, all the same.'

'You're not suggesting Paul had something to do with Abie's murder, are you?' The principal gazed across the desk suspiciously as he took the card.

'It's just a loose end we need to tie up,' said Phil. 'Probably nothing.'

'OK.' Allott seemed unconvinced. After taking so long to move beyond the stigma of association with a murder involving a student and a member of staff, the last thing the academy needed was more unwanted scrutiny.

————

Alexis Roper needed her ironing up to date because she wanted to get her packing done before she dropped off her two cats at the cattery in the afternoon. She and a friend were flying out early next morning for a girly week of sunning themselves beside a hotel pool in Crete and drinking too much. They had paid a little extra to stay at an adults-only hotel. They'd spent enough time in the company of children lately.

She had been tempted to ignore the call from the unknown number that morning. They were rarely anything other than an inconvenience. So this one had proved. A police officer – a detective, no less – wanted to ask her a few questions. She had been nice about it and reassured Alexis there was nothing to worry about but still. It was an unwelcome interruption to her tight schedule for the day. She'd better not take long. Or be late.

What on earth did a detective want to ask her questions about anyway?

The doorbell rang and Alexis glanced at the clock. If that was her, she was three minutes early. That was good. The steam iron hissed as she set it down and strode off to answer the door.

DC Hannah Short had found it quite easy to track down Paul Shirley's former girlfriend. Her last known place of employment was Shiregreen Park Comprehensive and she still taught there.

She had mentally rehearsed the questions she wanted to put to Alexis on the drive from the station. She wanted to be sure to do this right. Being part of the small murder reinvestigation team had done wonders for her confidence and she was desperately keen to contribute fully.

A woman of similar age – a couple of years older, maybe – answered the door. She wore a baggy t-shirt and sweat pants and had her brown hair loosely tied back. She had pretty features and Hannah was immediately on her side. Why would Shirley want to dump somebody as pretty as this to take up with a cow like Gemma Bales? Creeps like Shirley never knew when they were well off.

'Hi. I'm Detective Constable Hannah Short. We spoke earlier.'

Alexis responded with a forced half-smile and opened the door wider. 'You'd better come in.'

They walked through to the small living room. 'Excuse the mess, won't you. I'm getting ready to go away on holiday tomorrow.'

The two cats nuzzling next to each other on the sofa gazed up, wide-eyed, as a stranger invaded their environment. The ginger one shot off in alarm like it had been scalded but the black one decided the risk was minimal and settled back down to sleep.

'Anywhere nice?' asked Hannah.

Alexis, already inclined to be tetchy about this unwanted visitor, bit her tongue. *Why would anyone want to spend a week away somewhere that wasn't nice?*

'Crete,' she said.

'Lovely.'

Alexis sat on the sofa beside the black cat, which glanced at her through half-open eyes as she ruffled the fur on its head. Without waiting to be invited, Hannah headed for the single armchair which was in danger of being overwhelmed by an overgrown Yucca plant.

'So what can I do for you?' asked Alexis.

'It's about Paul Shirley,' Hannah answered.

Apprehension widened Alexis' eyes at mention of that name.

'Paul? Is he in trouble? Is he all right?'

'Nothing to worry about. It's only that we're taking a fresh look at the Abie Moran murder case in the light of new developments and there are a few details we need to clarify. Am I right in saying you and Paul were still together at the time of the murder?'

Alexis' concern soon passed and she stroked the cat's head again.

'That's right. I'd left Brincliffe but we were still seeing each other.'

'Do you remember him talking about the phone call he made to David Bales on the day of the murder? More specifically, do you remember him saying anything about a confrontation with a former pupil which was the reason why he decided to call Bales?'

She mulled over her response. 'Not really.'

'Didn't he discuss it with you? From the statement he gave us later, it sounded as if the incident upset him a lot.'

'No,' said Alexis, casually. 'To be honest, I only really knew what had gone off from reading about the trial.'

Hannah screwed up her face. 'That seems odd. He never talked to you about it?'

'I suppose by the time I saw him that evening the thing with the student had been overtaken by other events. That was Paul, anyway. He wasn't very good at communicating.'

'So what was he like when you saw him on the night of the murder? Did he talk about that much?' Hannah persisted.

'Again, he didn't say a lot,' said Alexis. 'He watched the coverage on the TV but he didn't really discuss it.'

'But him and Bales were good mates at school, weren't they?'

She shrugged. 'That was Paul.'

Hannah scribbled in her notepad for no better reason than to get her head around the concept of such strange behaviour.

'Can I ask, when did you and Paul break up?'

'Oo!' Alexis thought back. 'About two and a half years ago. It was early December in 2018. He sent me a WhatsApp message to say he wanted to end it.'

'Classy.' Hannah could not resist.

'Quite. That was a shit Christmas, let me tell you.'

'Did he say why?'

'Not at the time but when I eventually got him face-to-face he admitted he was seeing somebody else. He said it was someone he'd met at the new gym he'd just joined.'

'Did he tell you her name?'

'No. I didn't ask either. I didn't want to know.'

'Which gym did he move to?'

'The big one in the city centre on Broad Street. We both used to go to the same gym in Nether Edge but he decided he wanted to join this other one that summer because he said the equipment was better. I decided to stop at the other one. I guess that was a mistake.' Alexis checked herself. 'Actually, no, it wasn't. I was angry with myself for a while, but then I started to realise I was better off without him. She's welcome to him, whoever the poor bitch is.'

Hannah smiled. *Good for you.*

'Were you together long?'

'We started seeing each other a year or so before I left Brincliffe, so not far short of three years. That was my first proper teaching job and I was still a bit wet behind the ears. I don't know why I let him talk me into going out with him because he was a few years older than me, but there we go. I learned my lesson – eventually. Christ knows why I kept letting him string me along, actually, because everything was always on his terms. He's a very self-centred man. Commitment was an alien concept to him. I thought we might become closer as a couple when we weren't working at the same school anymore, but I guess I got that one wrong as well.'

She appeared lost in her memories but then snapped herself back to the present.

'Anyway, how is all this relevant to you? Paul's in trouble, isn't he?'

'We're not certain he's been telling us the whole truth,' Hannah confided. 'That's why I wanted to hear it from you.'

'Good luck getting the truth from him,' Alexis scoffed. 'Even at the time I was never sure I could trust him. How stupid was I to stay with him so long?'

'We all make mistakes, I suppose,' said Hannah closing her notepad. 'You've been very helpful, thank you. I hope you have a great holiday.'

Alexis watched as the young policewoman drove away. She hadn't thought about Paul Shirley for a long time but talking about him again reawakened a sense of disturbance within her. She hated the realisation she had been manipulated for so long. She shuddered.

This holiday was even better timed than it had been earlier that day. Roll on Crete.

CHAPTER
TWENTY-FOUR

The mood in the room was subdued. The compact confines of their surroundings meant there was no hiding from that. DI Clare Larson picked up on it as soon as she arrived back from her fractious interview with Gemma Bales and Paul Shirley and the mask she had hastily tried to paint on before stepping through the door became instantly transparent.

Hannah Short and Phil White were at their desks, apparently absorbed in whatever was on their computer screens. Neither looked up as Clare entered the room. She had hoped to be greeted by signs that either, or both of them, were eager to share the bounties of fruitful mornings but, clearly, her arrival was not so keenly anticipated. It seemed, instead, as if the two of them had already compared notes and neither had been able to make up for the disappointment experienced by the other. They were unmistakably flat.

'Hey, team. I tell you what, you did right to fix your appointments for earlier because the traffic's gone mad out there,' said Clare with strained cheeriness.

Hannah mustered a glance up and a stilted, 'Ma'am.' Phil offered a fleeting smile before returning to his screen.

Clare stood still and drew a deep breath. This could not be allowed to linger. However discouraging their mornings had been, they needed to get this out in the open.

'Look, I think we'd better debrief and see exactly where we stand. Drop what you're doing and let's get this done.'

Her car keys clattered and skidded across the desk as Clare cast them down and turned towards the wall-mounted white board. She wiped it clean with a thin yellow rag as Hannah spun in her chair to face it and Phil wandered to perch on the edge of her desk.

'Right.' Clare flipped off the cap of a black marker pen. 'What did we learn today?'

She scribbled at the top of the board.

BALES/SHIRLEY RELATIONSHIP

'They wouldn't tell me anything about how long it had been going on, so no surprise there. What did you get from Alexis Roper, Hannah?'

The younger officer flipped through her notes.

'She was very open with me, in fairness. She didn't have a great many good things to say about Shirley, actually. She said she never trusted him to tell the truth. He was selfish, controlling, and she was quite hard on herself for staying with him so long. They were together for about three years. Oh, and another thing that struck me as a bit weird, she said he never discussed the murder with her or wanted to talk about what was going on at school in the aftermath. That's not normal, is it?'

Clare shook her head. 'When did she say they split up?'

Another check of the notes. 'December 2018. He messaged her on WhatsApp.'

Phil shuffled uneasily and muttered, 'What a twat.'

'He told her later he'd met someone else at the gym. Alexis says she didn't know the name of the other woman. On my way back from seeing her I called in at the gym she said he'd joined the previous summer, the one on Broad Street, and the manager there was very helpful. She confirmed Paul Shirley joined in July 2018 and Gemma Bales had been a member there for several years before that.'

'That's a year after the murder and a month after the end of the trial,' said Clare, reluctantly writing *'start July 2018?'* under the heading on the white board. That did not fit well with their aim to prove the relationship had been going on for longer.

'This doesn't necessarily mean Shirley and Bales hadn't been seeing each other before they started going to the same gym, of course,' she added. It was important to retain the question mark after the date on the white board.

'Did the neighbours have anything to say, ma'am?' asked Phil.

'Well,' Clare hesitated. 'I remembered the neighbours opposite the Bales house from the time of the murder. They struck me at the time as the sort who didn't let much that happened on the street escape their attention, so I popped over to see them after I had my little chat today. They're both retired and I don't think they get out much because he's got some sort of medical condition I recall they described to me in too much detail once. Anyway, they told me they'd noticed Shirley coming and going for about the last two years and that his car has been more of a regular feature on the driveway for a year or so, suggesting that was about the time he moved in. They were adamant they didn't see him on the scene before two years ago. Obviously, that's not what we were hoping to hear either but, again, it doesn't categorically rule out them being in a relationship for a lot longer.'

The other two stared at the writing on the white board and said nothing. So few words. So little substance.

'Look, this just means we're going to have to do a bit more spade work to get to where we want to be. Let's start tracking down work colleagues for both of them. Friends, family – anybody they might have confided in. Also, we know Gemma loves to put stuff on social media, so let's have a proper trawl through her previous posts to see what she's had to say about herself and Shirley over the years. I doubt she's the type to keep her private life out of public view. Where did Shirley live before he moved in with Bales? He must have had neighbours there. Were any of them aware of his involvement with Gemma before July 2018? Let's see if we can talk to other people who have been using this gym for a long time and see if they can tell us anything. Were they members of any other clubs or societies? We need to dig a bit deeper.'

Phil stroked his moustache, which Clare knew was always a sign he was less than convinced about something. She understood his doubt but he was a good copper. He was thorough. He would figure out a way to get them the information they needed.

'How'd you get on with the academy principal, Phil?'

Clare turned and scribbled a second heading on the board.

THE PHONE CALL

'He wasn't exactly keen to revisit the subject of the murder, as you can imagine,' he began. 'I asked him if he would have been made aware, had there been disciplinary proceedings against Shirley because of the alleged incident with Liam Glover, and he said he would have, but that there hadn't been any action taken. I asked him to double-check their records for any mention of a complaint made against Shirley and he said he would but I haven't heard back from him yet. Early days, I suppose.'

Clare wrote, *No complaint submitted to school?'* Again, the question mark.

'You'll like this bit. Shirley's had a promotion since. He's head of maths. That was Bales' old job, wasn't it?'

'So he's seeing Bales' ex-wife, living in his former home and he's taken his old job,' said Hannah. 'Has he got some sort of complex? Bales envy?'

Her colleagues chuckled. They were in need of a little light relief.

'And you've gone through our records again to check there was no complaint made to the police by Glover?' Clare asked.

'I have, ma'am,' Phil confirmed ominously. 'There wasn't one.'

Clare wrote four double-apostrophe ditto marks under the previous words on the board and finished it with *'police'*. No question mark.

'Right,' she said with purpose. 'We still don't know for sure what happened between Shirley and the lad Glover if, indeed, anything did. I asked Shirley if he knew why Glover had decided to take no further action and he told me he'd sorted it. They were his precise words. Sorted it. It's imperative we track Glover down and find out.'

She wrote on the board *'How did Shirley sort it?'* and then, under that *'FIND GLOVER'*, underlining the words twice.

'I have made some progress on that, ma'am,' said Phil. 'Glover does have a record. We have a string of petty misdemeanours while he was a minor and he graduated from there to a few drug and handling stolen goods offences. He was sent down for twenty-six weeks for burglary of business premises in October last year and was released on licence in January. I'm trying to establish contact with his former probation officer to get a last known number and an address for Glover. That's one of my jobs for this afternoon.'

'Good,' said Clare. 'You need to get on to that and go to see him as soon as you can. We need to hear what he has to say about what happened that day – and after it. If we can establish Shirley made up or exaggerated the story behind the phone call, then we're a step closer to establishing he was part of some sort of ruse with Gemma Bales to get her husband out of the room. We've nothing to back up our theory there yet, so we need Glover.'

Phil nodded. 'On it, ma'am.'

'In the meantime, all of us need to do all we can to build up as complete a profile of Bales and Shirley as we can. Look into their pasts, separately and since they've been a couple – for however long that's been. They're definitely hiding something and, as it stands, they're still our most likely suspects. But we shouldn't lose sight of any other potential leads in this case either. We still need to work through as many names as we can on the list of original interview subjects to see if we can turn up anything that was missed first time around.'

Clare turned to face the board again.

'I know we haven't been able to come up with anything rock solid yet but we've already opened up some new avenues. There's too much about this case we just don't know yet and it's up to us to find it. We could use a few more bodies, we know that, but it's just us three for now, so we get on with it. Let's get to work.'

CHAPTER
TWENTY-FIVE

Brandon Carr. Poor troubled, tormented Brandon Carr.
The name had been echoing around Jane Featherby's mind since hearing it for the first time in years at David Bales' funeral.

She had not been able to put a face to the name at first but she had been under a lot of stress that day. Now she remembered him. She had thought about him a lot in the days since.

Poor Brandon. The sixth form student who took his own life, seemingly because the only person in his peer group to show him any compassion – maybe the only person of his own age all his life – was dead.

Poor Brandon. She hadn't realised he was so utterly besotted with Abie, to the point that he followed her like a frightened abandoned stray which had been thrown a few scraps by a stranger, too timid to leave the shadows but instantly and completely devoted.

Jane had not been made aware of this unhealthy dedication to the unattainable Abie at the time. How would she have handled it if she had? She would certainly have discouraged it. Stalking a fellow student, however innocent his motives, was not acceptable. It was harassment, even if it was always conducted at a distance. She would have had to be firm with Brandon about that.

How did Abie handle it? Was she even conscious it was going on? From what Megan told Jane at the funeral, it appeared to have been an open secret among the rest of the sixth form group. Did Abie know and choose to tolerate it?

Jane was upset to realise what had been going on. As head of sixth form, she should have known about it and acted. She rebuked herself for a duty not performed. It was another sign she was not as close to the group as she wanted to be. Not enough of a mentor, too much of an outsider.

But she had tried to help Brandon.

The first time she met him was early in the school year, shortly after his switch to Brincliffe Edge Academy for the final year of his two-year A Level studies.

The instruction passed on to her was that Brandon had been unhappy at his previous college because he had been singled out and picked on by a group of other students. Bullies. Such behaviour immediately ignited Jane's instinct to stand up for the victim and she wanted to take Brandon into her protection, but gaining his trust was hard work.

She recalled the first time they talked. They met in the small side room often used for counselling students, with its gentle lighting and comfortable chairs. She sat at ninety degrees to Brandon. No barriers, non-confrontational. He was still painfully on edge. For most of the session, the only view she had of him was the top of his head and his overgrown, naturally curly brown hair. His chin remained stuck to his chest.

Jane tried all she knew to coax him into conversation. She didn't expect him to reveal his inner-most feelings and only wanted to establish the most tentative of connections, but even that aim proved too much. Often, he would not answer her at all. Other times, he would shrug sulkily or mumble, 'dunno'. She ended the session early when it was clear it was going nowhere and he scurried eagerly away to the safety of solitude.

What had left him so badly damaged?

Jane made contact with Brandon's previous school, the one he went to before he left for his first sixth form college, and talked to Wendy, a sweet lady she had met a couple of times at union meetings. The picture Wendy painted was discouragingly familiar.

Brandon was exceptionally bright academically but a deeply disturbed young man. He was unable to build relationships, anxious among groups, had perilously low self-esteem and had, occasionally, suffered angry, flailing panic attacks.

Was he ever offered professional help?

Wendy said they had recommended to Brandon's mother that she take him to see a therapist and had offered to make the arrangements themselves but the mother would not listen. She insisted her son was only very shy and would grow out of it. They could not persuade her to change her mind.

But from researching on the internet, Jane knew there was more to it than that. What she saw in Brandon was so similar to the profile of a youngster with a recognised teenage social phobia.

The articles said it was common.

The articles said it was treatable.

The articles said sufferers didn't always just grow out of it.

The thought of the troubled young man growing up to be a troubled adult without an effort having been made to change his course was too much. Jane decided she should visit the mother herself.

———

Varey Street would have challenged any estate agent's skill at selling desirability.

It nestled in a forgotten dark island between three main roads, the constant noise of traffic and heavy pall of abandonment hanging over it like a permanent rain cloud. It's crumbling nineteenth-century terraces had escaped lasting damage during the Sheffield Blitz and had survived the scourge of the council planners when so many near-identical streets close by had been flattened to make way for the inner ring road. Quite why it was spared could not be explained. Perhaps it had simply been overlooked, hidden away as the construction workers loaded up their heavy machinery and moved on before anyone could point out they had missed a bit.

So it had remained, condemned to the slow decay of neglect. Even its main access road, off Shoreham Street, had long since been closed off. It had been left to wither and die.

The estate agents' art was not tested often because nobody wanted to buy a house on Varey Street to live there themselves. Most were owned by private landlords who saw opportunities to make regular easy money from those who depended on benefits for their only income. People stuck on the bottom rung of the social ladder who were too desperate to make demands about standards. There had been attempts to dress up some of the properties as student housing but the university authorities, concerned at the potential horror stories, soon put a block on that.

Jane shared their alarm as she edged her way along the street, peering through the early evening gloom for any sign that she was approaching number one hundred. The long, bleak stretch of conjoined dark brick houses, without sign of any personal touches to distinguish one from another, was almost hypnotic as she rolled by them. She liked to think she appreciated that not everyone in life got the breaks others took for granted but she hadn't realised somewhere so run down was so close to her own reasonably comfortable home. Less than a ten-minute drive.

So this was where Brandon Carr lived.

She spotted a number ninety-six and pulled in. The street seemed even more forebodingly menacing as soon as she turned off the ignition key and the reassuring hum of the engine, with its promise of a quick escape if needed, was gone. Jane clenched her fists and bit her lip. This had to be done. She opened the car door and climbed out.

Broken glass crunched under her foot as she set it down on the pavement. She looked around. Shards of whatever it once was glistened in the light of the feeble street lamp. Jane checked in case any others had been scattered on to the road close to her tyres. Being stranded with a puncture was the last thing she needed. She could not see any but was struck by a sudden fear of her car not being there at all when she returned. It was not a safe place. She locked it and checked twice to make sure it was secured, then reluctantly moved away.

She wasn't the first to take a chance on leaving a car there. Occasionally, someone would decide it was close enough to the city centre to make it a better option than paying for parking. Sometimes, lost football fans conscious that kick-off time was fast approaching would see it as a port in a storm. They would often be made to regret their choices.

It was just as well Jane was not aware of that.

Number one hundred had a cheap, wood-effect front door so flimsy it looked like it had been set up for a stunt man to dive through without any danger of harm. It rattled when Jane knocked.

Brandon opened it. He was still in the ill-fitting dark suit he wore most days for school but had taken off his tie.

'Hello Brandon.'

He opened the door wider, too uncomfortable to even attempt eye contact.

'Come in.'

She stepped straight into the front room and wiped her feet on the dirty mat. A woman was standing, ready to greet her. She was younger than Jane, thin and pale, with the dark rings of a burden-some life sitting heavy under eyes that had long since been drained of hope. She must have been very young when she had Brandon.

Barely a single strip of the faded flowery wallpaper in the room was stuck down completely and there were black flecks of damp in the corners, spreading onto the ceiling. The furniture was cheap and passed down but the effort had been made to keep it clean. What little they had they took care of.

As Jane moved towards the woman, Brandon locked the front door and slipped on a security chain, out of habit.

'Hello, Miss Featherby.'

They shook hands. 'Jane.'

The woman smiled, grateful for the small friendliness. 'Courtney.'

After a moment of awkwardness, she added: 'Which one is your car?'

It was not a question Jane expected. 'Er, the purple Micra,' she answered, pointing unnecessarily in the direction of where she had parked it.

'Go and keep an eye on it, love,' the woman said tenderly to her son, who bustled straight upstairs to keep watch.

'There are some dodgy types around here,' she explained. Jane tried not to let her increased agitation show.

'Come and have a sit down, please. Can I get you a cup of tea?'

Jane perched on the edge of a threadbare brown sofa which creaked as it accepted her weight. 'I'm fine, thank you.'

'You wanted to talk to me about Brandon going to university,' Courtney prompted.

'Yes, I –'

'I'm sorry but you might have had a wasted journey. We can't afford tuition fees and all that. There's no way.'

The objection had been anticipated. 'I don't know if anybody went through Brandon's options on funding at his last college, but there is help available for students from low-income families. Bursaries, grants. Money you wouldn't have to pay back.'

'Really?' Her eyes widened.

'Yes,' Jane added with enthusiasm. 'I'd be more than happy to help you secure as much of that as we could because I truly believe Brandon would benefit so much from further education. He has such a gift for maths and I honestly think he would excel. Brandon could have a very bright future.'

Courtney's shoulders slumped and she stared at her knees. Possibility was such a rare visitor that she didn't know how to behave in its company. She wanted to be carried along by the vision of her son escaping their desperate life and going on to succeed but she dared not.

'The thing is,' she said, faltering, lowering her voice. 'You must have seen that Brandon is not very… outgoing. He finds it difficult with new people and new places. I'm not sure he'd cope.'

The mother's pain was obvious. Jane nodded sympathetically. This objection had been anticipated, too. Behind it was the main reason she wanted to pay this visit in the first place.

She, too, spoke in hushed tones.

'Brandon is not unique. Lots of other young people experience what he's going through and it can be very distressing for them, but he doesn't have to put up with it and hope it goes away. He can get treatment.'

'I don't want them to drug him up. I've been through that myself after I had him. It was like they were trying to turn me into a zombie.'

Jane winced. How often it was that behind one sad story lay another.

'I think in Brandon's case what he needs is therapy. Look, I'm far from an expert on these things, but I've done a bit of reading about it and the impression I get is that lots of young people suffer similar anxiety. That's what it is – a form of anxiety. It can be very confusing for them because they don't really know what they're going through and have no idea how to deal with it, but there are experts out there who can talk to them and help them.'

'Brandon can always talk to me. I'm his mother.'

'But with respect, Courtney, you're no specialist and neither am I. I'm sure you're very close, the two of you, but you know how it is when you're Brandon's age. Sometimes, the last person you want to confide in is a parent. I've had parents tell me that if they didn't secretly spy on their kids' social media accounts they'd have no idea what they were thinking or doing. Now, I'm not suggesting you two have that kind of relationship. Far From it. All I'm saying is sometimes it's easier to talk to someone who isn't as close. Preferably someone who understands the condition and can give Brandon sound, practical advice for learning to control his emotions.'

Tears welled in Courtney's eyes. This was difficult to hear, but could it be true? She felt as if she had let her son down.

'If we get on top of this soon, there's no reason why Brandon shouldn't be able to grow into a perfectly well-adjusted young man. He could go to university, get a good degree and land the kind of job that could help him and you enjoy a brighter future. Just think of that, Courtney. Don't we all owe him that opportunity? Let us help him.'

A large watery blob ran down Courtney's nose and landed with a splash on the leg of her jeans.

'But what will I do if he goes off to university? I'd be all alone.'

They had arrived at the root of this mother's biggest fear. Brandon was a complicated teenager with needs neither of them understood, but he was her whole world. What else did she have? How can anyone sell a vision of a better life that depends first on making it infinitely worse?

'He doesn't have to leave. There are two excellent universities in Sheffield he could apply to. He could carry on living at home.'

Jane left shortly after with the belief they had made progress. Courtney promised to give what they had discussed serious thought.

The car was unscathed. The watchman had done a good job. Jane hoped she had done her best for him, too.

————

The Academy pulled out all the stops to land Brandon every bit of funding they could lay their hands on and he did secure a place at Sheffield University, studying maths. Jane was concerned at the lack of progress in getting him the psychological help she believed he needed, but Brandon did appear more settled the longer the academic year went on. Still the loner, but no longer the ticking time bomb.

No doubt, the kindness shown by Abie Moran played a large part in his improvement. Jane realised that now. Looking back, it was plain there was so much about the dynamic of that group she didn't know.

She had thought about Brandon a lot in the last few days and turned on her laptop to see what she could find out about his terrible premature death. As the ageing machine whirred through its laborious warm-up procedures, another memory flashed through Jane's mind.

Late in the school year, just before the start of final exams, Brandon came to her. It was so unusual for him to make the first move in interactions with anybody that Jane was a little startled when he first spoke. He wanted to know if he could go to Edinburgh University instead of Sheffield. Edinburgh? Jane explained that it was exceptionally late to contemplate such a move. That places at the top universities were difficult to come by anyway and that they would almost certainly be over-subscribed at this stage of the process. She reminded him that Sheffield was a really good university and that he would still be able to live at home, with his mother. She tried to put down the idea gently. He muttered something indistinguishable and shuffled away. He didn't raise the subject again.

Why Edinburgh? Then Jane realised.

Abie was going to study medicine at Edinburgh.

The laptop finally consented to allow her onto the internet and Jane keyed in the name.

Brandon Carr

She hesitated before adding one more key word to qualify her search.

Suicide

There was a result. A newspaper report of an inquest. It said he died on October the eighth, 2017. Jane worked it out. Almost three months after the murder and a few weeks after she had quit Brincliffe Edge Academy. Plainly, nobody had thought it worth passing the news on to her. That was how wide and how quickly the rift had grown between her and her former colleagues.

Brandon was found hanging around the back of abandoned industrial premises. The report said his body was discovered a day after his mother reported him missing.

What a terrible, desolate way to go. Poor Brandon.

Jane closed her laptop.

Once she began to reconcile herself to the shocking sadness of his death, she thought some more about Brandon. Thoughts on a different line.

The lonely, emotionally vulnerable teenage boy and the beautiful, self-assured teenage girl.

Girl shows boy kindness, boy becomes dedicated to girl but dare not express his feelings, boy begins to stalk girl, girl is murdered by an, as yet, unidentified assailant in an apparently motiveless assault – not for a reason that has been satisfactorily established yet, anyhow.

Then boy kills himself.

Jane thought about that a lot. Could it really mean what she was beginning to think it could mean? The more she considered it, the more it began to make sense.

CHAPTER
TWENTY-SIX

Detective Sergeant Phil White didn't usually feel nervous before conducting witness interviews but this was different.

Their lack of progress was not down to lack of effort. Between the three members of the team, they had gone through the list of witnesses from the time of the original case and had made contact with all of them. They had tapped into a new resource of friends, family, neighbours, work colleagues – anyone they could think of with any past connection to Gemma Bales and Paul Shirley – and had approached them all. Phil himself had dedicated hours to going through social media posts in an attempt to trace the source of their relationship back to before the time of the murder.

All this had turned up nothing. Nothing that took the case further forward anyway. Nothing that left them any closer to nailing their chief suspects.

At the same time, nothing they had heard had shaken their instinctive belief that neither Bales nor Shirley were the type you would like to invite to your house for tea. Not many people they talked to had a good word for either of them. In their general unpleasantness, they appeared a well-matched couple, but that didn't make them co-conspirators in a murder. Either they were very good at covering their tracks, or…

Or…

The looming probability remained unspoken between the three of them, but Phil had certainly thought it and he would have been surprised if the other two claimed they hadn't. The focus, for now, remained on exhausting every option before they had to turn to face what was increasingly likely. If that was where they stood after pursuing every possibility, then they would have to accept Bales and Shirley might not have been responsible for Abie Moran's death. That was the nature of the job sometimes. Sometimes, the clues lead you down blind alleys. Sometimes, you only arrived at the truth by eliminating other leads that appeared stronger at the time. All you can do is be thorough.

No stone unturned, right?

This knowledge could not insulate them against disappointment and morale had noticeably dropped within the tight confines of the glorified cupboard where they had spent so much time together recently. The DI was feeling the pressure. She had been irritable, snappy. Phil had worked alongside her for a few years and had never seen her so tense. They were all badly in need of a breakthrough and one real possibility remained.

Liam Glover. The disruptive former pupil Paul Shirley claimed to have tangled with on the day of the murder. The reason why Shirley said he needed to call David Bales. The call that prompted Bales to leave Abie alone in the room. The opportunity maybe for someone to enter the house through the rear conservatory and strangle her.

The hope that had sustained them so far had been drained almost dry. All that remained was concentrated on the chance that Shirley lied about the incident which had allegedly left him so distraught, so in fear for his professional future, that he had to call the one man he felt he could turn to in confidence. If they could only prove Shirley had lied about the confrontation with Glover, it could lend credibility to their theory that the call was made purely to get Bales out of the room and that the reason why Shirley wanted Bales out of the room was so his lover, Bales' wife Gemma, could sneak into the house and exact deadly revenge over her husband's young conquest. That way, so the theory went, she would be setting up David Bales as the only viable suspect in a brutal murder.

Only one person, besides Shirley and Gemma, knew the truth about the incident at school. Liam Glover.

Phil White had tracked Glover to a small town called Long Eaton, just off the M1 between Nottingham and Derby. The information came from Glover's former parole officer, who had provided a character assessment as well as a phone number. He said his former charge appeared a changed man for his brief experience of prison and was making a genuine effort to get his life back on the right course. That was encouraging. Phil hoped it would make him co-operative. The last thing he needed was to be met by a wall of silence from a man harbouring a stubborn dislike of authority figures. They couldn't compel him to tell them what they wanted to hear.

When Phil announced to the others that Glover had agreed to meet him, it was greeted with muted approval. None of them wanted to get carried away by this one piece of good news. They were glad it was happening and that was it. Nothing else needed to be said about the potential importance of what Glover might disclose. They all knew what was at stake.

———

Phil couldn't remember the last time he had been in a McDonald's. It was quite a while and he hadn't been in a hurry to change that, but it was Glover's suggestion and he went along with it. As neutral territory goes, he figured it was about as neutral as there was.

He stood back from the counter and looked up at the menu. It was lunchtime and he had flirted with the idea of eating but the pervasive whiff of overdone meat and cooking fat blunted his appetite. He ordered a coffee.

The staff in their grey and yellow uniforms were caught in a dance of synchronised bedlam behind the counter as an alarm signalled another batch of chips was ready to be raised out of the frier and numbers were called out for customers to step forward and collect their brown paper bags of food. Everybody appeared perfectly aware of what they were meant to be doing, though. Phil paid for his coffee and took his yellow and white paper cup to find a place to sit, as far from the smell of cooking as he could.

He settled on one in a line of tight booths and lowered himself on to the hard, easy-wipe bench where he could see most of the rest of the restaurant. The parole officer had emailed him a mug shot of Glover and the onus was on him to make sure they didn't miss each other.

There was no sign yet, but it was still early.

He checked around him. A man in the next booth was working intently at a laptop. Two overweight shaven-headed middle-aged men in matching fleeces to his right were discussing some detail about their work and, behind him, he could hear two older women talking too loudly to make sure they could be heard above the bland piped pop music. A young couple a little further away were absorbed by the sight of their small child, who must have been four or five, munching on a chicken nugget, cooing proudly as if the process was some sort of rites of passage initiation.

Then, peering back towards the counter, Phil saw him. Prison mug shots are never the most flattering of likenesses but it was certainly him. Glover was wearing a yellow high-vis tabard over an open black hooded top, scruffy jeans and heavy work boots. Everything he wore was covered in brick dust that almost seemed to hover around him in a cloud, like the character in the *Peanuts* cartoons. He was pressing his order into a touch screen monitor and, when he had finished, he turned to scan the room, unsure who exactly he was looking for. Phil tried to rise without banging his thigh on the dividing table and held up his hand to signal his whereabouts. Glover saw him and smiled an acknowledgement, then turned away to wait for his order to be processed.

Phil was relieved. A small part of him had feared Glover would change his mind and not turn up. He could relax about that now, at least. He took a first sip of coffee. Almost grudgingly, he admitted to himself he had tasted worse.

The man opposite snapped shut his laptop and hurried away. Barely had he left his seat when a staff member swooped with spray bottle and cloth to clean after him. As she turned to go, job done, Glover sidestepped past her with his brown paper bag and tall white cup.

Phil slithered along the bench so that he could rise properly. Glover was taller and far more sturdily built, much more naturally suited to tough physical work. His features were young, spattered with grime and erratic stubble, but his body, the way he carried himself, was older.

'Liam.' Phil held out a hand.

Glover hurriedly put his bag and cup on the table and wiped some of the ingrained dirt off his right hand by rubbing it under his armpit before offering it in return.

'You must be the copper.'

It was said in a friendly enough tone but Phil hoped it hadn't been overheard. He didn't want to attract any attention to the conversation he was about to have.

'Phil White,' he corrected. They sat.

'You not eating?' asked Glover, unpacking the contents of his bag.

'No, I'm good.'

The younger man plucked a handful of thin chips from the

paper sleeve and shovelled them into his mouth like he hadn't eaten in a month.

'The site I'm working on is just down the road from here and I haven't been able to keep away from this place,' he said, chewing. 'You wouldn't believe how much you get to crave eating this stuff when you're inside. You get obsessed. When you're locked in a shitty little cell for 22 hours a day with a bloke who can't speak English and wakes you up every night screaming like he's been set on fire, you've got a lot of time to think about stuff you used to do on the outside and dream of doing it again. I'm making up for it now.'

He unwrapped a hefty burger from greaseproof paper and took a huge bite.

Phil tried not to make it obvious how taken aback he was by the ferocity of the way the meal was being attacked.

'Thanks for agreeing to meet me. Did your probation officer explain to you why I wanted to talk?'

'Hmm,' Glover nodded, lifting his cup and sucking a drink up the straw to help clear his mouthful of food. 'He said it was about that murder at my old school a few years ago. I don't know what good you think I'm going to be but I said I'd come. Mr Johnson's been good to me, to be fair. He helped me get this job.'

'Mr Johnson had plenty of good things to say about how well you've adjusted since you got out.' It was an undisguised compliment but Phil needed his trust.

'I'm never going there again,' Glover replied with certainty. 'I did thirteen weeks in Nottingham and that was enough. There's people there who'll do you serious harm for no reason and not all the nutters are locked up, y'know what I mean?'

Phil attempted to keep his expression neutral.

'Anyway, I'm done with all the stuff that put me there. I'm thinking about going to college to learn how to be a proper builder. I don't want to be a labourer all my life.'

'Good for you.'

The young man glanced up, checking to be sure the encouraging words were sincerely meant. Satisfied they were, he bit off another chunk of burger.

'What I particularly wanted to talk to you about,' Phil thought it was time to explain, 'was what happened when you were caught back on the school premises on the day of the murder. I need to know who you saw and what you did.'

Glover's eyes hardened with suspicion. Was it in reaction to a situation he had no recollection of? Was he about to say he wasn't there that day?

'Is somebody trying to get me into trouble?'

'Not at all.' Phil tried to dismiss the suggestion with a shake of his head and took a sip of coffee in an attempt to keep it casual between them. In his haste to find what he needed to know he had jumped in clumsily. He couldn't afford to put a barrier between them.

'It's in connection with something we're looking into. Nobody's suggesting you could be in bother at all. I'm just hoping you might be able to fill in one or two gaps we have. Did you go to the school that day?'

Glover paused, considering. Phil held his breath.

'Yeah,' he said at last. 'I did.'

'Why? Why did you go there? You'd officially left by then, hadn't you?'

The young man was still contemplating how deeply he wanted to be drawn, but then his expression softened again and he picked up a single chip, twiddling it between his fingers.

'I was bored, I suppose. I'd been so full of wanting to get away from that shit heap that I hadn't thought about what I'd do next. I'd been hanging about with some other kids I knew, like I used to when I got excluded, but I must have been on my own that day, so I decided to go back and give it the big "look at me, you can't tell me what to do anymore". I was a cocky little sod then. I was doing it for a laugh. I wasn't looking to make trouble. I didn't want to smash stuff or nick stuff particularly. I was just being a pain in the arse, I suppose. That's what I was like then.'

Phil nodded. He was being introduced to the young, unruly teenaged Glover. 'Who did you see?'

'Ha!' The memory burst over him. 'Shifty Shirley!'

Did I hear that right?

'That was what the girls called him, you know? He used to creep them out. They'd catch him looking at them, letching. None of them used to like being in the same room as him on their own. I don't think he ever got handsy with anybody or he'd have been nicked for it, but they'd stay well away from him.'

'Is that right?'

'They used to reckon he only made out he was mates with Bales because the girls liked Bales and he thought they'd like him if they hung together. Bales was all right. He'd be fair with you. Shirley wouldn't. He'd be all over the smart kids like he was trying to be the cool teacher and all friendly like, but then if he didn't like you he'd be on at you all the time. He was a dick.'

Glover fed this burst of vitriol with another mouthful of burger and considered what he was going to say next as he chewed.

'So I'd just walked into the school and the first person I sees is Shifty Shirley and I'm thinking like, "Not that dick again" and he starts walking towards me all like, "What are you doing here? You're not allowed in here anymore. Clear off or I'll call the police". Obviously, I wasn't just going to do what he said because I was a cocky little sod and all that, so I started challenging him, like "Are you going to make me or what?" He said something about if I'd spent more time at school when I was meant to be there I wouldn't be such a waste of space, trying to get at me, and I came back with, "At least I'm not a paedo who probably only wanted to be a teacher so I could look at little girls" and that really got him.'

He paused, for dramatic effect. 'What happened then?' prompted Phil.

'He went for me. He shoved me against the wall and he got hold of me around the neck. He started swearing at me, calling me this and that and the other, saying what he was going to do to me.'

'What did you do?'

'I couldn't do anything. If he tried that with me now I could handle him. I'd put him down, no bother. I used to think I was a tough nut back then, but I was still only a kid really. He had proper man's strength. I was a bit scared, to be honest.'

Phil arched his eyebrows. 'I'm not surprised. Didn't anybody see this happen?'

'There was nobody about, as far as I could see. We were outside one of the main blocks…'

'In his statement, Shirley said it was in one of the classrooms,' Phil interrupted.

'Definitely outside,' Glover answered with an emphatic shake of the head.

'Anyway, sorry.' A hand gesture invited him to continue. 'What did he do then?'

'He must have realised he was proper choking me. I was gagging. I thought he was going to kill me. His eyes were mad, but then it kind of dawned on him what he was doing and he let me go. I was like coughing and trying to get my breath and he just kind of backed away a few steps and stood over me. He was still trying to be the big hard man but I could tell when I looked at him he was shitting himself. I picked myself up and started walking off, back towards where I came in, but I'm giving it all, "You've done it now, you wanker. I'm going to get you sacked. I'm going to get the coppers on you for this" as I'm moving away. I just wanted to get off, to be honest. I had some right bruises around my neck the next day.'

Phil took another sip of coffee. 'And was that the end of it? Did you make a formal complaint?'

'Nah!' He pushed in the last of his burger and wiped his fingers on his filthy top. 'I couldn't be arsed with all that crap.

Nobody would have taken my word against his anyway. That wasn't the end of it, though. Next day, he's round at my house.'

'Really?' This hadn't been mentioned before.

'Yeah. It was about eleven o'clock. I'd only just got up and there was a knock at the door. I thought it might have been one of my mates, but it was him.'

Phil sat back. 'That must have been a surprise.'

'Not kidding. I'm like, "What are you doing here?" and he's like, "Can I come in for a minute, Liam?" Liam! He'd never called me Liam before! I wasn't going to let him in the house. I thought he might have come to have another go at me, so I'm like, "What do you want?" and he's like, "I just wanted to clear up our disagreement yesterday". So I'm thinking he's realised I could land him in the shit here and so I started again with, "I'm going to get you sacked for what you did. I'm going to the coppers", just to make him squirm, like. He goes a bit pale, but then he says, "There's no need for that. I'm sorry for reacting like I did. I'd like us to come to an arrangement so I can make it up to you". I'm thinking, "What's he mean by that?" but before I could say anything he's reached into his coat pocket and brought out a roll of tenners.'

'Is that right?' Phil laughed.

'I went to take it off him but he pulled his hand back and said, "There's three hundred quid here. If I give you this, that's the end of it, right? You keep what happened yesterday to yourself". I'm thinking, three hundred quid! That was a lot of money to me then and, as I said, I had no intention of going to the coppers anyway. But I was playing it cool, like I was thinking about it, before I said, "All right. It's a deal". He hands me the money and I shut the door on him. That was the last time I saw him.'

Glover took a satisfied slurp from his drink. 'Do you think I should have tried to screw some more out of him?'

So that was what Shirley meant by 'taking care of it'. He paid the kid off. Everybody else in the school was in shock, comforting each other after one of their own had been killed the day before, and Shirley was saving his own neck. It added another sordid blot on the picture they had painted of the character they were dealing with, but Phil also understood the greater and far less palatable implication.

The story Shirley told them in his statement was, essentially, the truth.

They were back at square one.

'So what's all this got to do with that lass who got murdered?' Glover's question snapped him out of unhappy contemplation.

'As I said earlier, just dotting i's and crossing a few t's,' said Phil with what he hoped was a believable tone of casual dismissal. 'Nothing of any great importance. All part of an on-going investigation.'

Glover appeared unappeased. 'Are you saying Shirley had something to do with it, then? I thought it was Bales who killed her.'

'It's...' Phil was clearly fudging. 'It's not something I can talk about. Part of an on-going investigation, as I said. Nothing for you to worry about, though.'

The younger man's curiosity was stirred but he could tell he was being blanked. 'OK,' he answered in reluctant acceptance.

They stared at each other for a moment. Their conversation had reached a natural end.

'Anyway,' said Phil, slapping the palms of his hands on the table surface. 'I need to get off back to Sheffield. I really appreciate you taking time to meet with me, Liam, and for answering my questions. All the best with going to college, if you decide to go down that route.'

He shuffled along the bench and got to his feet to offer a parting handshake.

'No probs,' said Glover.

'Thanks again,' Phil added, awkwardly, before he turned to head for the door.

Outside, the long queue of cars waiting for the drive-through, which had snaked all the way back to the roundabout and the main road when Phil had arrived, had gone completely. For no perceptible reason, everybody wanted a takeaway half an hour ago and now no one did. As he walked back to the car park, it seemed to him to sum up rather too neatly how the course of the investigation had gone.

CHAPTER
TWENTY-SEVEN

Clare Larson stood outside the office waiting to be called through. She had declined the personal assistant's invitation to take a seat. She didn't feel like sitting. The PA, usually on friendly first name terms with the Detective Inspector, also quickly worked out that she didn't much feel like talking either. She could tell something was wrong.

Clare also suspected something was wrong. Detective Superintendent Haley liked to be kept informed but didn't very often insist on meeting with individual officers face to face first thing in the morning. That was not a good sign. She was pretty sure it was about the case. Of course it was about the case. But the urgency with which the meeting was called disturbed her. It suggested the DSU had something to tell her, instead of that he was keen to find out what she had to tell him.

That was why she stood, as awkward as the shy, sober stranger in the corner at a cocktail party, wondering what news she was about to hear and expecting it to be bad. Ready to fight her corner but knowing she was about to have to negotiate a deal armed with nothing more than a handful of shiny beads.

DS Phil White's interview with Liam Glover meant their number one line of enquiry was practically dead in the water. What made that harder to accept was that they didn't really have number two, three or four lines of enquiry. They were working hard to open them up, but had made no progress.

Obviously, Clare couldn't tell that to the DSU. He'd shut them down straight away. That would be especially bad because the one thing she was increasingly convinced of, since they had reopened the investigation, was it was unlikely David Bales was the killer. Her instinct told her it just didn't add up. But then, her instinct also told her Gemma Bales and Paul Shirley were guilty and look where that had led her. She had no proof it was them and no proof it wasn't David Bales. She was beginning to doubt the reliability of her instincts.

The internal phone buzzed twice on the PA's desk. It was the signal. The PA confirmed it with an arching of the eyebrows as an unspoken 'good luck' and Clare moved, full of false bravado, for the door through to the DSU's office.

'Take a seat, Clare.'

DSU Haley didn't look ready to tear into his Detective Inspector, so that was something. He rubbed his right hand over the few stubborn tufts of hair on the top of his head and sighed as he read the top sheet of a stapled bundle held in his left hand like he was about to deliver his line at a play rehearsal.

'Yes. The Moran case.'

Clare sat. 'We've got a really strong new lead on that, sir, and have been working hard to put together a solid case that has the wife at the core of a new scenario, in collusion with one of the original case's key witnesses who, as it turns out –'

'Can I just stop you there, Clare?' The DSU cut her off without taking his eyes off the sheet. She immediately fell obediently silent.

'We've received an official complaint from solicitors acting on behalf of Gemma Bales and Paul Shirley alleging harassment and intimidation. They say you personally visited their home and have made threats based on unsubstantiated allegations against them and that you and other members of the team have approached personal and professional associates of both Ms Bales and Mr Shirley, implicating them in serious crimes on several occasions. These are serious complaints, Clare. You and I both know this is likely to go to the Independent Police Complaints Commission.'

He averted his gaze from the papers for the first time and stared straight at the DI.

'Is there any justification to these claims?'

Clare was stunned. She expected Gemma, in particular, to respond aggressively to the investigation against them, but she hadn't anticipated they would go so rapidly through the formal channels. They knew Gemma lacked nothing in audacity but this was brazen, even by her standards.

'Well, none, sir,' she blurted, aware even to her own ear that she sounded unconvincing. 'DS White, DC Short and I have pursued our enquiries rigorously, as you would expect us to, but we've never overstepped the mark. We regard those two as suspects in an unsolved murder investigation and we've set out to follow up all available leads. It's no more than that, sir.'

Haley sat back and placed the papers on his desk, contemplating.

'I have no doubt,' he said at last. 'Should this matter go further, you will have my unreserved backing, but I need to know what we have on this pair.'

Clare went through it all, from first finding out that Bales and Shirley were a couple to formulating a theory about how they had conspired to commit murder and their motive for doing so. She told the DSU how they had come to doubt the validity of both suspects' accounts of where they were on the day of the murder and how information from the many new subjects they had interviewed recently consistently undermined the personal integrity of both.

'And have you been able to establish they were together at the time of the murder?'

Haley had cut straight to the key question.

'I feel certain they were, sir. They've been evasive whenever I've asked them about it directly and it's just too much of a coincidence to suggest they hooked up randomly sometime after the murder. I don't believe it happened like that. I believe they were lovers at the time and they needed David Bales out of the way. With him on the hook for murder, she had the house to herself and Shirley was free to move in.'

'Rather a drastic means to an end, though, don't you think?' The DSU had not taken his eyes off Clare all the while, staring at her, impassively but intently.

'It was the solution that presented itself, sir, and she's certainly capable, in my view. She's ruthless, cold, utterly selfish. Shirley has no moral compass and is completely dominated by her. I have no doubt he'd go along with whatever she asked him to do.'

Haley nodded and picked up the stapled sheets again.

'Yet the question of when they became a couple is key here, is it not? And in their statement issued by the solicitors with the complaint they directly refute any suggestion they were in a relationship at the time of the murder.'

He flicked through the pages until he found the passage he wanted.

'Here it is. It reads: "Ms Bales and Mr Shirley, while wanting to make it clear that they deeply resent the intrusions on their private life by the police, have nevertheless committed to an affidavit to clarify aspects of their relationship questioned during the current police investigation. Ms Bales and Mr Shirley wish it to be known that they did not enter into a personal relationship until August 2018. They first communicated directly at Billy's Gym of Broad Street in Sheffield, where Ms Bales had been a member for several years and Mr Shirley had only recently joined, having recognised each other from their attendance at the court trial involving Ms Bales' former husband. This trial had concluded more than two months earlier. While each was aware of the other through their mutual connection to Mr Bales, they did not have occasion to speak to each other before August 2018, let alone engage in a clandestine relationship, as alleged by the police. Ms Bales and Mr Shirley have entered into this sworn declaration of their own volition and ask that their right to privacy should now be respected." Then we have a copy of the signed document and such.'

Haley lay the sheets on his desk again with a resigned sigh.

'With respect, sir, I don't believe a word either of them says. They know what we're trying to prove and they'll do anything they can to stop us getting to the truth. If that means telling lies on a stack of bibles, then…'

'But do we have any evidence, Clare?' The DSU sounded as if his patience was being stretched. 'Do we have anything we could use against them to prove their relationship goes back further than they have said? Do we have any solid, verifiable evidence which would stand up to scrutiny if we were to go ahead today and charge them in connection with the death of the Moran girl?'

There was no point trying to pull wool over the DSU's eyes.

'Not yet, sir,' she admitted, dragging out the words as if they were barbed wire.

'Then there's the problem, isn't it?'

'We're still working hard to find what we need, sir, but with such a small team…'

Haley held up the flat of his hand.

'I understand and I don't doubt the three of you have put in plenty of effort through the last few weeks, but you know we need more than that. It's not just this,' he pushed at the papers contemptuously, 'have you seen the rancorous campaign Gemma Bales has been waging through social media?'

'Not all of it, but I'm well aware of stuff she's put on social media in the past. I'm sure it's pretty incendiary and not necessarily grounded in fact.'

'That's as maybe,' answered the DSU. 'But it's getting traction. She's alleging we're going after her in a desperate attempt to cover up for having made a mess of the case against her husband and, however unjustified we know that suggestion is, it's being picked up by the mainstream media now and used as a stick to beat us with – again. The same outlets that were calling us out only a few weeks ago for having prosecuted the wrong man in David Bales and demanding we reopen the investigation are now taking her side and accusing us of incompetence – again.'

Haley did a quarter spin in his chair and rose to his feet. He rubbed the top of his head.

'Now you know I'm not the type who will ever base police policy according to the latest mutterings in the tabloids, but it does present us with a problem, nevertheless. Those above me are taking notice and want to know what we have if we are to present a case against Ms Bales and Mr Shirley. What am I meant to tell them? Not everyone was so keen to launch a fresh look at the case in the wake of the unfortunate events involving DCI Pendlebury and David Bales. What have we got to show them as proof that we made the right decision? You see my predicament, Clare?'

Of course she did. She felt she had let him down. She bowed her head.

'I do, sir.'

He stood still and put his hands into his trouser pockets.

'I can get you another couple of weeks. If anything new comes to light in regard to the roles of Bales and Shirley, then do all you can to make it stand up. In the meantime, try to ease back on direct confrontation with them. Don't give them any more ammunition to fire back at us. I'm sure you've been through every detail of this case enough to be able to recite it in your sleep, but go through it one more time and view everyone as a potential suspect. If we cannot make any substantial progress in the case over the next two weeks, then I'll have to shut it down and reassign the three of you. I'll have no choice. We can issue a statement saying we're no longer looking for anyone else in connection with the Moran murder and if people want to read into that the suggestion we still believe David Bales was responsible, then so be it. Maybe he was. Maybe we went after the right person from the start and were just not able to get it over the line. If only we'd found the tie that was used to strangle her. That would have been the game-changer. That has long since been destroyed, no doubt.'

Clare stood to go. 'Thank you, sir.' She wanted to get back to the cupboard to let the other two know. No doubt, they would be on edge, wondering if they were about to be told to move on to other duties.

Two weeks! The DSU had been fair. She appreciated that. Others she could name would have been much less understanding. But two weeks! The pressure of time was piled on top of the pressure of her own expectations and weighed heavily on her shoulders.

Failure was looming. Worse still, it would be a second failure over the same case and that was intolerable. Maybe she should not have been so keen to get involved in the case again. Maybe someone not tainted by the original debacle would have made a better job of it.

Pull yourself together, woman!

It wasn't over yet. If two weeks was all they had, then they would have to make the most of every second. Clare pulled herself upright and strode purposefully to re-join the others. There was still work to be done.

CHAPTER
TWENTY-EIGHT

The man leaned against the wall in his three-quarter length leather coat and mirror shades, oozing casual menace and knock-off big brand aftershave. He was ready to explode into unspeakable violence at a moment's notice. *Lock, Stock and Two Smoking Barrels* meets *The Matrix*.

There appeared no good reason why anyone would loiter casually at that place at that time of the afternoon other than because they had been told to do so. Maybe the people on the other side of the white door to his left had told him to. From across the street, he looked quite young, even with his scruffy dark beard and neck tattoos. A foot soldier. Jane Featherby climbed out of her car and tried to glance across at him without it being obvious she was looking and saw enough to be sure she did not want to know what he had been stationed there to protect.

The man was less subtle in the way he made his assessment of Jane and her battered purple Micra, but seemed to quickly disregard her as both a threat and a potential customer.

The last time she visited Varey Street, around four and a half years ago, it was rough. It appeared to have gone downhill since then. Metal sheets covered the windows and doors of at least a quarter of the houses in this small section of the street. From the heavy black soot scars rising from the front window, it looked as if one had been burnt out before it was boarded up. She shuddered to think there might have been people in there when it happened.

Jane twisted the key in the lock of the driver's seat door and wished she hadn't noticed the car, twenty yards ahead, that had been systematically wrecked until not an inch of it had escaped being smashed or dented.

Do people really still live here? More to the point, did Courtney Carr still live here?

The sad fate of her son, Brandon, and thoughts of his last few months before he could see no better option than to take his own life around the back of abandoned industrial premises had absorbed Jane. She decided she had to see the mother to talk about it. She had to know. How had he behaved in those final weeks? Did he say anything to his mother?

The more Jane thought about it, the more important it became to her.

The visit could be considered an intrusion, she could see that, but Jane felt she had forged a sort of bond with Courtney the last time – the only time – they had met. She had proved she had Brandon's best interests at heart, with the work she put in to find him a university place, for instance, and so she couldn't be regarded as a nosey stranger. Besides, Courtney might be grateful for the chance to talk about her son with someone else who knew him and had tried their best for him. It could be good for her.

They might both get something out of it.

She remembered the route there. There were not many other streets left standing where once there would have been row after identical row, before work on the ring road began. The house number had also stuck in her mind. Number one hundred. She could even picture the insubstantial wood laminate front door which shook when she knocked on it.

But as she set off that afternoon, fearing what she might hear but compelled to find out, she had no way of knowing if Courtney Carr would still be at the house she used to share with Brandon. Their oasis in the chaos beyond. Would she have abandoned it as holding too many bittersweet memories? Jane had no idea where she would begin to start looking if Courtney had moved on.

At least the house wasn't one of those shuttered away and abandoned. She knocked, tentatively at first, and listened.

There was no sound. The occupier could be at work, of course. But then there was a voice. Apprehensive, trembling.

'Who is it?'

It was a woman's voice.

'Is it Courtney?'

No reply.

'Courtney, it's Jane Featherby. I was Brandon's sixth form tutor.'

Silence. The information was being considered. But then Jane could hear the sound of locks being turned and bolts being released.

The door opened only a sliver, wide enough for a pale, timid face to peer out. Stark frightened eyes surveyed the figure on the other side, suspiciously.

'What do you want?'

Jane was startled. What she could see of the woman sheltering behind the door bore little resemblance to the one she saw the last time. She recalled Courtney was younger than her but she appeared to have at least caught up. Life weighed heavy on the fragile creature she met before. Now, it was crushing her.

'Can I come in? I'd like to talk. About Brandon.'

The request drew another long, contemplative pause before, suddenly, the tiny space between door and frame was snapped shut. Jane was about to make plea for reconsideration when she heard the sound of the security chain being slipped off and the door was opened again, just wide enough for a person to get through this time.

'Quick! Quick!' said Courtney with a frantic wave of her hand. Jane hurried inside and the door was hastily locked and bolted behind her.

'They're all druggies around here. They knock and ask if I can lend them money. Lend them! What have I got to lend? I've got nowt.'

A dirty sweatshirt hung loosely over her slight frame and stained jeans were barely touched by the spindly legs moving beneath. Courtney had been a thin little bird before but now there was practically nothing to her. She moved quickly, jerkily, stooping like she had become too used to having to dodge bullets.

The stench of stale body odour made Jane flinch. She breathed as shallowly as she dare and suppressed the urge to gag. It was a warm August day, yet it felt as if the room had not been exposed to fresh air since April.

Around her, the same furniture sagged with age as the last of its usefulness was eked out and the same peeling flowery wall-paper clung on doggedly against the spreading invasion of black damp, but there had been little effort made to keep the room tidy any more. It was as if the whole house had given up trying.

The only difference to the room Jane could see, apart from the accumulation of mess, was the addition of a primary school photo, propped against the wall on the narrow mantle above the electric fire. A boy of ten or eleven years old in a red polo shirt with an embroidered school crest was smiling beneath a mop of naturally curly brown hair. It was a lovely photo. Jane didn't think she had seen Brandon smile before.

Courtney moved to the threadbare brown sofa without offering an invitation to join her and perched on the edge, hardly aware that another person was still with her. She started to rock, only a little but unmistakeably, and Jane wondered for a moment if the damage caused by losing her son had cut deeper than she had imagined it might have.

But then there was a flicker of life around the eyes again and she said: 'Where are my manners? Would you like a cup of tea?'

Jane saw the stained mug by the side of the sofa and declined the offer. She stepped carefully across the room to sit.

'Courtney, I'm so sorry it's taken me so long to offer you my condolences. I honestly had no idea what happened to Brandon until just recently. I left Brincliffe Edge Academy, you see, before – it was right at the start of the next term and I kind of cut myself off from everyone there. It was a bit of an acrimonious parting, to be honest. Anyhow, I can't tell you how sad I was to hear.'

'Oh, that's all right,' she replied with an unnerving lightness, like no one else had even bothered acknowledging her loss at all and she appreciated the novelty.

'How have you been?' Jane had to ask. The answer was evident.

'It's not been easy. I don't see people very often these days. I don't get out much. Just to go to the pharmacy. They won't deliver round here. I had to give up my job. I couldn't handle being around anybody. I knew they were looking at me. I knew what they were thinking. I couldn't do that anymore. Anyhow, I manage. It's just me now. It was only ever me and Brandon, you see. We never had anybody else, family and that. But, you know, I've still got my memories.'

Her forced cheerfulness was painful. Jane found it hard to hear.

'Didn't they offer you any support? The council or social services?'

Courtney shrugged. 'I stopped going. I didn't want to talk about it with strangers. I stopped going and they stopped sending me letters after a while. But that's OK.'

Jane recalled how they had tried, unsuccessfully, to convince her to trust counsellors to help Brandon deal with his issues.

'I should have taken him to see somebody, shouldn't I?' The admission was unexpected. It was as if she had intercepted Jane's thoughts.

'That time when you said. I should've listened and then maybe none of this would've happened. Brandon wouldn't have, you know, like he did.'

The pain was plain to see. It had been building, eating away, for four years. A mother's guilt that could never be erased by any amount of counselling.

'You did what you thought was right,' said Jane. She was never comfortable with physical contact but was compelled to move closer and lay her hand on Courtney's. 'You were entitled to think you knew what was best for Brandon. He was your son and, do you know what, for those last few months he was at Brincliffe, I would have said you called it right. He was becoming really settled and if you'd asked me then I would have agreed with you that he was starting to overcome his shyness and grow into being a fine young man, ready to move on to university and prove to the world who he really was. Do you proud.'

The tears were rolling freely down Courtney's face but the faintest of smiles tugged at the corners of her mouth as she stared at Jane's hand on hers. She was not used to receiving such compassion.

'You must have noticed that yourself. He was doing so well. He was making friends. Did he mention that at all?'

'Well, you know how Brandon was,' said Courtney with a half-chuckle of recollection. 'You did well to get two words out of him most days but he did used to talk about one person.'

She looked Jane in the eye, knowingly.

At first, Jane thought she might be indicating Brandon had formed a stronger bond with his tutor than she realised, but she couldn't perceive that to be true. This had to be spelled out.

'Who was that?'

Courtney rolled her eyes. Wasn't it obvious?

'You know! His girlfriend!'

Jane was startled but tried not to show it.

'Abie?'

'She was all he would talk about. What she'd said, where they'd been together, what she was into. Brandon had never had a proper girlfriend before. You know, not since he was little and that doesn't count, but he was really taken with this Abie and it sounded like she was keen on him. He told me she was trying to change her university so she could stay in Sheffield, like him.'

This was dumbfounding. The picture of obsession Megan Owen had painted for her at David's funeral was not even the half of it. Brandon was living out a whole fantasy relationship with Abie in his head. He was not only stalking Abie, she had become part of a whole new dangerous illusion.

'He didn't bring her home, of course. Who'd want to bring a girlfriend back to this? I'm sure I would have got the chance to meet her sometime, but then…' Her rage rose and brought a rare flush to her cheeks. 'What that man did to her was barbaric. They should've hung him. Prison would have been too good for him. That poor girl! And he got away with it! What kind of justice is that?'

Jane winced but ignored the question.

'So what happened to Abie must really have hit Brandon hard. Did he talk to you about that? How did he react when he heard?'

The ray of light that had briefly peeked through constant dark cloud was eclipsed again. Courtney's head dropped. Her whole body seemed to slump.

'I knew something was wrong as soon as he came home.' She was having to dredge back the memories from a place she hoped she would never have to visit again. 'I thought they might have had an argument, you know, like they sometimes do at that age. He went straight upstairs and shut himself in his room. He wouldn't come down. Wouldn't eat his tea. Wouldn't tell me what was wrong. Then I saw it on the telly. On the news.'

'So do you know where he had been that day? It was right at the end of term for the sixth form, so he wouldn't have been in lessons. Had he been with Abie, do you know?'

Courtney picked again through the wretched details of memory. 'I don't think he said they were seeing each other that day but he went out well before dinner and didn't get back here until, I don't know, about three? I thought he might have been meeting her. They seemed to be spending most days together.'

Only one of them didn't realise that.

'When he did finally come out of his room, what then?'

'Oh, he was there for days! I mean, I heard him sneak out to the toilet sometimes, but he wouldn't eat, wouldn't talk, just stayed in his room. When I did manage to talk him into coming down for some food, I tried to mention Abie but it just set him off again. He grabbed his food and went back upstairs. He was like that for weeks. I daren't mention her name again. I thought I just had to let him deal with it in his own way and then, when he was ready, I'd be there for him. But that time never came. He hardly said a word to me after that day for the rest of his life. It was horrible to see him suffer that way. Cruel. He was torn apart. He really loved her. The day before they found him was the first time I'd known him leave the house in months. He could've gone out while I was at work sometimes, I suppose, but he'd always be in his room when I left and always there when I got back. That night, when he didn't come home, I was panicking. I phoned the police to report him missing but they said to leave it until morning and see if he came back. I called back the next day and...'

Jane needed to let her dwell in the moment. It would have been churlish to interrupt it too soon. Surely, it must be the hardest thing any parent could face. She could see that, but she had to press on.

'When the police came to tell you they'd found Brandon, did they ask you questions about how he'd been – what you thought might have driven him to do what he did?'

She nodded.

'What did you tell them?'

'I told them he's been a bit down. I said he was a bit anxious about university and all that. I said he'd always been one to lock up what he was feeling inside, even with his mum. Do you know what else they asked me? Did I know if he took drugs? They obviously saw where he came from and assumed. That right got my back up. They found nothing in their tests, of course. My Brandon wasn't like that.'

'But what did you tell them about his relationship with Abie and how that affected him?'

The indignation stirred in Courtney by the drugs question was still in her eyes as she glared back at Jane.

'I told them nothing. They didn't need to know that. It was none of their business. I didn't want them going into Brandon's private matters and telling the world about it and getting it in the press and all that. Can you imagine what they would have said? Poor little lovesick kid. No, I wasn't going to let them do that to him. It was hard enough to deal with as it was. They could hold all the inquiries they wanted, it wouldn't make a blind bit of difference. It wouldn't have brought my Brandon back, so I decided not to tell them. I couldn't do anything for him anymore but I could stop them taking his dignity.'

There was no response Jane could think of for that. Inside, her mind was spinning. She thought about the inquest report she had read online. There had been no mention of anything to do with Abie's death. It was astonishing nobody had taken the time to look more deeply into the reasons why. What would she have told them if the police had come to her? She knew nothing about the whole Abie fantasy, but someone – one of the other students – might have been able to fill in missing background detail. Maybe the authorities were satisfied to take the easy route. Wrap up another sad story and move on.

Just another teenage suicide.

'I'll tell you one thing for certain, though, and I didn't need any inquest to pass judgement to know it. The bastard who killed that poor girl just as surely killed my Brandon as well.'

Courtney immediately checked herself and quelled the fury that had risen again, seeming to realise she might have said too much.

'I'm sorry, I didn't mean to... I know he was somebody you worked with. I shouldn't have...'

'I understand.' Jane attempted a reassuring smile. 'There's no need to apologise for how you feel, after what you've been through.'

'I've never said that to anybody before, but I feel like I can talk to you. You knew Brandon and you knew what a good boy he was. You've been so kind.'

Jane was actually touched. So much so that she was moved to pull Courtney into a hug. She instantly regretted it. Up close, the smell was overpowering.

'Look, I really have to go, I'm afraid,' she said, breaking free as soon as she could. 'I'm glad I called to see you and here...'

Jane reached down for her bag and rummaged through to find a pen. She also took out an envelope, tore off a strip of it and wrote on it.

'This is my number. Just call me if you want to talk.'

Courtney held the scrap like it was a precious secret. 'You sure?'

She smiled. 'Any time.'

Any time might have been going a bit far.

They both stood and Courtney took another half-step forward, as if she was ready for a repeat embrace.

'Anyway,' said Jane, quickly, drawing her bag to her chest. 'It's been good to see you again.' She made as if she was turning for the door but stopped.

'Actually, do you mind if I just use your loo before I go?'

'Of course!' Courtney replied with disproportionate delight. 'It's upstairs, first left.'

Each stair appeared to have its individual creak as she made her way up them and turned, walking straight past the bathroom towards the end bedroom. The one that gave a look-out's view over the street below.

There was no keyhole to suggest it could be locked from the outside but Jane pulled down the handle gently and slowly pushed the door when she felt the latch bolt free of its connection to the frame. It was stiff and she had to nudge her shoulder against it to get it open, desperate to avoid making any noise that could be heard below.

Finally, it swung free and she took a tentative step inside.

The room was tiny. Barely big enough for the single bed and sole battered wardrobe. It was unquestionably a boy's room, with a scattering of discarded clothes in the corner next to a lone shoe and an open rucksack. A hand-held games console and three cartridges lay on the floor at the near side of the bed. The duvet, with a cover far too child-like for a boy of eighteen, was still pulled back as if its occupant had climbed out only minutes earlier, but the musty aroma and taste of dust disturbed by opening the door told the real story.

This room had not been touched in years. She might not have been able to bear coming into it at all, never mind tidying it. It was a time capsule buried since October 2017.

Then Jane noticed the wall to her right, opposite the head of the bed. It was plastered with six-by-four photos. Only a few of them were posed. Most of them looked as if they had been taken surreptitiously by someone with a smartphone without the subject's knowledge. And they all featured one person.

Abie in the common room.

Abie in the library.

Abie chatting to friends.

Abie alone, her back to the camera, walking along the corridor.

Walking down the street.

He must have taken hundreds and printed what he considered the best of them in one of the self-service shops. He'd printed off dozens and dozens.

And there, in the middle of them, was half a sheet of lined A4 paper that looked as if it had been ripped out of a pad. On it were two words.

Thanks! Abie x

She had drawn a heart over the letter 'I' where the dot should have been. Maybe it was given in exchange for the maths advice Jane had been told Abie sometimes asked Brandon for, as a way of being kind. She almost certainly didn't think about such a small gesture again, but it plainly meant so much more to the recipient.

Jane shook her head as she took it all in. The implications of it.

She had come back to Varey Street in hope. It had exceeded anything she had dared dream of.

CHAPTER
TWENTY-NINE

Leather Jacket was still at his post but didn't even bother looking up this time. He was busy playing with his phone.

Jane was also preoccupied, her head buzzing with the new information as she wrestled to grasp the full extent of what it meant. She was in so much of a hurry to get back to the car that she almost broke into a trot. She wanted to run. She wanted to scream. She had not felt this pumped on adrenaline for years. This was huge! A game-changer!

Dropping into the driver's seat, she let her head fall back against the headrest and exhaled.

Just take a moment. Is this really what you want to do?

It was the possibility she had played over in her thoughts for days but it's so much easier to see it through when everything is in theory. This was real. Her finger was on the trigger. What she was about to unleash would have actual impact and, once it was released, there was no option to recall. Someone who had trusted her would get hurt.

Jane weighed up the potential damage against the likely gains.

No contest. This has to be done.

She took her phone out of her bag and scrolled to find the number. Her thumb hovered over the dial button. There were no more doubts. She was enjoying this. This was to be relished. It was all she wanted.

'Hello, Detective Inspector Clare Larson.'

Jane took another breath. Keep it together.

'Hi Clare. It's Jane Featherby. How are you?'

A sigh.

'I've had better weeks, to be honest, Jane. What can I do for you?'

This was it.

'I know you're going to think I'm just banging on the same drum here, Clare, but I think I've got something. You know how David always said whoever killed Abie must have sneaked in through the conservatory while he was on the phone in another room?'

Was that the sound of the detective's enthusiasm sinking to new depths? Jane smiled as she imagined the face of the woman on the other end of the line.

'Yeah, I remember.'

'I think I know who that person might be. I may have found your killer.'

Sit back and wait for it.

Now I've got your attention, haven't I?

'OK. I'm listening. What have you got?'

'I've just been to visit the mother of one of my former students. He was in the same year group as Abie and I found out only recently that he committed suicide three months after she died. The thing is, he was a difficult kid. Real social anxiety issues, very poor communication skills, but he was absolutely smitten with Abie. I mean, to the extent he used to follow her around all the time. Stalk her. I've just seen his bedroom and it's practically a shrine to her. One wall is covered with photos of her that were obviously taken without her knowing he was taking them. Look, I know it might be nothing, but I thought...'

'No, no, you did right.'

The rod was twitching. The float was bobbing.

'What was this kid's name?'

'Brandon Carr. He only came to us at the start of the final year of A Levels. Very bright boy but, as I said, he had challenges.'

'So Brandon killed himself, you say? Not long after the murder.'

'Just short of three months. There was something else that got me thinking. I'm not sure I should say...'

'Go on,' Clare encouraged.

'It was the mother. I think she knows more than she's letting on. They were very close, you see, it was just the two of them and I think Brandon told her what he'd done. I think she tried to protect him by keeping him at home until she could be sure her son wasn't regarded as a suspect, but then it got too much for the kid and he sneaked out to end it all. She told me she lied to the police investigating his death so that the truth wouldn't come out in the inquest.'

'Jesus!'

'He never registered to take up his place at university. He didn't even come to school to pick up his A Level results.'

Jane could hear the scratching of a pen as Clare tried to take all this information down.

'We need to talk to the mother. Have you got the address?'

'Yes. It's number one hundred on Varey Street. She's in now. I don't think she goes out much. She looks like she's really struggling to hold it all together to me but, as I said, she only trusted me to tell me so much. I hope I'm not wasting your time here, but I've just got a feeling.'

'Sure, sure. I appreciate the call, Jane. It needs to be checked out. Look, keep this to yourself for now. We have to do this properly – make a proper search of the house and especially the boy's room. It sounds promising and I guess we'll only know when we get in there and speak to the mother.'

Jane smiled. 'I hope it's helpful.' She turned to glance at leather jacket, still on his phone. 'While you're in the area, you might want to look into what's going on at the house with the white door opposite. It looks dodgy to me.'

'Got it. Listen, leave it with me. I have to go now. Appreciate this.'

The call was ended.

Jane brought down the phone from her ear and placed on it on her lap. That had gone well.

She allowed herself to bask for a few seconds more before putting the phone away and turning the key in the ignition. Time to go.

As she drove away, Jane could picture Courtney's horrified face as her squalid little home was flooded by policemen and women and she was led to a car to take her away for questioning. She thought about forensic officers in their white protective suits and latex gloves peeling off and bagging the photos off the wall. She imagined, most of all, the euphoria among the group as they discovered the one key piece of evidence that had eluded them for four years.

The woven silk tie in pale blue with a repeating pattern of six small white dots which David Bales had been wearing on the day of the murder and which had been used to strangle the helpless and tragic Abie Moran.

They were sure to find it.

She had left it in a place where they were certain to.

CHAPTER
THIRTY

I t was an especially hot day. I remember sitting in the corner of the staff room I usually avoided because the air conditioning was uselessly inefficient and, in that corner, the vents would either freeze you with icy gusts or roast you like you were staring into the face of a blast furnace. That day, though, the coolness was blissful.

I was eating alone. I preferred it that way. There were a few staff around – five or six, maybe. Others were on lunch duty and some, I heard, had nipped off to the pub. The term was almost over. Everyone was winding down, looking forward to the six weeks break. Exam time had been frantic and stressful, as it always was, but even the most hyper of the Year Elevens had come down off the ceiling by then and we had all begun to breathe a little more easily.

I looked up when David came in and I felt my face flush in a way that had nothing to do with the air conditioning. He wasn't a large man; just the right proportions, actually. He wasn't espe-cially demonstrative, either, in the way some of them were, breezing in and demanding attention like they were the only ones who ever had to deal with problems. David wasn't like that, but when he walked into a room, people noticed. He had a kind of aura. He drew attention without trying.

How he managed to stay immaculate on a day like that I've no idea. He was wearing a crisp plain white shirt and a pale blue tie. Shirt still buttoned at the cuffs, top button fastened, tie perfectly straight. He always dressed so nicely. Not the faintest sign of perspiration on him either. Hair beautifully groomed, always clean shaven. No wonder he attracted females. Males as well, probably.

I loved him. I'm not ashamed to admit that. I loved him. He didn't know that, though. Of course he didn't. We'd worked together for eight years and in all that time we hadn't had a single meaningful conversation, but I knew once he did take the time to get to know me properly he would love me too. I would balance him. I would never try to change him but I would provide him with the intellectual and emotional equilibrium he needed in his life and he would come to cherish me for that. We were a perfect match, in lots of ways.

It was a matter of finding the best time to begin the process of taking our relationship to a new level and because the end of term was almost upon us, my opportunities for having *the* talk with him were running short. I really didn't want it lingering through the six weeks holiday. Apart from anything, I was aware there was a possibility he would reject my proposal and, if that happened, I would have to leave Brincliffe Edge Academy. I couldn't bear to be around him if I knew we would never be together and I didn't want to make it awkward for David either. By letting him know how I felt at the end of term, I could allow him space to get in touch with how he felt about me and we could then either plan our lives together without distraction before the start of the new term or, if the worst came to the worst, I could put in my notice and find a new job.

The timing of it all made sense to me. All I needed was the

opportunity – and the courage to make my approach. It would be hard but I had to do it.

I tried not to make it noticeable I was watching David as he arrived in the staff room and walked straight over to the dispenser to pour himself a cup of water. Of course, Charlotte Maxted was less subtle. She was one of the PE teachers and thought she was it because she played semi-professional football for a team I'd never heard of. She always talked in staff meetings like she was one of those football managers giving an interview on *Match of the Day*, saying 'obviously' when it wasn't obvious and 'to be fair' when it was nothing to do with fairness. She preferred everybody to call her Charlie, so I called her Charlotte. I didn't like her especially.

'Hey, Davy,' she said, sidling up to him. She was the only one to call him that, as if there was a special intimacy between them. I don't know why he never corrected her. I would have.

'Are you staying with us today or eating at the Bales diner?'

David drained his paper cup and dropped it in the recycling bin. 'I'm going to head off home for a bit,' he said, not that it was any of her business. Because he lived only a few minutes' walk from school he often went home at lunchtime for a short break from it all. I can't say as I blame him.

'In fact, do you know what?' he said picking up his bag. 'I think I'm going to stay there. It's too nice a day to spend hanging around here. I haven't got anything scheduled this afternoon, so sod it.'

Charlotte tucked her hair behind her ear. She loved her hair. 'Sounds good. I might join you.'

He ignored that. She was so transparent. He smiled at her, kind of indulgently.

'If I'm needed back here, just give me a ring.'

With that, he left. Charlotte slinked back to do whatever she was doing on her laptop and I carried on eating my pasta salad.

A thought occurred. This could be the chance I was waiting for. Sudden fear squeezed my guts, but that was because it had been too easy to keep putting it off for too long. David was going to be alone at home all afternoon and I had nothing until period six, the last of the day. Would I get a better opportunity?

I gave myself a telling-off for hesitating. *Do you want this or not?* I resolved to give it quarter of an hour and then slip away. I was going to tell him.

Nobody noticed me go and I didn't invent an excuse for myself. I just went. I knew where David lived, even though I'd never been there before. I'd made a point of finding out. It wasn't far.

The sun was really fierce, but I felt a curious mix of hot on the outside and cold on the inside because my stomach was churning. I was by no means certain I could go through with it, but I pushed myself on and, almost before I knew it, I was on Stamford Road. It was a quietish estate and David's house was about a third of the way along. I approached it from the opposite side of the road and I'm glad I did.

She was there. At his door.

I didn't recognise her at first, in her tiny pink shorts and white crop top, showing herself off. I was used to seeing her in the business attire we expected our sixth formers to dress in. I stopped to try to work out what was going on and when she turned her head to the side to shake her flowing blonde hair I knew it was Abie Moran.

What the hell was she doing there?

I dropped back to watch from the edge of a driveway. David came to the door. She handed him something. They talked for a short while. He invited her in.

To be honest, I couldn't tell you how that made me feel. Confused, angry, frustrated, sick. All of that. I wanted to believe there was nothing in it. David was just being polite, that's all, because that's the man he was. That's what I was telling myself.

I decided to sit tight for a bit. She would be sent away soon and then, when I had watched her heading off to be so bloody perfect somewhere else, I could carry on with what I had gone there for. Should I mention what I'd seen to David?

But she didn't leave. I waited there for ten minutes, fifteen, nearly twenty. I was really anxious by then. I daren't imagine what was happening. Would David do such a thing? I still wanted to believe there was a perfectly innocent explanation, but surely he knew it was completely inappropriate for a sixth form student to stay so long in the home of a teacher, even if nothing untoward was happening. He could get in huge trouble.

What *was* going on?

I had to find out. I couldn't just turn around and head back to school not knowing. At first, I was going to stride straight up to the house and hammer on the front door, confront them, but then I realised that would totally embarrass David if all I'd interrupted was an earnest conversation about adapting to university life or such like. He wouldn't be in any mood to have our talk then. And what would Abie think if I turned up at David's front door, demanding an explanation? How could I explain that away? She might draw her own conclusions and it would be all over Instagram in no time. That would be awkward for both of us.

I needed to be more inconspicuous. There was a gap between the houses to the right of David's and I walked to where I could see down it. There was a path which seemed to lead to the back garden. I couldn't see a secured gate blocking the way. That could be my option. Go through to the back of the house and see if I could tell what was happening. If it all seemed reasonably above board, then fine. I'd sneak away again and I'd just have to try to get him to myself another day. I'd have to remind him at some stage how reckless he had been to invite Abie in, but that could wait until we got to know each other better.

What if it wasn't all above board? I didn't have a plan for that. I didn't particularly want to contemplate that possibility.

Around the corner at the end of the path, the garden was small, hemmed in by tall beech hedges, and most of it was paved.

THE MURDER OF MISS PERFECT   261

It was not a large space and the conservatory took up much of what there was.

I edged cautiously along the patio and peeked through the window closest to me. It was the dining room. There was no sign of anyone. I glanced through the next window, into the lounge, and couldn't see them there either. The conservatory doors were wide open but to get to them I had to crawl on my hands and knees, staying below the line of the glass so I was sure I couldn't be seen.

My hand pressed against a small sharp stone and I stopped to check it had not broken the skin. That was when I first heard faint noises, drifting out into the warm summer air from inside the house. The closer I crawled to the open doors, the clearer they became. I didn't need to catch sight of them anymore. I knew what was going on.

I could lay no claim on David then. There was no 'us' at that stage and so I had no right to expect exclusivity. He was married, after all, and I was still in a relationship as well. The ground rules of faithfulness and mutual respect were to be established once we both realised how we would be so good for each other. But, as I sat there on the patio, slumped against the outside of conservatory with my hands clamped against my ears to block out those soft mews of growing ecstasy, I felt betrayed.

Looking back now, I think it was a betrayal of the ideal image of David I had formed in my mind. I was wrong to believe any man could live up to that. They are such weak, pathetic creatures sometimes. Even with the benefit of time passed, however, it still disappoints me David could act that way with that... child. Didn't he understand how he cheapened himself to give himself away like that? Risking so much – and for what? A quick shag.

At that moment, I hated him for that. I hated myself for thinking better of him.

This should not be written off as jealousy. I didn't go there that day with the intention of seducing David. Of course I found him physically desirable. I was – I still am – a reasonably young woman, but it was about so much more than that. I had plans. Solid plans for a brighter future for both of us. Now those plans lay in tatters.

I don't know how long I sat there, wallowing in my disillusionment long after silence had fallen in the room not far behind me. Part of me just wanted to get up and leave, accept I had been fooling myself to believe David and I could be together, but I couldn't raise the will to move. I was paralysed by self-pity. It was the sound of the phone ringing that stirred me out of it.

It was impossible to hear what was being said because David's voice was so hushed, but I did make out him saying something like 'hang on a sec', followed by what seemed to be the sounds of him struggling to his feet. I heard her sleepy resistance to his movement, like she had been resting on top of him, and him reassuring her 'I'll be back in a few minutes'. As I twisted to sneak a look through the sliding doors into the lounge, I saw David, naked, heading out of the room and closing the door behind him.

The spell of my miserable contemplation was broken. I could have left then. Maybe I should. I just didn't want to.

You see, I've never been a quitter. Even when I can see the odds are against me, I never like to abandon a cause. If anything, I dig my heels even deeper. So, faced with the choice of accepting ignominious defeat or doing something about it, I chose to fight. I wasn't going to let that girl and her silly sexual fantasy beat me.

My strength was back. I rose to my feet and stepped into the conservatory, hesitating at the sliding doors until I could see where Abie was.

Clothes were scattered across the floor where they had been discarded in passion. On a sofa, against the outside wall just beyond from the exit to the conservatory, I saw her blonde head resting on a stack of red cushions at the end closest to me, with her slender tanned legs stretching out, just touching the far side.

Even then, I had no intention of killing her. If you'd even

suggested that to me I would have dismissed it as a preposterous over-reaction.

All I wanted to do was to wake her, shame her, threaten her with exposure. Threaten to ruin her, if that was what it took. As I saw it, the odds were very much in my favour then. Certainly, my presence there would be a surprise, but she was the young woman with the bright future and the flawless image and I figured she had considerably more to lose from news of this dalliance getting out. That, I reasoned, would be more than enough to guarantee her silence. I was going to tell her to get dressed, get out of the house and never go near or even speak of David again, or I would tell the world what a sordid little slut she was.

She would be gone by the time David finished his call and that would be the end of it. His little ego trip would be over and any thought of it ever becoming more than a one-off fling would disappear. Maybe he would even feel a little contrition and realise that men of his age, in such a position of responsibility, should not behave that way. I expected him to come to regret it ever happening.

I took my mobile phone from my bag. I was going to take pictures of her, lying there on his sofa with nothing on, to use as currency in my persuasion, but I became gripped by a whole new emotion.

Rage. I put the phone away.

The media came to call her Miss Perfect and that always irritated me. What I thought of her then, what I still think of her now, is that Abie Moran was a spoilt little tart from a privileged background who had been raised to believe she could take whatever she wanted. That was who I saw on the sofa that day and it made me angry. Angrier than I have ever felt before. She had taken what was rightfully mine and I wanted to punish her for that. Hurt her for hurting me. I wasn't necessarily determined she should die for the pain she had caused and the gross unfairness she represented. That just happened. My fury overwhelmed my rationality.

David's tie was at my feet and I picked it up, twisting the ends of it around my hands to give me a better grip. I held it taut as I stood behind her, so close I was sure she must sense my presence, but I didn't know what I should do after that. What is the best way to strangle somebody? I'd never done it before. Her head was nestled deep into the cushions, so I couldn't get the tie all around her neck. It was tricky. I didn't want to make a complete mess of it.

Just then, she let out a huge, contented sigh and raised herself in a stretch, her arms reaching high and her bare back arched in a lingering cat yawn.

That was my chance. I wrapped the tie around her throat and crossed my arms to trap her in a loop, then pulled her up until she was practically dangling. She let out this strange, gruesome gasping noise but didn't really resist in the first few seconds. I suppose it must have been a bit of a shock. When her survival instincts did kick in, she clawed at the tie to try to ease the choking pressure and thrashed her legs about, presumably in an attempt to get to her feet and fight me off, but I felt so much stronger than her. I leaned and pulled against her weight, wedging my feet against the base of the sofa. I raised her with my arms above my head at one stage, as I remember, until she stopped pulling at the restraint around her neck, stopped pedalling with her legs. I held the tension for a little longer, just in case, until I felt safe it was done. I released her. She dropped with her head falling over the arm of the sofa and her limbs limp.

When you've done an act like that, it leaves you with a weird sensation. The adrenaline drains from you suddenly, like sticking a knife into a balloon full of water, and you don't entirely know what to do with yourself. You feel odd. Out of place. Then it hits you what has actually just happened.

How did I react? I wouldn't say I felt triumphal. Atoned, maybe. There was no instant remorse and I wasn't panicked either, which some might consider surprising. Perhaps that should have surprised me, too, but I was calm, quite lucid. I didn't check Abie or even look at her. First, I stared at the tie, no tension in it now but still wrapped around my hands, and realised it would not be in my interests to leave it at the scene, so I stuffed it into my bag. Then I ran through a quick mental checklist in case I might have touched anything in or outside the house. I satisfied myself I hadn't and walked out back through the conservatory.

I returned to school. No one noticed me arriving. No one realised I had been gone. I was teaching a Year Ten group about the causes of the First World War when the pandemonium began.

CHAPTER
THIRTY-ONE

I learned a lot about myself that day, and in the four years since. First of all, I learned I was capable of taking a life. That was unexpected.

I also used to consider myself a person of great principle and high moral standards, but that, too, changed on Tuesday, July the eighteenth, 2017. Not only did I prove to myself I could kill, I later found it remarkably easy to cope with gambling with the lives of others if I calculated it would lead to personal gain. I could play this selfish game of strategy without being troubled by conscience.

I've never felt sorry for what I did to Abie Moran. She shouldn't have done what she did. I never felt sorry for her parents, either, who were all over the media and turned the court appearances into a circus. The mother treated the trial like a fashion parade. I could see where the daughter got it from.

Did I regret what I put David through? Those are slightly muddier waters.

As I walked away from the house that day, I did realise I'd left David in a whole heap of trouble. The police were bound to regard him as their prime suspect and, in truth, I wanted him to go through that. He deserved it. I wanted him to be scared. I expected him to be released, though, because I knew they had no evidence directly connecting him to the murder. It was ridiculous that it ever got to trial. Desperate on the part of the police.

When he was charged and remanded, I figured the whole ludicrous situation presented an opportunity. I saw a way I could have David by proving to him he needed me and that I was the only woman he could truly depend on. That was why I began my nuisance campaign of raising support for David's innocence, exposing the glaring flaws in the case against him. There was a risk that by putting myself in the forefront I might attract unwanted attention from the police later, but I saw it as hiding in plain sight. It's human nature that we often don't see what's right under our noses. By doing all I did for David and by visiting him regularly in prison, I was creating a situation whereby when his unjust persecution collapsed, as I knew it would, I would be the one he would turn to for comfort. It took longer than I anticipated, but I was proved right.

After his release, I picked David up and took him to my flat for safe haven. The experience had damaged him, which was to be expected, but I nursed him through his trauma and began to rebuild his faith in trusting the people who loved him. I thought we were making real progress. We were together, albeit in a flat I was still sharing with my partner at the time, and I was very happy. It was the beginning of everything I wanted.

When I came home that day to find he had left without a word of thanks or any clue as to where he had gone – well! I was hurt, of course I was. Massively. It shattered me, to be honest. It took me a long time to recover from what I saw as David's indefensible ingratitude and I grew quite bitter in my feelings towards him. I pledged to myself I would never allow him or any man close enough to do that to me again.

My partner, Mel, had to go, of course, and I was reconciled to being alone long before David phoned me, out of the blue, almost three years after he disappeared. I realised he only called because he was in trouble again and was desperate, but what was I meant to do? I couldn't just hang up, tell him to go to hell, because as much as I had tried to bury everything I felt for David in the three years since he walked out on me, I knew I still loved him. Does that make me feeble? A hypocrite? Possibly, but the frailty, the vulnerability in his voice, made me realise I would do all I could to try to save him again. I wish I could have reached him in time.

What happened to David was not my fault. Jim Pendlebury had no right to expose the new life David had made for himself and the thugs who attacked him are morons who didn't even have the basic sense to cover their own tracks. May they all rot in hell.

Maybe what happened was some sort of punishment for me. Maybe. I have considered that. Perhaps I should be made to pay for what I did but, do you know what, I won't be.

Thank you for that, Brandon Carr.

I must admit, I was concerned when I was told the police had reopened the Abie Moran case. I didn't believe they had anything to lead them to my door, but you never know. It only took one nosey neighbour to remember they saw me emerging from the path at the side of the Bales house or for one of my former colleagues to realise I wasn't in school for a crucial hour or so that afternoon. Thank goodness the police never bothered to check comings and goings on the school's CCTV.

When I picked up from media coverage that the police's attempt to implicate Gemma Bales and Paul Shirley was not going well, I reckoned the investigation could go one of two ways. Either it would be quickly wrapped up to save further embarrassment, or they would redouble their efforts to find someone else. I didn't want to take a chance that I would be their someone else, so I decided my safest option would be to intervene.

Having Brandon Carr drop in my lap was a godsend. Not only is he not around to argue his innocence, it was so easy to construct a scenario that has him stalking Abie all the way to David's, spying on them having sex and brutally killing her while he is blinded by psychotic jealousy. Unable to bear the weight of his deeds, he confesses to mother, she hides him away, but he hangs himself. The story is compelling and so, too, is the evidence.

It crossed my mind many times to destroy the tie I used to strangle Abie but I could never bring myself to do it. I don't know quite why. I'm glad I didn't now, of course. The police won't find a shred of DNA on it because I was careful and washed it several times with plenty of detergent. The internet can be such a useful teacher. It's not fit to wear anymore but the police will realise it is, without doubt, *the* tie and the fact that they will find it hidden in Brandon's bedroom is surely a clincher.

Case solved.

Should I feel bad about trampling on the memory of a tragic teenage boy? If I should, I don't. He makes a very good victim, if you ask me, and makes for a nice, clean ending. No one else will suffer unduly for what I've done, except his mother, I guess, and she's hardly worthy of consideration.

You know, it's often said history has been written by the winners.

The prize of victory was often the choice to dictate how history remembers you – and how badly it reflects on those you defeat. I tell this to my students all the time, so they understand there is so much more to history than key dates and the names of battles.

In my own case, Brandon Carr presented me with an opportunity to decide who should take the blame for the so-called Murder of Miss Perfect. Because of that, history will not condemn me. It will say Brandon did it. That's just the way it works. I was the victor.

Brandon's reputation may be trashed, but David's will be restored and mine will be preserved. Sorry Brandon, but the trade-off is worth it.

So this is what else I learned about myself that day, and in the four years since.

I learned I had the power to set my own course, my own destiny. I didn't have to be the little woman on the peripheries who nobody took seriously. I didn't have to live my life being buffeted by the wake of other people's decisions. I could take control. That was quite liberating.

I think what I will choose next is to give myself a fresh start. I think I'll get out of teaching. It's not for me anymore. Kids these days don't listen to what I say and that's fine. Let them find another voice and, through that, let them find their own.

I'll find something else to do and I'll find another place to go. I'll say goodbye to Sheffield. I've always fancied living by the coast, actually.

Scarborough might be nice.

ACKNOWLEDGMENTS

For a while, it has been an aim to partner up with people who know plenty more about the industry than I do.

I feel very fortunate that Sumaira Wilson has stepped forward to offer the faith and practical support I have been looking for. It has been a joy to work with her and the rest of the team on this, my first novel with SpellBound Books. I hope it is the first of many.

A special mention also has to go to Mark Brownless, for his great patience through the cover design stage.

Before the SpellBound alliance was sealed, Heather Fitt's guidance as editor was again valuable in whipping the draft novel into shape.

Leaning on the knowledge of others is such an important part of the writing stage and I have an over-abundance of medical specialists to turn to when the need calls – Jack, Cho, Ruth, Anne and Sue. Perhaps this is nature's way of telling me to write more medical dramas.

There are many others who help through the process from idea to finished novel with the encouragement they offer. To receive it from friends and family is great, but to hear kind words from relative strangers is, in a way, even more touching. I'm humbly grateful to you all.

Printed in Great Britain
by Amazon

86820693R00156